D0467009

Desperate
Hoodwives

An Urban Tale

Meesha Mink and
De'nesha Diamond

A TOUCHSTONE BOOK
PUBLISHED BY SIMON & SCHUSTER
NEW YORK   LONDON   TORONTO   SYDNEY

Touchstone
A Division of Simon & Schuster, Inc.
1230 Avenue of the Americas
New York, NY 10020

This book is a work of fiction. Names, characters, places, and incidents either are products of the authors' imagination or are used fictitiously. Any resemblance to actual events or locales or persons, living or dead, is entirely coincidental.

Copyright © 2008 by Niobia Bryant and Adrianne Byrd

All rights reserved, including the right to reproduce this book or portions thereof in any form whatsoever. For information address Touchstone Subsidiary Rights Department, 1230 Avenue of the Americas, New York, NY 10020

TOUCHSTONE and colophon are registered trademarks of Simon & Schuster, Inc.

Designed by Jan Pisciotta

Manufactured in the United States of America

ISBN: 978-0-7394-9142-3

For my momma, my brother, and my man.
I love y'all above all others.

—Meesha

For my Baby Alice—I'll miss you
for the rest of my life.

—De'nesha Diamond

Miz Cleo

When Godfrey and I *first moved into Bentley Manor in June of '69, it was supposed to be a temporary stop until the financing for our first home came through. Thirty-seven years later, I'm still waiting. My husband's wait ended in '71 when he suffered a massive heart attack while working at the Atlanta Steel plant.*

That day changed my life forever.

Hopes and dreams withered away like rose petals in a snowstorm. I worked three jobs to support and raise four children. When my oldest got strung out, I hustled just like everyone else during the infamous '80s to take care of my grandbaby. Now I don't know where the hell she is.

Living paycheck to paycheck has a way of making the years roll by. Afros turned to Jeri curls, then to box fades, then twisted cornrows, and then finally back to Afros.

Between you, me, and the lamppost, I've seen just about everything under the sun in this slowly dilapidating apartment complex. Me and my best friend, Osceola Washington.

Osceola brags that she was Bentley Manor's first tenant. She says she still remembers the original color of the carpets. I have a hard time believing they were ever any other color than puke green, but she swears otherwise.

Over the years, or rather over the decades, Atlanta as well as Bentley Manor has gone through some changes and is currently suffering through head-shaking fads. Did you know they call this city A-T-L now? Bentley Manor started off as a regular apartment complex, but in the late '70s it was the ghetto, in the late '80s, the projects. Now, it's the hood.

Atlanta was once called as the black Mecca and played host to thousands of college students for Freaknic in the '90s. Now rappers decree it the capital of the Dirty South. Don't try to wrap your mind around that; it will all change before you know it.

You can't tell them young folks nothin', mainly because they're hardheaded and they know everything. In my lifetime, I've gone from being a nigger, to black, to African American (though I don't know nothin' about Africa). Now nigga *is back and there are more than a few of those running around Bentley Manor.*

I pretty much spend my days sitting out on the stoop with

Osceola—watching and, yes, sometimes snickering. Misery loves company, after all.

This place is hard on folks—the ones coming in and the ones clawing to get out. But it's hardest on the women. The little girls, the disillusioned teenagers, and The Desperate Hoodwives . . .

1

Aisha

Look, I don't want to keep up with the fucking Joneses. I *am* the Joneses. Especially when it comes to these fools living in Bentley Manor.

See me. Envy me. Want to be me.

That's all these broke, welfare heifers and food stamps–loving bitches can do for me as far as I'm concerned. Fuck 'em.

Now I'll admit when I first met my husband, at sixteen, I was living in Hollywood Court projects with my mother and two brothers, and just straight struggling. No designer clothes. No nice rides. No money. No nothing.

I used to be ashamed of my tore-up shoes and high-water pants with the faded knees. I was shy and quiet as hell, just trying to make people forget I was around so they wouldn't notice how fucked-up my gear was.

The only thing I felt I had going for me back then was my looks. Light complexion, green eyes, long hair, and a bangin' body. I had curves for days. And that's what drew Maleek Cummings to me that hot summer day in 1998.

He was a big-time drug dealer sitting behind the wheel of his green Lexus SC400. He caught my eye and motioned for me to come to him. Humph. My silly ass was so surprised that he was talking to me that I actually looked behind me first to make sure. Once I saw it was all me, I slid on a shy smile and made my way to him. A little conversation, lots of flirting, and ten minutes later he invited my grown ass to go for a ride. Damn right I got in.

We just rode around cruising the different neighborhoods. I had my window down profiling like crazy. I didn't think about the police pulling us over and maybe getting locked up because Maleek had work—drugs—in his car. I didn't think about someone wanting to hurt him and shoot up his ride while I was in it. I didn't think about him being twenty-one and I was just sixteen.

All I had on my mind was how lucky I was to be riding with Maleek. But I was smart about shit. I already knew that no matter how fine he said I was, no matter how many times he licked his lips like LL Cool J and gave me that I-wanna-fuck-you look, I was not giving up the goodies that easy. My momma been taught me that it was up to a woman to always make sure a man had more to give a woman than just a wet ass.

And it worked. Just two weeks later the shy girl with the raggedy clothes became Maleek's girl.

My life ain't been the same since.

From no name to name brand. Riding the bus to getting dropped off at high school in Maleek's Lexus. Being broke as a joke to laughing my fine ass all the way to the goddamned bank. From watching my momma struggle to being able to help her take care of my little brothers. I felt like the world was mine.

Six years later I went from wifey to wife.

Maleek was the kingpin and I reigned as his queen.

My only complaint was that he moved us from one bull-shit apartment in Hollywood Court to another in Bentley Manor.

When he first told me to go and fill out an application, I was like, "What the fuck?"

Don't let the name fool you. Bentley Manor is a low-rise project that has seen better days. The red brick has graffiti all over it. The parking lot has more potholes than a freeway. Tiny shards of broken glass litter the street like sparkling confetti. Crackheads and dope fiends battle with the rats and roaches for prominence.

It damn sure ain't my dream of a nice home in a gated community.

Far the fuck from it.

I wanted to be in a home. My home. With my husband and my kids—the ones I won't have until I'm thirty.

Once a week I'd drive by Whitewater Creek—a gated community near Peachtree City—and long for the day I'll lay around in one of those half a million-dollar homes. But Maleek didn't want to draw too much attention to himself with such a big house and neither of us working. "Let me get something legit off and poppin' first," he said as we lay in bed together smoking a blunt. "And then Whitewater Creek's yours."

So fuck it. My man's in the game moving major weight and I feel if his big, black, sexy ass was in Bentley Manor, then I'd be right up in there with him.

Shit, better me than the next bitch.

And tricks are always trying to get at my spot, but I have that shit on lock for sure. I made sure to give my man the three p's to a happy relationship: pussy, pussy, and more pussy. If the wind blew and made his dick hard I made it my business to drain that motherfucker of every last drop.

Our sex is that type of freaky-deaky, stop-before-you-give-me-a-heart-attack type of shit. There's nothing we don't do to or for each other. When it's on it's on.

Maleek taught my ass very well about what he likes and don't like. Hell, when a nigga's taking care of his wife as good as Maleek takes care of me, what's a little request for a rim shot or a hot lick of his ass?

Fuck it. That's how we get down.

I park our silver chromed-out Benz in the first spot I

come up on in the crowded parking lot. Before I get out I reach into my Gucci crocodile purse for my compact and double-checked my makeup. I wink at the almost identical image of Lisa Raye looking back at me. Matter of fact, that chick from *Player's Club* ain't got shit on me.

When I stepped out my apartment that morning I knew all eyes around the Manor were always on me. Bitches straight-checking for one sign of me slipping. One clue that I was wobbling and ready to fall, but that was nothing. Them hos needed to fall back because my game would forever and always be tight.

My Mary J. "Be Without You" ring tone echoes from my purse. Damn, Mary can sing. I'm feeling her because I didn't wanna be without *my* baby.

Like always, I let the whole ring tone play before I flip my phone open.

"Hello."

"I need a favor, Aisha."

Usually I hate a begging ass . . . but this is my mother. Still, a little greeting would've been nice. No hi, hello, how you doing? Just straight asking for something. But I couldn't refuse her. I wouldn't.

"How much, Ma?" I ask, climbing out the car and locking the door.

"You know I hate to ask, but I want to get some groceries in this house for the kids."

My mother works every day of her life but she always

has one of those living on a shoestring budget kinda jobs: cashier, clerk, school aide, janitor-type shit. But when me and my baby brothers we're growing up she always kept food on the table and the best clothes she could on our backs. I have to give her credit because she didn't chase men, drugs, or parties. She stayed home with us. She just didn't have the skills or the know-how to step up her cash game. Where she falls short, Maleek and me step in.

Ma is well aware Maleek make his money via his street game. She loves him to death and don't give a shit 'bout how he make his money. Especially when he's so free-giving with her.

"I'll stop by on my way home."

"Tell my son-in-law I asked about him and thank you, baby."

"You welcome, Momma."

I will *never* tell her no.

Right now I have it all compared to what she has. I'm used to having everything—what I want when I want it.

Everything, that is, except my husband.

Sadness fills my eyes and my soul at the very sight of the Jesup Federal Correctional Institute.

Behind those walls—those bars—is my man. Locked the fuck up like an animal.

I walk into the building feeling sick to my stomach.

Three months already gone and God knows how many more to go before his trial. Some kind of joint police bullshit or another investigated him and some other dudes he dealt with all up in New York and Virginia for nearly three years before a federal grand jury handed down a forty-five-count indictment. They all were charged with everything from conspiracy to possession and distribution of crack cocaine, drug trafficking, money laundering, and gun charges.

Maleek is looking at a ten-year bid.

I hate that there's a stupid fucking point system. He can only get eight days of visits a month—time I have to share with his mother and sister. I hate the shit I have to go through to get inside just to look in his face and hold his hand.

I take a deep breath trying to calm my damn nerves as I walk into the lobby with the other women and kids. Getting checked in makes me feel like I'm the damn criminal. The ID check, the photo they take every fucking time, the invisible hand stamp, and the metal detectors. Only a plastic purse. No more than a twenty-spot. No sexy clothes. Thank God we don't have a baby because them motherfuckers count how many diapers and shit you bring in. They even admit they peep out the bathroom to make sure no woman smuggled in drugs.

Shit, like I'm going to push a balloon filled with dope up my pussy. What the fuck ever. Maleek would never put me at risk like that.

So there's a lot of bullshit—starting with a helluva five-hour drive from Atlanta—but I will do it for the next ten years or more if I have to. Maleek is worth that to me.

As the officer leads me to the visitation room I block out where I am. I try to pretend I'm not inside a prison.

Even when I walk into the visitation room and take my seat I don't look around at the other inmates and their visitors. I find a blank spot on the wall and keep my eyes glued to it, trying not to think of what Maleek might have to deal with.

I mean, damn, what if some of dem niggas try to get at him while he in jail? Maleek ain't no punk but what if a gang of 'em go out *American Me*-style on him?

Every time I think about it I have to remind myself that Maleek is well known and well respected. Nobody is stupid enough to fuck with him. I couldn't let movies or rumors of men leaving jail livin' life on the down low get at me.

"Hey, baby."

My body nearly melts at the sound of his voice. Tears well up in my throat as I look up at his handsome square face and buff body in these whack-ass prison khakis and Rockport shoes from the commissary. I stand up and wrap my arms around his neck as we press our lips together. I moan and suckle his tongue as long as I can before the officers will step in.

This is my marriage. My life.

God help me.

2

Devani

I'm so sick of Tyrik's shit I don't know what to do. Here it is nine o'clock and his ass is still not here. Hell, he hasn't even bothered to call. Let me pull some sorry shit like not answer my cell and he would be all over me like white on rice.

"Humph. Looks like somebody is all dressed up with nowhere to go."

My mother's cackle, like always, bounces off my last nerve and I pull away from the grimy window to give her my best "don't-fuck-with-me" glare, but she ignores me and takes another hit off one of Koolay's famous fat blunts and lowers her eyelids to half-mast.

"Don't go gettin' mad at me 'cos I tell it like it is." Another hit and Mom passes the blunt to Koolay. "A nigga is a nigga is a nigga. Your fancy NFL nigga ain't no different than the nappy-headed ones runnin' around here."

"Word." Koolay, with his lost-in-the-eighties ass, chuckles and untwines his skinny, vein-protruding arm to take the blunt.

Encouraged by her boyfriend's agreement, Mom finally succeeds in finding my glare, but she hardly takes it as the kryptonite it's intended to be. "That nigga is never gonna swoop in here and take you away from all this. So stop dreaming. You ain't special."

"And neither is that tightly guarded coochee you got," Koolay grunts.

That snaps my Mom out her glossy-eyed high and she quickly smacks the back of Koolay's head. "What the fuck you doing thinking about her coochee for?"

Koolay ducks and turns on his wide-eyed innocent act to full volume. "What? I had your back."

"Fuck you, motherfucker." Momma jumps to her feet and starts waving her long slender finger like a policeman's baton. "If I ever find out you been putting the moves on my daughter, your ass is out of here!"

Momma is in her element. The only thing she likes better than good weed and good dick is a good argument. Shaking my head, I stroll out the front door of the small apartment and walk out to the front stoop.

It's a hot, muggy night with enough humidity to wither my kitchen area, but I'm past caring whether I need to make an appointment with Keisha. I'm still wondering why the hell Tyrik stood me up two nights in a row. Not like I want him to meet my momma, but still.

Maybe my momma is right. Maybe Tyrik is no better than the other niggas running around like cockroaches in Bentley Manor.

Shit.

I suck in a deep breath and will my tears to disappear. This can't be happening. I played my cards right. I don't act like some loose booty around him. I was careful to be aloof about his money and fame. I cared about him, not what he had.

He ate that bullshit up because I served it on a silver tray with a smile. So where the fuck is he?

Standing outside like an idiot, I gaze around at my old, red-brick prison, complete with a wrought iron security gate. A joke really, since the worst of the worst lived in Bentley Manor. Who exactly is the gate supposed to keep out . . . or keep in?

I have to get out of this place.

I know clinging to a nigga like he's the Messiah is sorry as hell. I've tried to save myself, working three jobs to put myself through some sorry tech school that promised job placement after graduation. But that shit turned out to be a joke. Everybody and their mommas ended up with a computer degree. The motherfucker barely qualifies you to turn on a computer, let alone rake in the six-figure income the dot-comer revolutionists promised from every glossy-paged business magazine.

"Yo, Devani!"

I make a quick swipe at my tears, disgusted with myself for acting like a weak bitch in front of the whole damn neighborhood. I turn to see Junior lumbering up the cracked sidewalk. Junior, Tyrik's cousin and struggling rapper—though he can't flow for shit—bounces up the stoop and stops before me. "Whatcha know good, gurl?"

"Nothing. Just hanging out."

His unkempt bushy eyebrows—which look like one long fuckin' hairy caterpillar—leaps at this. "Since when does your bougie ass hang out wit us common Negroes?"

I'm not in the mood for Junior's needling and I flash him my DFWM glare and he quickly tosses up his arms. "I'm just sayin'. I figured you'd be over at Tyrik's party, shakin' dat fine ass before some other hood rat jumps on dat rich, NFL dick."

No shit. My heart drops to my Gucci knockoff shoes. "What party?"

Junior looks at me as if I suddenly spouted an extra head, but then just as quickly his face cracks with an understanding smirk. "Ah, dat nigga didn't tell you?"

"Fuck!" I explode, tossing my hands up in the air. My mind scrambles for a plan, a move, or tactical military maneuver to get my ass back into the game. "Junior, I need a ride."

He scrunches up his face. "What the fuck? This ain't Drivin' Miss Daisy Incorporated."

"Nigga, you can't spell incorporated." Snatching his arm, I storm down the steps. Junior apparently knows I mean business since he doesn't offer any further resistance. "What is Tyrik celebrating?" I ask under my breath, but the question was voiced loud enough to reach Junior's ear.

"Farewell party. He's been traded to Pittsburgh."

If my heart wasn't already in my shoes, I swear it would have fallen again. Still, it takes everything I have to keep my burning tears in check. Tyrik is planning to leave me in Bentley Manor.

The realization is like fuel on a fire blazing inside of me. He's not leaving me. Not if I have anything to say about it.

I jerk open the passenger door on Junior's long-ass Chevy Caprice and pray the mysterious odor wafting from inside wouldn't kill me before we make it to Tyrik's mansion out in the suburbs.

Junior starts up the car and the damn thing roars to life like one of the city's garbage trucks. If the engine isn't sufficient enough to cause ear damage, his top-of-the-line stereo system—which is worth ten times more than the car—booms enough bass to rattle my teeth.

"You know, you owe me for this one, right?" Junior asks, lighting a roach he retrieved from the car's ashtray. He takes a hit and passes it over. I need something to calm my nerves so I hit it for a few puffs. It's laced with something I can't name, but at the same time I don't care.

"I'll hook you up with some gas money later in the week," I answer belatedly. I know that's not what he wants. Hell, I can feel what he wants because his hand is on my thigh and is caressing it like it's some long-lost friend of his.

"C'mon, Devani. We got about twenty minutes before we reach dat nigga's place. I've already hooked you up twice. You can't tell me you ain't feelin' good right now."

Actually, I am feeling damn good.

"I scratch your back, you scratch mine."

"Junior, cut the shit. I'm in a hurry."

Anger polishes Junior's black eyes. To my surprise he pulls the car over into the emergency lane of I-285, and then reaches across my lap to open the car door. "Get the fuck out," he barks.

"What? We're in the middle of the highway."

"Good. Then you'll have no problems hitchin' a ride," he says unconcerned, and pulls out a fresh blunt from his shirt pocket.

I glance around, noting all the cars rocketing down the dark highway to unknown destinations. No way am I going to hitchhike all the way to Alpharetta.

"Fine." I slam the door and turn toward him. "What do you want?"

Junior crackles under his breath. "Do you really have to ask?"

"I'm dating your cousin," I inform him, unable to stop my face from twisting in disgust.

"Doesn't look dat way to me."

I'm not fucking him. I may have attended community college but I'm not jumping on community dick. Junior has a reputation of fucking everything that isn't nailed down and I refuse to gamble with sexually transmitted diseases.

"Forget it." I open the car door. I'll take my chances hitching a ride with a mass murderer.

"All right. All right." He takes another puff from his magic dragon and passes it to me.

This time, I wave off the offer.

"How about a hand job?" He unzips his jeans without waiting for an answer. What he pulls out shocks the shit out of me. His large—no, massive—nearly blue-black cock is the prettiest thing I've ever seen. This nigga is seriously missing out on a career in porno.

"Let me see you," he says, pushing my skirt up again with his rough, calloused hands.

This time, I actually get a little wet, but I rein in my senses to push back his hand. "Drive."

Junior snickers, but does as I ask. "I just want a little peek." His hand glides expertly up and down his pretty cock and I have to admit I'm more than a little fascinated.

"C'mon, li'l ma. Let me see what you're holdin' out for only those niggas wit the fat wallets. I bet you keep dat shit shaved, don't you?"

Actually, I sport a cute little Mohawk straight down the center. A woman's body is more than her temple . . . it's her most powerful bargaining chip. That's why I eat right, which is hard to do on my income. All the crap that's bad for you is cheap and guaranteed to put you in an early grave. And, of course, I'm an exercise fanatic.

Every woman should carry a compact, their favorite tube of lipstick, and a gym membership card. I don't mean one to some rinky-dink gym that only obese people attend with enough clothing to cover every inch of their bodies. I mean a real gym where you're not only inspired by the muscles rippling around you, but turned on as well.

I met Tyrik at a Gold's Gym.

"Shit, baby. Let me take a peek," Junior groans as irritation ripples across his features. If I don't do something soon, he's going to try to put my ass out on the side of the road again.

I lean back a bit; ignoring the fact I'm drifting to the area with the mysterious odor, and hike up my dress to show him a little thong action.

"Ah, pink." Junior grins. "I love pink." He reaches over and brushes his finger across the lacy material.

I slap his hand back. "Don't touch."

His grin only widens. "Open your legs so I get a good look."

I roll my eyes but do as he asks.

"Move the thong," he orders, snubbing out his blunt.

Again, I obey.

"Oh, look at you wit the pretty kitty." He licks his fingers for a little lubrication and begins pumping his cock. Unbelievably the damn thing grows bigger.

"Give me your hand, li'l ma."

I know I shouldn't, but damn, I'm Curious George at the moment and I want to touch it. I inch closer to him and wrap my slender fingers around his exotic work of art and, no shit, my fingertips just barely touch each other. Now that's a thick brother who can cause some damage.

Junior moans as my fingers tighten and relax while I take over pumping his cock, and a few times I have to remind him to watch the road. Despite my warnings, two houses in Tyrik's neighborhood lose their mailboxes.

One thing for sure, Junior has impeccable timing. Just seconds before rolling to a stop outside of Tyrik's mansion, Junior's orgasm erupts like a California geyser.

"Shit," he gasps and then winks at me.

I cringe at the thick gooey mess all over my hand, but before I can utter a complaint, Junior magically produces a dingy towel from the backseat and tosses it over. No, the damn thing isn't clean, but it will do in a jam. I quickly clean up and scramble out the car just as one of the hired valets offers to park Junior's monstrosity of a vehicle.

Rufus, another one of Tyrik's cousins, spots me and is a little slow to react when I jet past him without an invitation. When I enter the house, I realize this is more than just a party—this is the party of the year.

"Devani," Rufus calls, coming up behind me. "You can't be in here."

"Where is he?" I ask, rounding on the four-hundred-pound man. My DFWM glare is in full effect and Rufus quickly drops his gaze.

"Look, I'm just doing my job, Devani. Invite only."

"Fuck your job." I turn and dart away again before the large man has the chance to react. I perform a quick walk-run sort of search in hopes of spotting Tyrik before another member of his sorry entourage kicks my ass to the curb.

With no sight of Tyrik downstairs, I rush up the circular staircase. The atmosphere is a hell of a lot looser upstairs as women's titties spill out of their dresses and men are planted here and there between their legs.

Tyrik's ass better not be up here.

My fervent threat quickly becomes a soulful prayer, but when I open the door to Tyrik's grand-size bedroom, God makes it clear he isn't in the prayer-answering business tonight.

There, sitting on the bed, with his head thrown back in ecstasy, is my one-way ticket out Bentley Manor and planted between his legs is an exotic Latina hoochie with her mouth wrapped possessively around Tyrik's cock.

Shit.

3

Lexi

Good sex always messed me up.

A good lay made a sistah like me forget a man was broke or cheating, using or abusing, lying and denying. There's plenty of times I had sold my soul for good sex. I loved nothing more than climbing on ten good inches and riding it until I passed out.

Yup, a good nut beat out good sense damn near all the damn time.

Or at least it used to. But I knew I had to get over it because it wasn't about just me. It took some time for me to buy a clue, but now I see everything quite clearly. Yes, I have five kids and four baby daddies, but I'm married now. Luther Mitchell stepped up and did what none of the fathers of my children would: he married my behind.

Finally a good man. A loyal man. An honest man. A hardworking man. Finally.

Luther makes me see more out of life than what I'm used to. Like getting out of Bentley Manor. I never really thought about moving out in the past, but he makes me see there is so much more to life. This brotha has dreams and he wants to share those dreams with me and my kids—well . . . *our* kids, like he always says.

He works as a mechanic until he's tired and grimy and then comes home and still makes time for us as a family. He takes the kids to the movies and stuff like that. He talks to them and tries to teach them wrong from right.

After my baby girl was born I swore I wasn't having any more kids, but after Luther came into our world I wished I hadn't tied my tubes. I want nothing more than to have his baby.

Not that we aren't struggling. Between my stamps, our jobs, and my steady child support from one of my kids' father, we doing all right. Still, clothes, shoes, toys, birthday gifts, Christmas gifts, and all the normal costs of five kids isn't anything to play with. Luther is right there with me helping me get it all done. We'll go lacking to make sure the kids don't.

I always knew there were good men in the world. I just knew it. And now I got one who is all mine. Finally.

I'm sitting on my couch sipping on a glass of orange Kool-Aid and watching the Maury Povich show that I

TiVoed earlier while I was on the cash register at Wal-Mart. I hear a child holler out in play. I damn near drop my drink as I jump off the couch, but then I remember my kids are spending the night at my sister WooWoo's apartment over in Building 230. And there's no way my kids are outside at ten at night. Now, some of the other mothers at Bentley don't have rules and regulations for their children, but I have mine in check.

When I speak all five of my kids freeze and listen. They know Momma don't play. With five kids I have to check them before they gang up and check me.

I love my children. They are mine. All mine. Even though each one is a symbol of yet another one of my failed relationships, I never put my feelings for their fathers onto them. They would catch plenty of hell if I did.

I hear the metal door of our apartment swing open and slam shut. I look over my shoulder to see my oldest boy, Trey, stroll in. He's growing up so fast. Thirteen. Already taller than my short self. Voice cracking. Pubic hairs growing. Two or three hairs on his upper lip. Girls calling my phone all time of the night and day.

"Hey, Momma. I left my new game," he hollers over his shoulder on the way to his bedroom.

Just moments later he's strolling right back out. "'Night, Ma."

"Straight back to WooWoo's, Trey," I call over my shoulder to him.

"I am."

The metal door squeaks open and slams shut behind him.

"Lord, don't let him be like his no-good daddy," I whisper, my words echoing inside my glass just before I take a deep sip and get lost in my memories.

Sixteen years old. It's 1994. Me, my grandmother, and my baby sister are just a week strong staying in Bentley Manor. It's a Saturday and I had nothing on my mind but catching the eye of one of them hot boys sitting on the hood of an abandoned car in the parking lot. I always loved to get the attention of boys and usually I did. Petite, body tight, behind juicy in my jeans. I strolled right past them on my way to nowhere.

"Damn, cutie, let me holla at you for a sec."

That was the first thing Calvin Jefferson III, aka Junior, ever said to me. One picky-head seventeen-year-old Negro telling me I was fine and one month later I was cutting school and giving up my virginity on my rickety twin bed.

"I'm scared, Junior," I admitted, as he kissed my neck while we laid on the bed.

"I'm not gone hurt you, baby," he whispered in my ear.

I shivered but I wasn't cold. In fact my whole body was warm. Very warm. The spot between my legs throbbed and my heart raced like crazy.

Junior kissed his way up to my mouth and a moan escaped me as his tongue circled mine. I liked kissing him. It always felt so good and it always made me wet.

My heart swelled with love for him.

I gasped as he raised my Calvin Klein t-shirt over my head and looked down at my small plum-sized breasts in my white cotton bra. I closed my eyes as he raised the bra above my breasts. A cool draft made my nipples even harder.

"Damn," he swore.

Seconds later, for the first time in my life, I knew how it felt to have my titties sucked. I squirmed and cried out.

He stopped. "That hurt?"

I opened my eyes and looked at him. "It felt good," I admitted with a shy smile.

He raised up to pull his white tee over his head. He lay down flat and worked his pants and boxers down his skinny legs.

My mouth dropped as his thing stood straight up. Thick, dark as my favorite candy bar (Snickers), and hard as a bat. He want to put all that in me? I wondered.

He laughed at the expression on my face. "Big motherfucker, ain't it?"

I swallowed over a lump in my throat and nodded.

Junior shifted down to take my nipple into his mouth again.

I raised my hands to his woolly short 'fro, pressing his square face closer as he licked away at my nipples.

I didn't resist as he unbuttoned my jeans and worked them and my moist panties off. I even raised my hips to help him. His fingers touched my stuff.

"Damn, girl, you wet," he said, sounding a little in awe.

I tried to bury my face in his neck but he moved to squat on the bed between my open legs like he was looking for something he lost. "Stop, boy," I complained, trying to close them.

"Junior," I snapped.

He looked up at me and wiggled his thick eyebrows.

I reached down to pull him back up to lay beside me.

His head dipped and I felt his cool lips suck my stuff before his tongue circled some spot that caused my hips to fly up off the bed. My eyes bugged out and my heart slammed against my chest. My hands moved from his shoulders to the back of his head.

Another first. Junior was eating me out! I couldn't wait to tell my friend Red. It . . . felt . . .

I cried out as first my toes and then my thighs started to tingle. I closed my eyes and I felt like stars were bursting before me. My body trembled but I felt like I was floating on waves and free-falling through space all at once.

"Junior!" I cried out as he sucked harder.

I was still trembling like a fiend as he moved up my body and used his hand to start pushing his big thing in me. I pushed at his shoulder. "Wait, Junior, wait."

"Okay, let me know when," he said, leaning down to kiss me. He sucked my tongue like a lollipop.

I relaxed and enjoyed the feel of his kisses.

Junior raised his hips and pushed his thing inside me all at once. I cried out and nearly bit his tongue off. I felt nothing but pressure and the sting of pain. I started slapping him on his shoulders and all upside his head.

"Hey," he cried out, reaching up to hold my hands.

"Did you hear me say when?" I snapped with attitude.

"I'm sorry," he said. "Felt so good I couldn't wait."

He kissed me again and released my hands to rub my titties.

Okay, damn. That felt good.

I didn't even realize he had started to move his thing inside me at first. Between my legs was still tender and felt swollen but his kisses and the feel of his hands on my titties was good as hell.

I thought of the feel of his tongue between my legs and I actually moaned.

"Feel good, don't it?" he asked.

I wrapped my arms around him and even raised my legs to wrap around him, too.

I nodded. It did feel good.

His body got stiff above me and I looked up at him scared that I did something to hurt him.

"I'm cumming." He buried his face in my neck. With each pump of his hips he grunted. Once. Twice. Three times.

I felt the sticky wetness between my legs.

"I love you, Lexi," he said, his heart beating like a drum.

My heart swelled. "I love you, too."

Being in love and having sex opened up a whole new

world to me. The more we did it the better it got. I was hooked like an addict. And my drug brought me way more than I ever was looking for.

Six months after that first time my nana walked in on me taking a bath and knew the secret my baggy clothes had been hiding. Two months later I had a baby boy to take care of. Three months after that I caught Junior's cheating ass giving all that good dick to my enemy Basheemah. And then my cousin Kimmy. And then my best friend Red.

Not only was he cheating, he didn't even help with our son. Too much tears and too many damn fears so I kicked that d-a-w-g to the c-u-r-b.

I got on the grind and took care of my child. I ain't had no choice with my nana. My mother was somewhere cracked out and she left me and WooWoo on my grandmother to raise. Nana wasn't going to let me skip out on mine. I went to school and worked. When I turned eighteen almost ten years ago, I moved into my own one-bedroom apartment here in Bentley Manor. Ten damn years.

Luther's right, it's time for a change.

There is always some drama. The he-say-she-say. The women fighting each other because some man is sexing both of them. The drug hustling right in the parking lot. The addicts running around like roaches. The roaches running around no matter how clean you keep your damn apartment. The constant fight to keep mice from lounging up in your apartment like they pay the rent. The halls that can get pissy as hell at times.

And the walls are so thin. One night Luther and I got hot laying in bed listening to Mr. Miller give Mrs. Miller the best that he got in the apartment above us. We all came at the same time. A damn shame. Okay, it was one hell of a good time for Luther and me but it still was a damn shame.

On top of that I did the right thing (some say it would be the stupid thing) and added Luther to my lease so that easy eleven dollars a month I used to pay went up to over two hundred. Not that two hundred is the highest rent in the world, but it irks me that we one of the few paying full rent. Still, where the hell would we find a four-bedroom for two hundred a month? Nowhere. So for now Bentley Manor it is.

And then there's Junior and his wife, Molly the hungry-hungry hippo, living in the building across from me. Poor thing doesn't know a blessed thing about Junior sexing everything up in Bentley Manor. Junior's still a no-good, always begging for pussy, screwing any woman with her legs open, wannabe rapper, half-ass-child-support paying, fat-white-chick-for-a-wife having, no good son of a bitch. She married a stone-cold whore and couldn't buy a clue if someone gave her a million dollars.

And this isn't gossip.

Junior's always trying to get some more of me, but he

might as well get over it because Luther's the man for me. Over the years I have given in to the occasional Junior booty-call special now and then. A sister has needs and he knows how to lay it down. Sue me. But those days are over now that I have Luther.

"Maury, I'm one thousand percent sure Quentin is my baby daddy! He's the only man I been with. And all I know is soon as we hear these results I'm suing his no-good ass for child support."

I focus my eyes at the television and shake my head in shame at some young black girl clasping her hands, crying and rocking with her mouth balled up. Her body moves back and forth in the chair like she's on a rocking horse.

Now see, I wouldn't ever carry myself on Maury's show trying to find out who the father of my kids . . . especially if I wasn't sure. I'd hate to see her shame if it isn't his baby. Just like all the rest she'll go crying like a fool while she ran offstage. One girl was up to sixteen different men getting tested for paternity—and she still didn't know!

I use the remote to turn up the volume. I'm on edge on my seat like these is *my* damn test results.

"With a result of 99.99 percent, Quentin, you are . . . NOT the father. . . ."

Sure enough, Quentin did the running man, the audience exploded with oohs and aahs, and the dead-wrong baby momma goes screeching off the stage.

I hear the metal front door of the apartment open and then close again. I look over my shoulder this time to see my husband, Luther, stroll in. I'm happy to see him. Big Friday night, not quite ten and he's already home after hanging out with his boys after work. He's still in his black and gray mechanic's uniform but there's no mistaking his Ginuwine-like good looks. I shift over so that he can plop down onto the sofa next to me. "Hey, baby."

"Whaddup."

"You want something to drink or eat?" I ask, falling into my role of a good wife.

"Naw, but I know something else I want," he says, leaning over to playfully bite one of my itty-bitty titties through the white wifebeater I had on.

With five kids we never have time to do the do unless it's in the bedroom at night with the TV blaring—no need for them to know Momma makes they new daddy holler like a bitch.

"Where the kids?" he asks, putting out his Newport cigarette.

"I sent them to WooWoo's for the night." I drop my panties and raise my jean skirt up to my waist as he drops his pants.

I climb onto his lap, the back of my thighs pressed to the top of his. With his thick dark lips he sucks at my titties. I reach between us to stroke his dick slowly with a tight grip just the way he likes it.

If nothing else, Luther has a tongue that reached his chin and he knows what to do with it.

"Yes, Luther, suck 'em," I moan, raising one hand to press the back of his smooth, bald head closer. I shiver as I feel my clit swell with life. He circles the whole breast wetly like he's starved as my heated pussy moistens from my own juices.

I arch my back causing my long weaved hair to tickle the middle as he cups both smooth, firm breasts with his hands and sucks the thickened nipples at one time.

I'm ready to fuck. Horny. Hot. And ready to cum. "Gimme that dick," I whisper into the heat between us.

His hands move down to grip my ass tightly as he lifts me up and slides my pussy down onto him. "Want that motherfucker, don't you?" he asks, resting his head on the back of the sofa to look up at me.

This is where I take the lead, leaning toward him and circling my hips to bring the hard shaft of his dick against my slick, throbbing clit.

"Damn, girl. Damn," he whispers against my chest.

I feel his heart beating like crazy and so is mine.

My pussy got wetter. His dick got harder.

I pick up the pace, working my walls as I ride him fast and furious like I'm about to lose a race.

I cry out as I feel my nut building all in my thighs and stomach as I close my eyes and ride the waves.

"Best dick you ever had?" he asks.

"Yes," I lie, shifting his hands up to my breasts for him to squeeze and massage my nipples while I cum—just the way I like.

"Cum on this dick."

I holler out roughly. It feel like my pussy explodes as my heart hammers in my chest and my throat gets dry from gasping for air.

"I'm cumming," I moan.

"Me too," he roars, his grip on my ass tightening.

"You big dick son of a bitch," I lie as we cum together. His nut fills me as mine soaks him.

That's why I like to ride. No matter what kinda dick you're working with a woman can—and will—always come when she's on top.

No, Luther isn't the best lover I had. He's the worst.

No, Luther's dick isn't the biggest I ever had. It's the smallest.

For me, sex is the one weak spot in our marriage. Luther knows nothing about different positions. Sometimes he cums so quick it's over before it ever starts. Besides that tongue he doesn't have nothing else going for him in bed, but I refuse to put my pussy before my heart anymore.

4

Devani

"Ah shit, Dee!" Tyrik jumps from the bed with his big-ass dick springing free from this bitch's mouth.

"Fuck this," I snap, and I swear to God I launch into Tyrik's room like a goddamn NASA space shuttle. Before I know it, I have one fist of silky hair and the other fist pounding all over Mami's little ass. These Latina bitches make me sick and if you ask me they're the biggest threat on our niggas with their white-girl hair and black-chick attitudes.

I'll beat this bitch back to the border before I let her take my spot. Case you don't know—I'm like my momma. I love good weed, a good dick, and good fight, too.

"Rufus, get the fuck in here!" Tyrik shouts before locking his arms around my waist; but before he lifts me off J-Ho, I grab hold of one of her gold loop earrings and snatch that son of a bitch clean off.

I smile in satisfaction as the bitch's scream fills the room. In the next second, she springs toward me but not before Rufus barges in and plucks her out the air as if she weighs nothing.

"Yo le mataré, puta! Yo le mataré!"

"I like to see you try," I snap back. Bentley Manor is filled with all kinds of niggas, you know. Black, white, and Hispanic—one doesn't live around them without picking up a few things.

"Get her out of here!" Tyrik yells at his cousin, because he's quickly losing his grip on me.

I want one more good lick at the bitch. I squirm and wiggle my way free and then launch another attack before Rufus is able to clear the door.

The heifa grabs a good hunk of my weave, but I knuckle up and bust her nose wide open.

"Goddamn it, Dee!" Tyrik wrestles me away again. "Calm the fuck down. Calm the fuck down."

Ain't this nigga got some nerve? "Calm the fuck down?" I turn on him and smack him dead in his mouth. "What the fuck is your dick doin' in her mouth, huh?" I hit him again and then the next thing I know I'm wailing on him for all it's worth and daring this fucker to hit me back.

If he did, then it would really be on in this motherfucker. I'm talking about some "NFL player killed in his own home—film at eleven" type of shit.

Our fight becomes a wrestling match. We're knocking

over lamps and tables and the only thing I can think of is trying to hurt this nigga as much as he's hurt me. How he's gonna leave me standing at Bentley Manor waiting for him while he's throwing a big-ass party and shit? Why didn't he tell me about the trade?

I'm grabbing, smacking, and scratching the hell out of Tyrik and I'm realizing he's ripping my clothes off. When he tries to kiss me I chomp down on his thick lips for all it's worth and draw blood.

"Bitch!"

I receive my first hard slap across the face and like I say I don't play that shit. I'm now tryna kill this motherfucker, but Tyrik Jefferson has a few tricks up his sleeve. Next thing I know, he ties me down to the goddamn bedpost and this nigga is trying to rip my left nipple off.

I scream and try to buck him off of me, but he stays on like I'm some damn rodeo ride.

"Come on, Dee. You know you want this shit," Tyrik snaps. "Ain't that why you came here? Huh?"

"Get the fuck off me!"

His answer to that is to cram his big-ass hand into my soppy wet pussy. Hell, I can't help it if this shit turns me on. Anger is passion, too.

"Ah, now that's what I'm talking about." He pumps his hand in and out. I'm fighting but loving what he's doing. My pussy is slurping and smacking while I'm gritting my teeth and rolling my eyes.

"You hear that, baby?" Tyrik asks. "Your pussy is all hot and ready for me, ain't it?"

"Fuck you!"

"Ah, Dee. Why you been holding this shit out on me, huh? I've been rubbing up on you for three months and I haven't so much as sniffed this shit yet." His eyes widen as if he's just had his first idea. Tyrik repositions himself after locking down my legs and literally takes a good whiff of my coochee.

"Now that's what I call some prime pussy."

He winks at me above my sexy trimmed Mohawk and then dives into me like he's at an all-you-can-eat buffet. Fuckin' delicious. If I'd known this nigga was this skilled I would've been feeding him morning, noon, and night . . . and a few midnight snacks.

Before Tyrik, I didn't know nothin' about football and to be honest, I'm still a little shady on the details. The only important thing to know is that Tyrik makes some serious paper. It doesn't hurt that he's also fine as hell. Six foot four, about two hundred and twenty pounds, and skin the color of a Hershey's dark chocolate bar.

Hmmm-hmmm-hm.

All that shit is good, but the first thing I noticed about Tyrik that fateful day at Gold's Gym was his smile. He had dimples the size of raisins on both cheeks and his teeth were so white and straight I doubt he's ever had a cavity in his life.

Yet, Tyrik insists there is another part of him that I don't know about. He brags about a violent past and being from the street. Usually he's popping off this nonsense when he's hanging with his paid entourage and trying to downplay the silver spoon hanging from his mouth. How hard can you be when your father is a black reverend in the Bible Belt?

No one buys the act. Tyrik is as hard as Will Smith. Hell, Tyrik even had a one-hit rap song a few years back, trying to prove his bad-boy image. Shaquille O'Neal would've squashed his ass in a head-to-head rap contest.

No, my man isn't a hard-ass and he wouldn't last a weekend on my side of the tracks, but that's not why I love him. Okay, maybe I'm not in love with him. Hell, I don't love anybody.

Love makes women weak.

Tyrik Jefferson, a clean-cut, Bible-thumping, suburban momma's boy, serves one purpose: to get me the hell up out of Bentley Manor.

"Oh, shit! Oh, shit!" I'm cummin' all over the place and his tongue and lips are still smacking away. He spreads my ass cheeks and slides in his thick finger.

I got a freak on my hands.

Just as I'm about to douse his face with another orgasm, the door bursts open, music fills the room, and Junior spills inside with a couple of giggling hoochies locked on each arm.

I scream, because I'm naked and I have my legs spread as far as the eye can't see.

"What the fuck, Junior?" Tyrik shouts, not bothering to get out of bed. "What the hell are you doing in here?"

"Sorry, cuz," Junior smirks. "I thought this room was empty. My bad." His hands slither down the women's asses and give them a hard squeeze, but Junior takes a long look at my gaping pussy and licks his lips.

Fuck, I grow even wetter, remembering that black marble of a dick I pumped out in the car. Can I even fit something that big inside of me without requiring a visit to the emergency room?

The way the women gaze at the bed, for a sec, I'm afraid Tyrik is about to issue an invitation for the group to join us.

"Tyrik," I hiss and try to kick.

"Y'all get the fuck out of here." He waves them off, disgruntled for not having a full-out freak party.

"All right," Junior says, directing the women toward the door. "Your loss." He winks at me. "For now."

My pussy throbs at his veiled, yet bold, invitation as he closes the door.

"Now where were we?" Tyrik asks, turning back to me and licking his lips.

"You were going to let them join us," I accuse.

"What? No I wasn't."

Bullshit. Right then and there while he's flashing those

big dimples at me, I know I have to up my game if I want to keep him.

"I don't want another nigga eating this good pussy." He dips his head low again, but I no longer want an appetizer. Thinking about Junior's big, black dick, I need the real thing—Now!

"Fuck me," I command harshly. No tongue can satisfy the ache I'm experiencing now. "Fuck me, goddamn it." I'm bucking, struggling, and pulling and about to snap off my wrists.

"All right, baby. All right." Tyrik chuckles and reaches over to the nightstand and opens the top drawer. "I'm going to hook you up, baby girl. I'm going to hook you up real good."

At this point, I'm sure I'm going to come the moment he sticks it in.

He removes a condom and a wave of disappointment stabs at my heart. I squirm my ass against his rock-hard dick. It's a good size, but nowhere near as thick and beautiful as what his cousin is packin'. Yet at this point I'll settle for anything hard.

I hear the rip of the condom packet. "Do you have to, baby? I want to be able to feel you inside of me."

Tyrik pauses. For a brief moment, I see he's tempted.

"I'm clean, baby. I swear. I just want to feel you." I'm wiggling for all it's worth, but Tyrik banishes the temptation with a firm shake of his head.

"I can't take no chances knockin' you up, baby girl." He slips the condom on in one quick swoosh and then jacks my legs up to Jesus and plunges deliciously into my pussy.

Any lingering thoughts of Junior vanish as Tyrik proves he knows how to handle his equipment. He beats every square inch of my pussy into submission and I can hardly breathe while wave after wave of ecstasy crashes through me.

At one point, I fold like a burrito with my knees tucked near my ears and Tyrik has to do deep knee squats to fuck me in the ass. I've lost count of how many orgasms I've had, but I can now smell my own scent and his growing musk. It's a potent aphrodisiac and I'm determined to stay in the game as long as this playa is on the field.

My wrist free, I peel off his cream-filled condom and then lick and suck his glazed dick and balls as though my life depends on it. In a warped way, it does. Tyrik whimpers, squirms, and calls on his Savior when his final orgasm hits and I swallow every drop like the sex soldier I am. After two hours, a swollen jaw, and a tore-up pussy, Tyrik Jefferson finally rolls his big, muscular ass over and goes to sleep.

I, on the other hand, prop up against a stack of pillows, light a blunt and contemplate my next move.

5

Molly

White trash. Coon whore. Nigger lover.

I've heard it all. I wish I could say that sticks and stones may break my bones but words will never hurt me. However, anyone who's ever been called anything knows that's a lie. Words kill you softly.

The sad part is I chose this path. The moment I said, "I do" to my husband, Calvin Jefferson III, aka Junior. But you know what? I would do it all again because I love my man.

That's right. I love him.

All these black bitches can kiss my ass, talking that shit about white women stealing their good black brothers. All is fair in love and war. When I first hooked up with Junior, I thought: *What the hell? It's the twenty-first century.*

I quickly learned that little has changed in Jim Crow's

South, at least as far as attitudes go. There's no lynching, but I have a feeling the desire still crosses the minds of the overflowing redneck population.

My father included.

No sooner than the image of my father surfaces in my mind do I feel a sudden sting of tears. My once doting father has owned and operated the number one Ford dealership in the Southeast for the last twenty years.

Right up until the moment he discovered me having sex with Junior in my bedroom, I'd always thought of my father as an honest, fair, and caring man.

Sure, any father would've hit the roof after catching their seventeen-year-old baby girl in bed with a boy, but the monster my father turned into the moment his gaze took in Junior's coal-black complexion and his long Mandingo cock was like nothing I've ever witnessed.

Back then, Junior used to pack a hot .45 in his baggy jeans. To me, it added to his dangerous street vibe and gave me bragging rights about dating a rap gangster. However, that night, Junior's .45 didn't stand a chance against my father's power rifle. Junior knew it, so he didn't bother making a grab for it before diving out my bedroom window.

Despite my begging and screaming, my father chased after him. For a full hour I remained sobbing on the floor of my pink princess room, listening to the occasional shotgun blast. I just knew my father had killed Junior, the love of my life—my soul mate.

Instead, when he returned to the house he'd nearly killed me.

White trash. Coon whore. Nigger lover.

That was the first time I'd heard those words. They were shouted with venom each time his fist crashed against my ribs, jaw, lips, and eyes. I had also felt the sharp point of my father's favorite steel-toe cowboy boots at every unprotected part of my body.

I begged him to stop, but in the end all I could do was curl into a fetal position and try to protect myself the best I could. Even then I wondered if Junior had gotten away or whether he was lying in a pool of blood somewhere on the property.

How did two kids from the opposite sides of the railroad tracks meet? Believe it or not—at a downtown Taco Bell. I know it's funny and not nearly romantic, but I like to think it was fate. Before the night Junior asked if I wanted any special sauce with my order, I'd never given a thought about dating a black man, let alone falling in love with one.

But I did and paid one hell of a price.

That night, my mother . . . well, let's just say that there was really nothing she could do but wait until my father grew exhausted kicking and punching me. Afterward he declared I was dead to him and once he left the house, she managed to get me dressed and take me to the emergency room.

There, when the doctors inquired about my extensive

injuries, my mother coerced me to lie. The next thing I knew I was filing a false police report about being raped.

It made me sick to turn something so beautiful into something so ugly. I gave a generic description of a black man who'd supposedly raped me and to my horror—because of my father's status in the community—the police sketch was splashed across the local news for three days.

A few innocent black men were hauled in for questioning and then forced into a lineup where I pretended to be confused and couldn't make a positive ID.

After that, reporters moved on to the next groundbreaking news story and I was left alone.

To my amazement, my father calmed down—well, after Pastor Robinson spent a week praying over my soul and I was forced to repent for the sins I had committed with my body. Before God and family I vowed never to lay with a disgusting black serpent again.

It was a vow I couldn't and wouldn't keep.

Despite the constant check-ins my father required, I grew creative with my hookups with Junior. I wasn't going to stop seeing him for nothing in the world. Besides, his record deal with So-So Def was all but a done deal—according to his NFL cousin, Tyrik.

All we had to do was hold on a few weeks or months tops. But that isn't how it played out. Nothing went according to plan.

One night, when I was supposed to be spending the

night at my best friend Kimberly's house, my father followed me to Bentley Manor. This time he fully intended to kill both Junior and me. However, he miscalculated by rolling into the projects in the middle of the night, thinking he was about to kill himself a nigger.

He barely got out of Bentley Manor alive, but this time I really was dead to him. It was a year before my mother started talking to me again—but only secretly.

I lost everything: my parents, friends, and even my college fund. I wanted to be a journalist—the future Katie Couric. Now, I don't know. Maybe with the advance money Junior will eventually get with his record deal I can attend Perimeter Community College.

Sighing, I stop peeking out the closed slits of the venetian blinds and glance around the small cramped quarters of our one-bedroom apartment in Bentley Manor. I wrinkle my nose at the sight of the plaid hand-me-down sofa Junior and I picked up at the Salvation Army. It, along with everything else, was supposed to be temporary.

Temporary is now three years and counting.

"It's all going to be worth it in the end," I remind myself. The words are hollow tonight like they are every night Junior stays out late. I'm not going to trip. I know my man is working late at the studio, trying to get his hustle on.

I trust Junior and all these whispering haters can kiss my lily-white ass—and that includes his baby momma, Lexi, who lives across the way. That bitch isn't fooling me, switching around with her five damn kids and all them different daddies. I know she wants Junior back, but I'll go Jerry Springer on her ghetto ass if she crosses one toe out of line.

I hate the fact she has something I seem to be incapable of giving Junior. Babies. It isn't for lack of trying. Junior says it doesn't matter and that he doesn't want any more children anyway, but I'm confident he will feel differently once our baby arrives—if a baby ever arrives. I went off the pill over a year ago.

With each prompt menstrual cycle, I can't help but think about the night of my reported rape and wonder about the damage those steel-toed cowboy boots may have caused to my internal organs. It's either that or perhaps the fifty pounds I've put on since we've gotten married.

I'm no longer the perfect blond, blue-eyed cheerleader with a slamming body. I'm soft and round, but Junior has never uttered a single complaint. Now tell me that's not love.

Since I know Junior is capable of producing a child, that can only mean I'm the problem. I'll give it a couple more months before I go to the clinic to get checked out. I want beautiful brown babies—the more the better. Maybe I'll get a little more respect from the people around here.

But I doubt it.

Racism runs wild on both sides of the fence.

Despite my pep talk and nightly affirmations, I cross

the room and pick up the cordless phone with the itch to dial Junior's cell. He'd promised to come home early tonight but the last thing I want to do is nag him to death.

I, at least, want to know whether he dropped off the rent payment. We're already two months behind and the last thing I want is to call my mother for help again. I hate to ask and my mother hates doing things behind my father's back.

My baby sister, Shannon, is my father's new princess and he now goes on about his life as though I've never existed. And that's fine with me.

White trash. Coon whore. Nigger lover. And proud of it.

6

Aisha

I softly sing along with Keyshia Cole as I head north up Piedmont. I pull to a stop at a red light and double-check my makeup in the rearview mirror. A-town is all the way live as people move up and down the streets, but I don't pay no mind to who's who because I'm headed to Phipps Plaza for some serious shopping. Nothing like Nordstrom and Saks Fifth Avenue to help ease the my-man-is-on-lock blues.

The sun glints off the two-carat solitaire of my engagement ring. I swallow back the guilt I feel. I'm out and about, living life to the fullest and my man, my lover, my husband, is locked down in a cell.

"Damn, I miss that nigga," I admit, the look in my eyes shifting to sadness in the mirror.

And I mean I really miss everything about his ass. His smile. His touch. His dick. His scent. His body. His warmth. His protection.

Boom . . . boom . . . boom.

The heavy bass of a car system jars me from my thoughts. A-town's own Dem Franchise Boyz '06 "snap" anthem "Lean Wit It, Rock Wit It" is echoing all through my car. A badass, milk-white '68 Cadillac sitting on shiny twenty-two-inch rims pulls to the light beside me. I'm shocked as fuck to see my husband's friend Kaseem leaned back behind the wheel with its funky Gucci logo interior.

Damn, Kaseem got a new whip? Shit, he was just pushing a Tahoe when I saw him last week.

He turns his head, catches sight of me and his face frames right up with a smile as he leans forward to turn the music down. "Whaddup, Aisha?"

"Look like you what's up. Nice ride," I tell him, ignoring the car horns behind me blaring as the light turned green.

"Yo, pull over. Let me holla at you for a sec."

I make a right at the light, park my car, and wait 'til Kaseem can pull over. I hop out my Benz knowing Maleek would be proud that I still dress and present myself as his queen even while he is looking at a bid.

Kaseem walks up to me, his jeans nearly falling off his narrow hips, his white Air Force 1s looking fresh out the box, his white tee crisp as a new hundred-dollar bill and his jewelry gleaming like a motherfucker. He hugs me to him and I'm surrounded by the scent of Tommy cologne. The same cologne Maleek wears.

For one precious second I hug Kaseem back, inhaled deeply of his scent and imagine he's my Maleek.

But it doesn't work. Kaseem is a sorry-ass substitute. Too thin and too tall. For me no man can compare to my Maleek.

Tears fill my eyes but I blink them away as I step back from him—or at least I try to step back. Kaseem's arms are still wrapped tightly around my body like he tryna mold me into him.

"I get to see Maleek every Friday," I tell him. That's a signal and a half for his ass to get the fuck up off his friend's woman. If that don't work I am more than ready to give his ass a nice two-piece and I ain't talkin' 'bout no chicken.

Luckily for his nuts and his grill he lets me go.

"How that nigga doin'?" he asks, looking down at me with squinted eyes as he crosses his arms over his chest.

"No worries. Our lawyers working hard on his case. So you know it ain't nothing but a small thing." I speak with more confidence than I feel.

"No doubt. No doubt. I would visit him but you know I got a record."

Convicted felons ain't allowed to visit those on lock. Guess the government figures they ass should feel blessed not to be in that motherfucker anymore. "Maleek know what's up."

Kaseem reaches in the front pocket of his jeans and pulls

out a rubber-band-wrapped wad of money big enough to choke a elephant. Quickly, I calculate he got at least five grand in twenties, fifties, and hundreds, but I don't get excited or start salivating and shit because I rolled with a nigga like Maleek.

That five grand is chump change up against the tens of thousands we've fucked on.

"We're straight for money, Kaseem," I tell him as he counts off some bills that still hold the curve of the roll.

He laughs and winks at me. "Oh, trust I know Maleek straight and this grand ain't shit but my way of lettin' him I know I ain't forgot a nigga, that's all."

I hesitate. I know Maleek wouldn't want nobody thinking he needed them sending him money like he's hurtin'. But if Kaseem's just tryna to stay in Maleek's good graces then who am I to block him. I take the money out his outstretched hand.

Kaseem peels off more bills. "And this is for you, just to let you know I got you on my mind, too."

My eyes dart down to the bills and then up to his face to catch him eyeing my size 36DDs with a suggestive lick of his lips. WTF? "No thanks, Kaseem. My husband laced me with enough money and dick to keep me straight 'til he gets home."

He has the audacity to look offended. "Come on, Aisha, I ain't even trying to play you like no two-bit ho who would fuck around on my boy."

"I know you see it," I tell him with much attitude.

Kaseem shoves the money back into his pocket. "Don't get me wrong. You fine enough to make a nigga sweat you, but I didn't mean to come off that way."

I nod and smile. "As long as all the niggas know that while my king is on lock, Aisha Cummings's pussy is on lock, too. Ya heard me?"

He laughed with the diamond grille on the bottom row of his teeth gleaming. "I heard you. I heard you. Tell Maleek I said to keep his head up." He gives me another look before he turn and strolls back to his whip. Soon the motor purrs to life. The *boom . . . boom . . . boom* makes the street vibrate beneath my Jimmy Choos. He honks twice before he whizzes past me up Lenox, causing my skirt to fly up.

I ain't have no doubt in my mind his eyes is watching my thick-ass thighs in his rearview mirrors.

Two thousand dollars and four hours later I drive away from Phipps Plaza. I definitely downsized my usual shopping sprees. It used to be nothing for me to blow five grand. Maleek would lace me with one or two outfits and maybe a new designer purse. I'm proud of myself for cutting my shopping budget in half.

Shit, Maleek encourages me to rep him to the fullest and I love how he likes the finer things in life. He showed me the finer things in the first place and let me know straight up this is what I deserve. Yeah, we live in that fucked-up, bullshit-ass Bentley Manor but we drive a nice car (which thank God Maleek put in my mom's name or the Feds woulda snatched it up), we have a low-income apartment but it's filled with luxury (leather furniture, top of the line electronics, 1,000-count sheets, and a $3,000 mattress), we eat at nice-ass restaurants (sometimes we couldn't even read the damn French menus), and we rent luxury suites at the best hotels just to blaze trees, relax, and be together.

I look out my windshield at the Ritz-Carlton Buckhead. It is *the* hotel in Atlanta. Wealthy and famous niggas stay here when they're up in A-town. And this is our spot.

I don't know when my ass decided to steer my vehicle toward the Ritz-Carlton, but I did. I pull to a stop by the valet, grab my purse as I climb out the car and smooth my skirt over my hips. It's February, the end of winter, and the air is cool at night. Goose bumps race up my bare legs.

I hurry inside the hotel lobby and soon I'm surrounded by the luxury that is so different from Bentley Manor and Hollywood Court. The difference between Bankhead and Buckhead. Without him I would have never seen—shit, enjoyed—this side of life. I wouldn't have ever known that this life is the life this badass bitch is meant to live.

❖   ❖   ❖

"Baby, Momma would die if she could see this." I pressed my face to the glass and looked out at Buckhead at night. We were just twenty minutes away from our hood but the suite in this top-notch hotel was a gazillion miles away in wealth, class, and style.

Shee-it, my baby was a straight baller and on our wedding night there was no other way to do it but big. We were married at the courthouse that morning and that afternoon we threw a helluva barbeque in the hood to celebrate. Plenty of good food and good liquor. We had a ball and everything was all good but when Maleek grabbed my hand and told me "let's ride," I was more than ready to follow him anywhere. I just never guessed this suite would be my surprise.

"You like it, baby?" he asked, coming up behind me to wrap his strong arm around my waist.

"Damn real I like it. I only seen shit like this in the movies or in videos."

"Get used to it, baby." He turned my slim, trim, and sexy-as-hell body around and pressed me up against that glass. I looked up into his fine-ass face and twisted my fingers in his dreads to pull it toward mine.

"Thank you, baby," I whispered, looking into his eyes as I traced his thick lips with my tongue. He tasted like weed, Crown Royal, and promises of a good dicking down.

Maleek moved his hands up to squeeze that juicy ass of mine that he loved so much. Not that my ass was all he loved. My looks. My bomb-ass pussy. Me period. He loved me. This *motherfucker was mine. My husband. My lover. My man. My baller.*

And nothing or nobody was gone to take him from me.

And I believed that all the way up to the day I got the call telling me Maleek got busted. I honestly believed nothing or no one would—or could—come between us.

"Can I buy you a drink?"

I turn my head to see some sucker-ass Opie-fucking-Cunningham-looking fool smiling in my face. I start to cuss him the fuck out for trying to play me but Maleek always taught me when you're on their turf you have to chill on the type of shit you would say or do like we home in the hood. So instead of telling this cornball to roll out my face before I roll on him, I just say, "No thanks."

"You look like you could use some company for the night," Opie says, with a friendly smile.

What the fuck?

I give him the nastiest ghetto/country girl Bankhead stare. He disappears quicker than a yard full of hot boys when somebody hollers out 5-0.

As I watch him walk away I notice quite a few eyes on me. Shit, I look good so I'm used to the hot stares of men and the even cooler stares of women. But here in this place with these mostly pale-ass faces and without my chocolate warrior by my side I feel hella out of place.

It was stupid to come here. What made me think coming here would make me feel closer to my husband. I turn and throw on my aviator shades as I leave the hotel lobby. I quickly pay the valet and soon I am turning off Piedmont and eating up the drive to west Atlanta.

I use my thumb to work my diamond ring around my finger as Bentley Manor comes up before me. I take in the run-down buildings. Women and they badass kids with no man in sight. Old people who done gave the fuck up on life and gonna die right up in this project. The hot boys chillin' like they ain't have shit else to do 'cause they ain't have shit else to do. Motherfuckers ain't making no real money. They asses happy for enough cash to buy a new pair of kicks and a fucking jersey.

And their customers: junkies dumb enough to get hooked on that shit. The women who look like damn shadows of themselves willing to suck and fuck they way to another crack high. The men who let themselves get treated like less than men—some of they cracked-out ass willing to suck and fuck these homo-thugs on the DL. Yeah, these heads' money keep smart businessmen like Maleek in the loot to keep smart bitches like me in the shit I love.

I don't belong here but with Maleek on lock I ain't going anywhere anytime soon.

I turn my gleaming Benz into the parking lot and as always all eyes are on me. I don't even bother speaking to nobody even though some of them throw they hand up at me. Fuck 'em. I park my car and get out. I push my shades up sending my long—and 100 percent real—hair back from my face as I walk to the rear to get my shopping bags from the trunk.

I know them niggas behind me is talkin' about me, wishing they can be my man, wishing they can afford to send me on shoppin' sprees, wishing they can get up in all this good pussy. Yeah, okay, what the fuck ever.

I close my trunk and use the remote to activate the alarm. *Beep-beep.*

I turn and walk into my building, jumping back as I nearly bump into somebody coming out the building.

"Whaddup, Aisha?" Junior says around the lit blunt in his mouth.

I roll my eyes. Junior: resident male jump-off of Bentley Manor. If a woman is looking for some good dick on the low then Junior's the trick to call. He's worse than some skank 'round here fuckin' like it's going out of style. He's a bold motherfucker though 'cause he's the only one who even tries to step to me knowing Maleek would sing they ass to sleep with his nine. I look at him with much attitude from head to toe. His clothes: typical jeans, hoodie, and Air Force 1s. His face: cute enough—especially if he does something with them bushy-ass brows. His haircut: in need of a trim but passable. His situation: married to some low-level white bitch. Everything about this nigga says he ain't even on my level. So why the hell he all up in my space? Like he can compete with Maleek.

"Hey, Junior." I move past him and he steps in my path.

He reaches out to grab my hand. "Aisha, why you be trippin'? You know how much I like you."

I pull it out his grasp and put my hand on my purse ready to reach for my box cutter if this nigga tried to flex. Not that I'm scared of him. He's harmless. The only things on his mind is fuckin' pussy, blazin' trees, and faking the funk 'bout his bullshit rhymes. Still a bitch should always be prepared. "Junior, don't play with me."

"Check this out," he says, wiggling them brows as he looks down at himself.

I look before I can catch myself and my eyes get big as shit when he makes his dick jump up in his pants. And that motherfucker is down by his thigh.

Okay, it has been long time since I had a Maleek special and I have to admit this nigga makes my pussy lips jump to life. My nipples got hard like pebbles and the seat of my lace panties is moist as hell. The stairwell gets hot. *I'm* hot up in that stairwell (shit, I'm human). I heard that motherfucker could throw that dick like a pro. But none of that ain't have shit to do with me.

"Nigga, you stupid as hell," I tell him, walking up the stairs slow and easy like I own the apartment complex. Junior and his big dick are already forgotten.

I walk into my apartment and drop my bags by the door. I kick off my shoes and plop down on the custom-made leather sofa. With the remote I turn on the flat screen and flip through the channels. I stop on a show about real estate and I think about the house Maleek and me will have in one of them ritzy-ass neighborhoods.

My eyes drop to our big 11 x 17 wedding photo on the coffee table. I smile and touch Maleek's face. Our time is coming and I can't wait for Maleek to get out so we can get the fuck up outta here.

7

Lexi

That Wednesday morning I get up early as hell excited about it being Valentine's Day. The skies are cloudy and the news called for rain, but nothing can kill my good mood. Luther and I always go all the way out on V-Day. I can't wait to see my gift this year. Maybe a gold charm bracelet like last year or a nice Juicy Couture outfit like the year before that.

To be honest it isn't about the gifts for me. I know we're saving for our house and even if he doesn't give me nothing but a card I will be happy. Plus, I'm excited enough about my plans for him. Since I lucked up and have the day off from work, I'm going all out.

A nice T-bone steak dinner with all the works (Oh, I throw down in more places than just the bedroom), red satin sheets and candles for the bedroom, flower petals for the bath I will give him, chocolate scented massage oil, a nice piece of black lingerie for me and satin boxers for him, whipped cream (to go on the strawberries and me), champagne (it isn't Dom or Cristal but that bottle of Andres will do just fine), and last, my old lady friend Miz Cleo from the building in the rear agreed to watch the kids for me since my sister WooWoo has her own plans for the night.

I take a quick shower and throw on my red velour sweat suit. I have a few more errands to run for tonight and I want to get an early start. I grab my short leather jacket and walk out the bedroom looking through my purse for my keys.

The sweet scent hit me before I even look up and see the glass vase filled with a dozen beautiful red roses. For me everything else in the apartment fades to black: the nice neat and warm decor of our small living room, the dozens and dozens of pictures of the kids neatly arranged on the walls, the bright white and green decor of the kitchen. All I see is flowers.

I step into the kitchen and pick up the card leaning against the vase. The smile on my face spreads like melted butter. "I will always love you, Lexi. Luther," I read out loud. Short. Sweet. To the point. But it speaks volumes for me. Luther is a man's man. A southern boy. He's not a thug but he isn't one of those men with flowery words. For me his actions speak a whole lot more.

I open the front door to leave the apartment and find

Junior standing there with his hand still raised to knock. I release a heavy breath and cross my arms over my chest. "What do you want, Junior?" I ask, sounding tired and aggravated. Humph. I am tired of his butt aggravating me.

He wiggles those crazy brows as he breezes past me to walk into the apartment. He smells of some cologne and weed. "I'm on my way to the studio and decided to stop by and holla at you first. Happy Valentine's Day, Sexy Lexi."

I let the front door swing closed and turn to him. "Yeah, I remember the last Valentine's Day we shared together. Do you?"

It was 1996, and I was eighteen and living in my small one-bedroom apartment in Bentley Manor. I only have a bedroom set, a 19-inch television set, and a sofa my nana bought for me from the secondhand store, but it was good enough for me and my baby boy Trey (Calvin Jefferson III). The rent was based on my income (welfare) so I was good to go between my cheap rent, my food stamps, the Medicaid, my check, and my child support (I needed a source of income to get the apartment so I applied for welfare and the state sued Junior for child support).

I'll never forget how pissed Junior was when he got served his papers, especially since we had started kicking it again a few months ago. With us both living in the same apartment complex it was inevitable that we hooked up again. We wasn't living together—even though I offered—but we were definitely back on.

He said the right words. Made the right apologies. Told me he loved me more than anything. Said he wanted his family.

I gave him another chance. I believed him. I loved him. We were good together.

So I had my own place. My son. My man.

I was in the kitchen singing along with Monica's Miss Thang *CD on my little boom box and frying some steak and onions for dinner. It was Valentine's Day and I planned a sweet romantic dinner for me, Junior, and Trey. We were celebrating it together as a family. Later, after we put Trey to sleep we would celebrate on a whole different level.*

Junior had went to the mall to get my present and I was waiting on him to get back. I looked at the cheap Dollar General clock hanging on the white wall of my kitchen. It was three o'clock.

I turned the steaks on low and slid the tossed salad into the fridge. I laid on my lumpy couch next to Trey taking a nap.

Three o'clock became four and then five and then six. No Junior. I beeped him. He didn't call back. I called his friends and nobody seen him. I kept looking out the window to see if he was hanging out front but Junior was nowhere to be seen.

Night turned into morning and he never showed. I went from anger to worry until I felt like I was going crazy. I cried. I paced. I threw out the dinner. I regretted throwing out the dinner. I woke Trey up just to hug and love on him. I rocked Trey back to sleep because I was too aggravated to take his tears.

Around seven I pulled on some jeans and one of Junior's hoodies before I dressed my sleepy baby. I was gonna leave Trey with Nana and borrow her Lincoln to go looking for him. I wanted answers.

And I got them. Unfortunately.

I had just turned the Lincoln out the complex when I saw a green Escort hatchback pulled to the curb up the street to my left. I was about to make a right and do a drive-by of the house of this bitch I know Junior used to mess with. I looked left again to make sure no traffic was coming and saw Junior hop out the Escort, hitch his pants up by the waist as he walked around the front of the car, and leaned down to kiss the girl sitting behind the wheel.

My nana always said when you go looking for something be ready because you might just find it.

My heart broke into a thousand pieces and I wasn't hardly ready for that.

I found out I was pregnant for him just one month later. Seven months after that our daughter Danina was born.

So this man standing before me fathered children with me . . . twice, and broke my heart . . . twice.

"Trey wants a new pair of sneakers and Danina needs a uniform for cheerleading," I tell him, holding out my hand. One sure way to get rid of a tired man is to ask for money.

Junior sticks his hands inside his leather racing jacket, cocking his head to the side to look at me. "Damn, you used to beg for this dick 'til you met that sucka husband of yours. Now the first thing out your mouth is to beg me for money."

"We're not a couple and we haven't been a couple since I caught your ass that morning and tossed your two pairs of raggedy drawers and your CDs out my window into the parking lot. *Thus* the only conversation we need to have is concerning our kids, and right now we're chitchatting about our son needing a new pair of kicks and our daughter needing a cheerleading uniform. So save your Valentine wishes for that stuck-on-stupid wife of yours. Matter of fact, tell her dumb ass to pay your child support so I can get a check."

He laughed as he steps up and takes my hand in his. "You shoulda been my wife."

I snatch my hand away. "And have me around looking stupid like her dumb ass? She around here watching me like a hawk like I have a 'give me Junior's dick when I want it' pass, but she needs to be watching *your* slick behind."

He reaches down and unzips his pants to release his snakelike dick and licks his lips. "You can get that pass fo' sho, Sexy Lexi."

I swallow over a lump in my throat as he begins to massage the full, thick, dark length of it before he teases the tip with his thumb. I think of the times that dick would make me cum until I thought I would pass out.

Yes, he cheated on me. Yes, he left me with two kids to support. Yes, he had other girlfriends over the years. Yes, sometimes I had a "friend" of my own. And yes, I used to still give up my drawers to him. I would sex him and make him tell me my pussy was better than his bitch of the moment. I would suck his dick while he was on the phone with his girl. I would make him eat me out while I was talking to my "friend." There was a time I just couldn't say no to Junior.

"That busta-ass husband of yours can't fuck you like I can," he says.

Sad, but so very, very true.

I can't look away from the way he plays with himself. His dick swells in size until his finger and thumb no longer touch. The rhythm is hypnotic. I imagine it's my pussy walls sliding up and down the length of that dick instead of his fingers and my clit jumps to life like it's nudging me to just say, "Fuck me, Junior."

Okay, he is turning me on.

"You know you want this dick, girl."

I'm kind of breathless and weak and my pussy is aching so bad for the kind of pleasure I know he can give me. Sex was never our problem. Never. And I know that I can give in to him just this once and get the kind of good dicking down I'm yearning for.

I know his thrusts will be deep and hard.

I know he can twist and turn and position my body until he is hitting parts of my pussy that I don't even know exist.

I know he can make me cum until I coat his dick with my juices until it's slick and wet.

I know Junior will have me sweaty, climbing the walls, and shouting to the rooftops while he blows my back out.

I press myself against the wall and take deep breaths as he picks up the pace until I think he will snap his wrist.

"Come on girl, give me some of that of pussy. Don't let all this hard dick go to waste." He reaches out with his left hand and gropes my breast teasing the nipple the way he knows I love.

And I let him. I did. I let him tweak and twist and pluck my hard and long nipples. *God, this is wrong. This is soooo wrong but it feels sooooooooooooo good.*

What am I doing? It's Valentine's Day. I'm about five lousy feet from the bouquet of roses my husband bought for me. My loving, faithful, honest husband who doesn't deserve me having a freakfest with one of my baby daddies in our home.

"No," I cry out, twisting my body away from him and breaking his hold on my breast. "No, no, no, no, no, no. No. NO. NO!"

"Shee-it, I'm gone get this motherfuckin' nut," Junior says, pressing his back against the opposite wall of the hall as he bit his bottom lip.

I knock his hand off his dick. "Not in here you ain't."

I snatch open the front door and get behind Junior to push him and his tempting erection out.

The door of the apartment up the hall from me opens and Aisha Cummings stands there taking in the sight of me, Junior, and his hard dick with a haughty-taughty roll of her eyes before she closes her door and strolls away like she's the Queen of Egypt. That chick is forever acting like she's better than everybody else.

I notice Junior eyeing her ghetto booty. I ain't even mad. "Please, she don't even think you on her level so don't embarrass yourself."

Junior put his now limp dick back in his pants and zipped up as he looks down at me. "I don't want that snotty ho. Man, fuck that bitch."

"Better her than me. Good-bye, Junior," I say with a big fake smile. I push him out the way, slam and lock my front door and walk past him to move down the hall.

"Damn, Lex, you gone leave me hangin'," he hollers behind me.

"Sneakers and cheerleading uniform. Don't leave your kids hanging," I holler back, not breaking my stride as I leave the building.

It's the end of winter in Atlanta but the morning air is

still cold as hell—well, if you consider 53 degrees cold like I do—and it won't warm up until later this afternoon. I hop into Black Betty, the 1991 black Lincoln Continental I inherited when my precious nana passed away when I was twenty-one. Aisha the Diva is in her Benz. The car looks out of place in the projects. I don't miss the disdainful look she shoots me and my car before she backs up and whizzes away with ease. If she thinks she put me to shame she's wrong. My nana's car was purchased with hard-earned money and not the cold, hard cash of killing black folks with drugs and crime.

Okay, Betty isn't in the best cosmetic shape. There are a couple dings in the side. A little rust around the bumpers. The leather seats are pretty torn up. With five kids the interior can use a good cleaning. Luther has it in great running condition so I have no worries that when I turn the key the car will purr to life.

I look out the moist window at the front door of WooWoo's first-floor apartment in the building next to mine. When Nana died, WooWoo was nineteen and working three days a week as a receptionist for a plastic surgeon in Buckhead. Her age and pay stub was enough for her to take over the apartment. That was eight years ago and that left just me, my kids, and WooWoo. Well, and now Luther. We are all the family we have in the world.

WooWoo's door opens. She pokes out her fuchsia-colored hair and waves. My sister has a bad habit of always running late. She's everything I'm not. Single, kid-free, free-spirited, lively, wild, ghetto as hell, and sometimes crazy as hell.

She steps out and locks her door, running over to me in her pink, lightweight bomber jacket, and pink and white Air Force 1s. As soon as she gets into the car I can smell the weed all in her clothes.

"Girl, I know you ain't smoke a blunt already this morning?" I ask her as I put the car in reverse.

"Shee-it." Her eyes are half shut like she's Chinese and I know she's feeling nice.

As long as she doesn't smoke around my kids I let her be.

"Turn up the heat and let me tell you the latest shit buzzin' around here." She rubs her hands together, her two-inch nails painted with every imaginable neon color and plenty of rhinestones.

"Do you know everybody's business?" I ask her as I pull out the parking lot.

"Nope, not everybody. Just those dumb enough to let their business get out. Once it's out it's like community property. God bless America."

We both laugh.

WooWoo is the only thing about Bentley Manor that I will miss.

8

Devani

The thing about Koolay's constantly high ass is that he's always whipping out his dick and massaging it as if it is the most natural thing in the world. Usually he's on the sofa with a blunt, a beer, or the remote control in one hand and his dick in the other. In the year that he's been living with me and Momma, I'm accustomed to ignoring his wrinkly uncircumcised dick.

Sometimes, like today, it's a little harder than usual. The moment I open my eyes, Koolay is standing at the door of my bedroom, "massaging" and making annoying sucking sounds between his teeth.

"What the fuck are you doing in here?" I yank the top sheet down over my exposed ass cheeks, since my pajamas consist of a pair of Wal-Mart thongs and a short tee that asks: "Got Milk?"

"Yo momma wants you in the kitchen," he says, rolling his eyes as if he's hit a particular sweet spot.

"Fine. Now get the hell out of here."

A second later, he turns and heads back to his beloved sofa. He didn't cum. In fact, I don't think the motherfucker ever cums. It's just hours and hours of rubbing, caressing, and massaging. Like that damn energizer bunny, he just keeps going and going.

Annoyed, I jump into a pair of form-fitting workout shorts and my ratty pair of house slippers and shuffle into the kitchen. My mother, with half of her hair braided and the other half a frizzy mess, is scrambling a skillet of government powdered eggs and pasteurized cheese with one hand and sipping Hennessy with the other. Why she's cooking breakfast at one in the afternoon, I have no idea.

"You wanted me?"

"Yeah, I need you to go to the store for me. I need a pack of Philly blunts and a box of tampons."

"What the fuck? How come you can't send your man to the store?"

On cue, Koolay unlocks the series of door locks and jerks open the front door. "Be back," he hollers and then slams the door behind him.

"He's making a run to see M. Dawg," Momma says, flipping over the bacon in the back skillet.

"Fine. Whatever. Give me the money." I hold out my hand.

"Spot me and I'll hit you back later."

"What the fuck?" My hands grip my waist. "You got money to get some weed from M. Dawg, but you can't buy your own tampons? What makes you think I got some damn money?"

"Stop trippin', Devani. I know your NFL nigga broke you off some chomp change. At least he better have. I've told you about laying up with these no good bastards and not gettin' something in return."

"You're laying up with Koolay and his ass ain't got a pot to piss in or a window to throw it out of."

"Goddamn it, Devani." Momma shoves the eggs skillet toward the back of the stove and hot grease from the bacon splashes everywhere. "We ain't talking about me. We're talking about you. I'm tryna to teach your hardheaded ass not to make the same mistakes I've made, but I can't tell you shit 'cos you run around here like you know every goddamn thing."

The last thing I'm in the mood for is a lecture. "Fine. Whatever. I'll buy your damn shit." Might as well, I'm not going to win the damn argument. "When in the hell are you going to hit menopause, anyway?" As I storm back to my room to get ready, Momma dogs my heels.

"You want to know why I'm with Koolay?"

"Not particularly." I snatch open my bottom chest of drawers and grab a pair of jeans.

"It's 'cos he's simple . . . easy. He ain't out runnin'

around here tryna to fuck anything with a hole and he understands me."

Okay, now she's delusional. Koolay would fuck me in front of my momma, if I let him.

"When the sun rises in the morning, Koolay is there. When I lay my head down at night, he's there."

"Where else is he going to be? The nigga ain't got a job."

"You'll understand when you get my age. When you get tired of believing all the lies these niggas tell you. 'Ooh, baby. I looove you.'" She shakes her hips, careful not to spill her drink. "How about: 'You're the only woman for me' or my personal favorite: 'Sure, baby. Stick with me I'll take you away from all of this'? That one came from your damn daddy and I ain't seen his black ass since he knocked me up."

"Okay, Momma. I got it."

"Do you?" She steps farther into the room. "You only get so many chances before your looks go and your figure is shot. After that, niggas don't want shit to do with you."

Not the first time I've heard this speech, but there's something in my mother's voice that catches my attention. For a moment, I'm thrown off guard by the teary gloss of her sad eyes and the defeated slump of her shoulders. Vulnerable is not a word that usually describes Momma, but one would have to be as blind as Stevie Wonder to miss her frailty today.

"When you get my age, all that's left are these stragglers

who ain't never done shit, ain't doing shit, and ain't planning on doing shit." She folds one arm across her body and takes another gulp of her drink. "Which is fine," she continues without missing a beat. " 'Cos all I want now is a warm body and a good buzz to help me forget about all the wrong turns I've made."

One of those wrong turns was a brief stint in jail some years back. One of her many boyfriends hid a gun used in a convenience store robbery in her car. Momma failed to have the good sense to rat the nigga out—despite having two kids waiting for her at home.

Maybe if she'd been home, my twin sister, Dynia, would've never hooked up with the wrong crowd, become addicted to crack, and die at fifteen of an overdose while riding the Marta train home.

"I better get to the store so I can get back. I have a date with Tyrik." I know why I changed the subject. I'm uncomfortable around this "vulnerable" woman. Give me the loud, argumentative Momma any day of the week.

"Tyrik," she mumbles under her breath and then takes another sip. "That nigga is running a damn game on you and you damn well know it."

"He's not like that, Momma." I run a brush through my hair and bunch it all into a clip at the nape of my neck.

"There you go being hardheaded again. Let me ask you this: has he asked you to move to Pittsburgh yet?"

The question is a punch to the gut, but no way I'm lettin' my nosy momma in my business. If I do, she's just going to tryna work the situation to her benefit.

"He hasn't asked you, has he?" Momma throws her head back with a high cackle. "You're one dumb-ass bitch, Devani. I swear."

I kick off my slippers and jam my feet into my Nikes. In the next move I try to bum rush my way past her to get the hell out the apartment, but Momma grabs my arm with amazing strength.

"Don't let this nigga run over you, baby."

Her words are slurred, but it's that damn teary gloss in her eyes that disturbs me.

"If you want that nigga and you want to get out of this place, then you got to play your cards right. You gotta think outside of your coochee, baby. Every bitch on the street got one of those. They come in different shapes, sizes, and flavors. And the sky is the limit with a nigga with some money. You need an ace in the hole if you want to play this game. You need something he can't walk away from."

What the fuck is she talking about now?

"You can't eat off love—but a baby is a good damn check for at least eighteen years."

Literally my mouth sags open. Not because I would never think of such a thing or stoop to such a level, but because the advice is coming from my momma.

"Getting knocked up didn't help you sink your claws into my daddy."

"That's 'cos your damn daddy was another nigga without a pot to piss in." She shoves my arm back at me. "Had I listened to my own momma I could of saved myself from that mistake."

And I wouldn't be here.

"When does Tyrik report to training camp?"

I start not to answer but I know she will needle it out of me. "July."

"It's February. Not a whole lot of wiggle room." She folds her arm again and takes another sip of her drink. "Of course, all you need is one night. And tonight is Valentine's night. I wouldn't mind being a grandma by the holidays. You just make sure you hook your momma up when you start gettin' those big checks."

I knew it. "Your bacon is burning, Momma."

"Shit." She takes off for the kitchen and sure enough the kitchen and the living room are filled with choking, white smoke. Because cooking isn't my momma's strong suit, that sorry-ass smoke detector doesn't so much as emit a single beep.

I grab my jacket. "I'll be back," I holler and bolt out of the tiny apartment.

The day is cloudy but I can't tell whether the gray is from the promise of rain or because it's the general mood at Bentley Manor. But sunshine, snow, or rain, Miz Cleo and Miz Osceola are parked out on their stoop at the center of the U-shaped complex and staring at everyone like two hawks, waiting for their first meal.

Miz Cleo is a handsome, five-foot-seven, Mahalia Jackson look-alike, with stunningly beautiful silver hair. She may be in her seventies but her skin is as rich and smooth as any thirty-year-old and is a true testament that black don't crack. Miz Osceola is three inches shorter, three shades lighter and with a spray of freckles and small moles over her face.

I tell you, not a damn thing gets past those two old birds and every once in a while they feel the need to wave you over and read your ass like they kin to you or something.

I glance around the complex and spot crackheads and streetwalkers creeping and shuffling around like those goon dancers in that old *Thriller* video. Ole Eddie, an ex-boyfriend of my momma, is sitting out on his own stoop sipping on his usual cheap Mad Dog and getting fucked up. People say he's been drunk since the day he returned from Vietnam. If you ask me, there are faster ways to killing yourself than pickling your insides.

I step out onto the glass-littered parking lot and literally have to jump out the way when two kids bolt out from behind a few run-down cars.

"Hey!" I shout.

The tallest boy is thin and lanky with oil-black skin. I don't know his name but he has the habit of running around like he owns the damn place. In another couple of years he'll undoubtedly make his grand debut in juvenile court.

"Watch where you're going," I tell him.

"You watch where you're going," he snaps, looking me over and staring at my titties as if he's still being breast-fed. I swear these damn kids at Bentley Manor think their asses are grown. Only Lexi Mitchell's kids act like they got some damn sense. As I turn and head down the street, the boys behind me make crude yet flattering comments about the amount of junk in my trunk.

Goddamn kids.

Junior's loud-ass hoopty whips into the complex. My pussy muscle twitches a bit at the memory of his beautiful cock, but it isn't Junior who hops out the car, but his clueless, trophy white-trash bitch.

"Hi," she says, catching my stare.

I roll my eyes in the opposite direction. I ain't got time for fake hos wanting a free black pass just because they rockin' some black dick—even a big, black dick in Junior's case.

Fuck her.

I walk through the wrought-iron security gate (which is always open, by the way). Down the block at the neighborhood Circle K gas station, niggas are clustered together because they ain't got nothing better to do.

By the large ice machine, an even larger group of Latinos in dirty, paint-splattered clothing scan the streets for almighty whitey, who hates them for being illegal in the country, but loves the cheap manual labor. In a lot of ways Mexican niggas are no better off than regular niggas.

"Hola, Mami," one calls out to me.

I promptly ignore his ass. I'm trying to get ahead of the game, not take two steps back.

Shakespeare, who earned his nickname back in junior high for spray-painting what he called "some serious knowledge" on a few highway underpasses, glides up beside me and follows me into the store. "Whatsup, Devani?"

"I'm just runnin' an errand," I tell him.

"Yeah? Where's your rich nigga at?"

"What the hell are you doing all up in my business?" I ask, cutting a glance over my shoulder.

Shakespeare licks his thick, juicy lips and curls a mischievous smile. "You know I've been sweatin' you since we were in elementary school."

This is true. I remember back when he had to wear funny shoes and thick Coca-Cola–bottle glasses. He's definitely come a long way. He has a nice-cut body and since he got rid the weird shoes and converted to contacts, he's generally considered a pretty boy. Now, if he only had his shit together and had a job he might be worth something. Instead, he's just another nigga smokin' his dreams away.

There's no shame in my game when I grab a small box of tampons. Shakespeare tries his best to suppress a knowing smirk, but fails. I just shake my head and march up to the counter. "A pack of Philly blunts," I tell the Indian cashier. At least I think he's Indian—he could be Arab. Who the fuck knows? I just know they own all the convenience stores, liquor stores, and Dairy Queens in the black neighborhoods.

"I'll take care of that for you." Shakespeare tosses a few dollars on the counter and I give him a saucy smile as thanks and even sway my hips a little harder as I walk away.

"So you got plans with your nigga tonight?" Shakespeare asks as we walk past his boys.

"Of course. It's Valentine's Day." And I'm gonna fuck Tyrik so good he won't dare think about moving to Pittsburgh without me.

Shakespeare nods and casts his gaze off in the distance.

"What about you?" I ask. "You got plans this evening?"

"Nah, nah. I got a few chickenheads on standby— nothin' serious."

I nod and we both fall silent as we walk down the busted-up sidewalk and pass large patches of Georgia red clay. That's another peculiar thing; grass don't grow in the projects. But there are plenty of crushed beer cans, cigarette butts, and everything else that belongs in garbage cans.

"You know I'm going to get out of this joint one day," Shakespeare says suddenly.

"Oh yeah?" Bullshit.

"Yeah. I got some plans in the works. I just need a good woman in my corner. Someone like you."

I laugh and cut another look at him. "And what is that supposed to mean?"

"It means I'm tryna get in where I fit in. If things don't work out between you and your nigga . . . " He struck a pose so I get a good look at him.

"What the fuck ever."

"Nah. Nah. I'd like to be the one to take you away from all of this."

I laugh again and walk through the security gate. The first things to catch my attention are the two police cars. Shit. I swear the po-po spend more time in Bentley Manor than at the police station.

"Who are they sweatin' now?" Shakespeare asks, exasperated. When he sees his older brother, Smokey (you get one guess on how he earned that nickname), he jets from my side to find out the 4-1-1.

I just shake my head and go about my business. Smokey's arrest can only mean someone called about him beating his wife's ass again. Probably Miz Cleo. I don't why she would do that—Keisha ain't never gonna press charges.

"I'm back," I holler out the moment I walk back into the apartment. There's still smoke, but at least all the windows are open.

Momma and Koolay jet from out their bedroom like I'd announced they were the winners of the Publishing Clearance House sweepstakes. They probably hid when they saw the po-pos' blue lights through the open window.

"Give me the blunts," Koolay demands, already pulling the bag of weed from his pants pocket.

Momma pops him on the back of the head.

"Ow. What?"

"Nigga, go close the window."

Frowning and rubbing his head, Koolay shuffles toward the windows while mumbling under his breath, "Play too damn much."

I can't help but laugh, but Momma's next words sober my ass.

"Tyrik called while you were out." A sloppy smile curves her lips as she snatches the brown bag from my hands. "He says he has to cancel your date this evening. Something came up."

"Probably some better coochee." Koolay laughs.

I slice my don't-fuck-with-me glare in his direction and make sure I meet his half-lidded gaze. "There's no such thing as better than this."

That shut him up. But as his gaze roams my curvy body, he makes the mistake of licking his lips. I doubt he ever saw Momma's left hook.

9

Molly

Valentine's Day is almost over and Junior is still not home. Dinner was done two hours ago, more than half the wicks in my army of ninety-nine-cent candles are burned out, and I feel ridiculous in this pink, fake lace teddy I bought from Super Wal-Mart. I keep crying and fucking up my mascara to the point I now look like Tammy Faye Bakker's stepchild.

How could he do this? He knows how special this day is to me. I know our money is funny and all. Since we've been together, we've never really been able to go all out like we want to, but Junior hinted that this year was going to be different. I imagined roses being delivered or even a stuffed teddy bear with a big-ass balloon with the words "I love you." That would have been nice and romantic. But who am I kidding? Bentley Manor is a red zone—meaning no one made deliveries here—except the cops serving warrants, subpoenas, and eviction notices.

My eyes zoom to our folded copies of this month's eviction notice sitting on top of the television set. It's a damn shame we can't afford a hundred and ten dollars a month. Of course, if I had a baby we could get more government assistance and probably even qualify to get this rat hole for free.

If only.

Another hour slips by and I've chewed my nails down to the nubs. That's a new habit for me, which is my first line of defense before grabbing a half gallon of Mayfield's ice cream from the freezer.

I get up from the rickety kitchen table and make a beeline across the always-sticky tile floor. I mean it. I've tried every product imaginable on this floor and the damn thing still feels as if it's coated with sugar.

Which also attributes to this apartment's roach problem. Until I moved here, I'd never seen a cockroach. Now, I'm in a war against these nasty, six-legged creatures that seem as pointless as the one in the Middle East.

There are small ones, big ones, ones that can fly, and ones that can outdistance Olympic sprinters. The first year I moved here the damn things nearly turned me into a schizoid, thinking that they were always crawling on me. These motherfuckers drink Raid like it's fuckin' Cristal, get high off foggers, and treat bait traps like vacation houses. Nothing kills these bastards.

Nothing.

"He's not coming home." Fresh tears roll down my face. "Maybe he's getting a lot done in the studio." My heart drops so low I swear it's pulsing in my toes. I've maxed my limit with keeping open food out and begin wrapping everything up. When I'm through, I blow out the rest of the candles and power off the CD player.

Stealing a peek out of the dust-covered blinds, a light drizzle of rain sprinkles across the windows. However, that doesn't stop the night crawlers from prowling the street. Men are arguing down the way and, unbelievably, children are still playing in the street and somewhere in the building, a baby is crying.

I hate this place.

And I hate not knowing where my husband is.

A familiar face appears out of the darkness and I almost turn away from the window but then I realize Devani is crying and I'm stunned. The woman treats me like something stuck under her shoe no matter how nice I am.

I can't imagine what's pierced that steely bitchiness and has her crying where the whole world can see.

This is a Kodak moment.

Seconds later, Devani drifts back into the shadows and my loneliness returns. I start to chew on my nails again, but they're already raw and I have one cuticle bleeding. Fuck it. I need that ice cream now.

I snatch a new carton out of the freezer and grab a large spoon. No bowls necessary at this pity party.

When I pull the top off the carton, a loud squeak startles me and I look down in time to see a fat, long-tail rat scurrying by my feet.

I scream and drop the lid but manage to hold on to the prized ice cream. As if sensing my fear, my unwelcome guest stops halfway across the tile and, I swear to God, glances back at me as if stunned to see me standing in his kitchen.

I plop the ice cream carton in the sink and rush to grab the broom. "Get out of here. Get!" I jab at him with the hard straw end of the broom. Instead of running away this damn thing charges at me.

Screaming, I back up against the sink and then jump up on it when the ugly bastard keeps coming. Terrified, my heart is beating like it's trying to escape my chest.

Then suddenly, the rat disappears beneath me.

"Hey!" A voice hollers from above and thumps down on my ceiling. "Keep quiet down there!" Another thump and pieces of plaster drift around the kitchen like snow.

I close my eyes and try to slow my racing heart. Before I know it, more tears sting my eyes. I hate living like this. I want to go home.

Visions of my childhood home, a brick, Georgian-style house, fill my mind. The heavenly scent of baked chocolate chip cookies always drifted through every room and, more important, our housekeeper kept everything spotless. No cockroaches. No rats.

Slowly I'm aware of my butt getting cold and it hits me that I'm sitting on top of the open carton of ice cream.

"Shit."

Drawing a deep breath, I finally open my eyes to the disheartening nightmare that is my kitchen. After scanning the floor beneath me for my tormentor, I slide my butt out of the sink. I move away from the sink and glance underneath it. Sure enough, there's a sizable hole where Mr. Rat must have ducked.

Snatching a few paper towels, I quickly wipe the ice cream off my ass and then rush to the back of the apartment to search for something to stuff the hole. I'm trembling and shaking, wanting to hurry before the fat bastard comes back out.

But I can't find anything. In the bathroom, on top of the clothes hamper, I spot a pair of Junior's socks and make a snap decision to use it. When I return to the kitchen, my heart begins hammering again. I try to be quiet but the sticky floor announces my every step. Needless to say the idea of getting on my hands and knees to stuff a sock in a rat hole fills me with terror. But I squat down anyway and crawl toward the hole.

What if I get bitten? Couldn't I get rabies or something?

The front door rattles and I freeze. Is it my husband or

some crackhead, looking for a quick score? Mr. Rat takes advantage of my temporary distraction and jets back out of the hole toward me.

Screaming, I'm back up on my feet and running into the living room.

Thump. Thump. "Bitch, I said keep it down!"

The front door swings open and Junior has less than two seconds to prepare for my launch into his arms.

"The fuck?" He drops the box he's holding and catches me in time.

Squeak. Squeak.

Junior jumps back as Mr. Rat races between his legs and out into the hallway.

"Shut the door! Shut the door!"

My baby chuckles under his breath, causing the wide span of his chest to rumble. I love that.

"Damn, li'l ma. It's just a rat." He moves into the apartment and closes the door.

I lock my arms around his neck and inhale the masculine scent of musk, weed, and beer. "I was beginning to think you weren't coming home," I murmur against his ear and squeeze him tighter.

"Don't be silly. 'Course I was coming home."

Turning my head, I stare into his coal-black eyes and my entire body pimples with goose bumps. Cautious of the fact that I could give him a hernia, I slide out of his arms but keep my hands locked behind his neck.

"Where have you been? I thought you forgot what night it is."

"Aw, now. Don't start sweatin' me. You know I was at the studio." His thick hands roam over my hips and make a straight dive for my crotch and I'm instantly hot and wet. "What's this shit you got on, gurl?"

Finally, I step back and strike a pose. "You like?"

"Uhm. Uhm. Uhm." He licks his lips like I'm a bucket of KFC and pulls me close again to plant a sloppy kiss against my lips. He tastes funny, but I quickly dismiss it when he roughly grabs my nipples and twists them painfully.

"You like that shit, baby?" I don't, but I say I do since he clearly gets off on it. "You bought this lingerie for me?"

Again I nod.

"How many times have I told you I want you naked when I come home, huh?"

He twists my nipples so hard I suck in a sharp gasp between my teeth.

"I told you I always want you wet and ready when I come home, haven't I?"

Another nod.

"Then take that off."

He steps away from me and I have a hard time figuring out whether he's angry or just annoyed. It's always hard gauging my man's mood. He can be playful one minute and irritable the next.

I peel the thin spaghetti straps off my shoulders and shimmy out of the one-piece teddy.

"Now that's what I'm talking about." He steps to me and slides his hand back down into my crotch. "Open up for me, li'l ma."

I spread my legs and he dips his fingers inside me.

"You've been waiting for me, baby?"

"You know I have."

"Tell me what you want, li'l ma. You want to get fucked, is that what it is? You want some of your man's black dick?"

"Oh, God, yes."

"On your knees." He commands unzipping his pants.

He doesn't have to tell me twice so I drop to the floor and feel my mouth salivate at the sheer size of him.

"You love me, baby?"

"You know I do."

"Show me."

With the challenge before me, I open my mouth wide, knowing damn well there's no way I can fit all of him in my mouth, but I'm going to do my damn best. But I don't get more than the tip in my mouth before backing away from the strange bitter taste.

"C'mon, li'l ma. Don't tease. I'm just a little sweaty. You don't want my sweaty dick, is that it?"

"No. Yes. I mean it's okay." I take his beautiful, long

cock and shove it back into my mouth. I don't like the taste, but that's okay. I can handle it.

"Ooh. Now, that's my baby girl." He spreads his legs a bit and begins pumping his hips.

I force my throat muscles to relax and he goes deeper, pressing the thick head to the back of my throat.

"Aw, shit. Aw, shit." He holds my head still and ignores the fact I'm literally gagging. "That's right, baby. You know how to suck this shit the way I like it."

I love the praise and allow him to fuck my mouth any way he wants to. Soon, he holds my head still and rams my throat so hard, I swear at any moment I'm going to pass out. But then his hot cum explodes into the back of my mouth and rushes down my tight throat.

"Don't spit it out. Swallow that shit, baby."

I do so gladly.

At long last, he pulls out and I suck in desperately needed air.

"That's my girl." He strokes my hair a little and then leans down to kiss the tip of my nose. "I love you, baby."

His words warm me like sunshine and I'm willing and able to let him go another round. Instead he helps me up and then picks up the box he'd dropped on the floor earlier. "Happy V-Day, baby."

Suddenly, I'm giddy again as I reach for it. "I have something for you, too," I say, setting the box down on our chipped coffee table and then turning toward the kitchen. When I return, I hand him a small square box and hope like hell he likes it.

A thrill tickles through me as he rips open the package and his eyes widen at the sight of the beautiful gold chain I bought at the Shane Diamond store. I had to pawn some of the jewelry my father bought me on my sixteenth and seventeenth birthdays—but it's well worth the look on his face.

"Damn, baby. This is the shit here." He pulls the chain out of the box and I help him fasten it behind his neck. "I'm gonna take a look." He goes to the bathroom and checks himself out.

While we're in there, I quickly brush my teeth and then rinse with the Listerine.

"Shit. This is straight fire, li'l ma. You did good." He turns and plants another kiss on me that gets my pussy sloppy wet.

"Can I go open mine now?"

"Sure."

When I turn, he gives my ass a firm slap and I giggle my way back into the living room. I pick up the heavy box, wondering what it can be.

Junior plops down on our sofa and reaches for the TV remote.

Slightly annoyed, I tear into the box and frown when I read: Payless shoes. "You bought me shoes?"

"No. Don't be silly. Open it up."

I do as he instructs and then I'm so stunned that I have sit down as well. Inside the box are two forty-ounce beers. Beer?

Junior reaches over and grabs one. "Happy V-Day, baby."

10

Aisha

It's funny how when you're separated from the man you love something as common as holding hands becomes the most important thing in your marriage. During every moment of my visit I hold this nigga's hand like it will save my life. Like it will make up for missing him. Or needing him. Fucking him. Kissing him. Smelling him. Stroking him. Sucking him. Blowing him. Tracing his tattoos with my tongue and my hands. Just holding him.

That Friday I ignore anything and everything in the visitation room but him. Maleek is hella fine like Tyrese. Smooth and dark-complexioned, strong, handsome face, toned-up body that is getting even more ripped with every passing month he spends in jail. His sexy dreads are gone but the baldhead he wears just brings out his fine-ass face even more.

I hate to think about my warrior not beating this shit. I mean damn, what if?

Fuck that. I need my man home like yesterday.

I swallow back the tears 'cause I wasn't gone be one of them whiny, wimpy wives. I can't hold him but I will at least hold him down.

I squeeze his hand a little tighter and make myself smile. "What the attorneys talkin' 'bout?"

Maleek uses his free hand to wipe his mouth before he looks up and locks his eyes with mine. "More money."

My nails nearly bite into the palm of his hand as I lean forward and whisper, "I already gave 'em thirty grand like you told me. What the fuck more they want?"

Maleek's eyes turn cold and he lets my hand go. "He wants to get me the fuck off. He wants to get me out this motherfucker. He wants me to be free so I can piss and shit and eat when the fuck I want. So I can walk outside when the fuck I please. So I can come the fuck up out that fucking cell. So I can wear some fly-ass gear like your ass and come out *this* bullshit."

"And you think I don't want that." I lean back in my chair and cross my arms over my chest.

My feelings are hurt and I'm afraid of the coldness in his face. Was being locked up changing him? I have seen Maleek be hard but he never went there on me.

He stretched his arms across the table to unlock my arms and take both my hands in his. "Aisha. Baby, I'm sorry. A'ight? I'm sorry. It's just this jail got me fucked up. I'm not used to this shit."

I hold his hands tighter than ever. "So what you want me to do, Maleek?"

"I need you to take the attorney another twenty grand."

I'm not one of them book-smart bitches but there were two things I'm good at. Counting money and spending money. "How's Aunt Darla?"

Translation: Do you have money stashed anywhere else?

"She ain't doin' good at all."

Translation: No.

Damn.

I give him a serious look. "Yeah, I heard she ain't doin' good, either."

Translation: That thirty grand that went to the lawyers already hurt the stash you left me like a motherfucker.

"Damn."

I'm feeling a lot of fucked-up things in that moment. I'm suddenly realizing that with his whole operation shut down there is no money to come in to cover the money that is steadily going out. "I'll go see the attorney Monday," I tell him.

"That's my queen," he says, his thumb tracing circles on my wrist.

"And you my king," I say, more out of habit than anything even as my grip on his hand loosens up a little bit.

✧   ✧   ✧

As soon as I walk through the door that night I go straight to my bedroom closet and pull out this old wool coat we bought from a secondhand store. My heart is beating like crazy as I drop to my knees and lay the coat on the floor. I tear the stitched lining from the coat and fling it back. Small plastic covered stacks of hundred- and fifty-dollar bills were taped over the entire inside of the coat.

Our stash. I now know this is all the cash we have in the world. This is it. I counted it quickly. $27,500. Maleek needs twenty grand.

I sit back on the floor and pull my knees to my chest. Reality is setting in like crazy.

I still have a life to live.

I still have to put money in Maleek's commissary.

I still have to help my momma and my brothers.

I still have bills up the ass.

"Damn." I drop my head on my knees.

I woke up that next morning a bitch on a mission. Ordinarily I didn't really get down with Maleek's family. They're always relying on him to take care of them. Pay this bill. Pay that bill. Whup this nigga's ass. Take care of that motherfucka. And I feel like they disrespect me when they get money from his ass and not even ask about me. Or think they can drop by the apartment whenever the mood hit they ass and not even speak to me. Family or no family, I'm his wife and I've had to check them on more than a few times 'bout respecting mine—especially his older sister, Hassana. That big, sloppy bitch thinks she is Maleek's momma. Me and her done had plenty of run-ins about her tryna run shit up in my house.

So I usually steer clear of they ass and they steer clear of me. In the last three months I ain't seen them but twice and that's two times too many. But today I'm making it my business to go straight to them. It's time to shake a few trees and see what the fuck falls out.

I take a quick shower and grab a silver Baby Phat sweat suit to put on. I pull my hair into a ponytail and skip my usual makeup. This casual thing wasn't me but my mind is stuck on doing what I got to do.

Maleek gave his parents the loot to buy a small house in his father's hometown of Newman just twenty-five minutes outside of Atlanta. This is straight country: cows crossing the road at any minute, damn deer dashing back and forth into the woods. Ditches. No stop lights. Juke joints. Dirt yards. Woods for miles with God knows what in it.

Some real bullshit.

I grab my shades and my Gucci hobo. It was mid-March and the Atlanta weather is warm during the day so I don't bother with a jacket. I leave my apartment and pause at the sound of children, loud TVs, and God knows what else coming from apartment 3B down the hall from me. Lexi. Humph. I thought she was a goody-two-shoes wife but look like the bitch back fucking Junior.

All them fucking kids? She needs to sit her hot ass down somewhere and be glad somebody married her.

Focus, Aisha. I walk down the hall and out the door. As soon as I step out the building I eye this bitch name Reema sitting on the hood of her red Honda Civic with her two flunky friends Kelly and Jase.

I'm well aware that Reema think she can steal my shine with her ghetto booty and well-known deep-throating ass. She actually thinks she bangin' enough to replace me with Maleek. Dumb bitches think dumb things.

I look at all three of 'em like they shit on a pair of my Manolos as I unlock my car. All together the three of 'em probably have on a hundred dollars' worth of clothes. These broke bitches don't get enough of that cheap-ass It's Fashion store.

"I can't stand that stuck-up bitch."

Reema's voice is intentionally loud enough for me to hear. The parking lot is kinda crunk and there ain't no way I'm letting this bitch play me. I open the door and slip my blade from my purse. These bitches tryna flex and I just happen to be dressed to give a beat-down? Cool wit me.

"And I can't stand jealous-ass, tricking-ass, welfare-ass, stank-ass bitches!" I say loud as hell, already moving back toward them with my hand on my blade in the pocket of my sweat jacket.

People in the parking lot are already stepping closer at the smell of a girl fight.

"Dayum!" Somebody yells out.

I can see the look in Reema's eyes that she is shame and her two cronies are looking scared.

"Your man like *this* ass," Reema says, hopping off the hood to turn her ass to me to shake before she taps it twice.

"I like that ass, too."

That sounds like Junior's no-good ass but I don't even pay none of these niggas 'round me no mind.

Two steps and I yoke that bitch up by her neck and throw her on the hood of her own shit. BOOM! I know that shit is dented. Before she can blink I got my blade to her throat. Her two cronies jump the fuck back. *Way* back.

The lot got quiet as shit.

I feed off the fear in this bitch's eyes as I stick my fucking face in hers. "Don't fuck wit me, bitch. Don't fucking play yourself and get fucked up."

I grab a fistful of her hair and slam her head down on the hood. "My man wants your ass? Huh, bitch? Huh? Tell me that fucking lie now. Tell me that damn lie. I *dare* your ass."

"Stop playin', Aisha," she whispers nervously, looking up at me scared as shit. This bitch knows I have her life in my hands.

"No, bitch, *you* stop playing," I spit at her, edging my blade closer to her throat until the tip presses into her flesh just enough not to break the skin. One wrong move and her ass is grass.

"Ya'll children break that up 'fore I call the police."

I know that's one of the two old ladies who live in Building 220. They stay in them two chairs by the door of the building from morning to night and never miss shit. I ain't had no doubt they would call 5-0.

I jump off Reema and stick my blade back in my pocket. "Don't make me have to fuck you up," I tell her, reaching out to nudge that bitch in the face one last time before I turn with no fear of retaliation and walk back to my whip.

I ain't even look back as I pull out Bentley Manor with a squeal of my tires. When these bitches gone learn?

I turn my car into the driveway of Maleek's parents' house. It's been over a year since I last visited with Maleek but wasn't a damn thing different. Same dull brick house with the yellow shutters. Same dogs running loose in the dirt yard. Same broke-down cars in the backyard. Same-o-same-o.

As soon as I step out the car the front door opens and big Hassana steps onto the porch looking a hot mess in a t-shirt with no bra. The nipples of her sagging titties are down by her fat belly. I can tell by the look on her face she ain't any happier to see me than I am to see her.

"Whassup, Hassana? Your momma here?" I walk up the wooden steps.

"Well, well. Miss High Saddity comes for a little visit."

"Sure did. Running a little errand for Maleek."

She rolls her eyes and turns to walk back into the house. The screen door nearly knocks me in the face. Now see, I'd hate to have to flip her big ass on her back.

The house smells of soul food. I have to admit that Mr. Cummings can throw down in the kitchen.

"Queen Aisha's here," Hassana calls out with a nasty tone before she shoots me one last nasty glance and strolls into her bedroom slamming the door behind her.

Mrs. Cummings comes out of the kitchen wiping her hands on a dish towel. She's a hard-looking bitch, like she lived too much and seen too much. They say Mr. Cummings—who is a sexy older version of his son—is a bad motherfucka with the ladies and that's why they moved back out to the woods. Heard he was in Atlanta runnin' straight buck wild and fuckin' out of both his pants legs. She smiles at me but I know it's fake as hell. "How you doin', Aisha?"

"I'm good. I saw Maleek yesterday. He wanted me to stop by and see if you needed anything," I lie, laying out the bait.

Her smile becomes a little more genuine. Money always

makes these motherfuckas nicer. "No, we don't need a thing but thanks for checking up on us. You remember Hassana and me going to see Maleek next Saturday?"

"Yes ma'am," I say, but my mind is stuck on her turning down my offer of money. That means she has her hands on some.

We both are still standing. No offer was made to sit down and I made no move to sit down either. "Yeah, he told me yesterday the lawyer needed another twenty thousand with the trial coming up."

Mrs. Cummings damn near sways off her feet and she moves to sit in a leather recliner. "Well we have—"

Hassana's door flies open. "We don't have nothing. Use my brother's money for something besides clothes and shit."

"Hassana!"

"Excuse my language, Momma, but she only came here to see if we got some of Maleek's money." She turns on me with hostile eyes.

Now I'm pissed. "Hassana, why don't you mind your business? Ain't nobody talkin' to you."

She steps closer to me. "But I'm talkin' to you."

I step up too. "And? And? And?" I have my arms stretched out like I dare her to touch me.

Mrs. Cummings moves in between us. "Just go on home, Aisha."

I'm ready to straight knock Hassana the fuck out but I'm

not gonna disrespect Maleek by fighting in his momma's house.

"If she know like I know she *better* go home."

I walk to the door. "I'll see you another time, Hassana," I tell her with pure threat in my tone.

I leave before she can say something else. One of their dogs comes sniffing around me. I raise my foot and nudge it away from me hard before I climb into the car.

Nothing went down the way I want but I'm pretty sure they have money. Questions are: How much? And how do I get my hands on it?

I back out the yard and pull away with a soft purr of the motor. My cell phone is buzzing with a voice mail message.

I dial it and steer the car with one hand.

"This Aisha. Holla at your girl."

Beep.

"Aisha. Call me. I need you. The police just came for Nasir talkin' 'bout he raped some white girl. I don't know what to do, Aisha. We can't leave him in there. What we gone do?"

My stomach feels tight as I listen to my mother. She's hysterical. My brother's locked the fuck up. Rape? No way.

My mother's words echo even as I speed back to Atlanta.

"What we gone do?"

We. That's the story of my life.

11

Devani

I'm not a stalker.

I'm just keeping a closer eye on what belongs to me—and Tyrik's fine ass belongs to me. That bullshit move he pulled on Valentine's Day last month proved to me that Momma (and I hate to admit this) is on the right track on how to get this nigga on lock. I don't know who he was fuckin' that night and I didn't ask because a lie ain't nothin' for a nigga to tell.

I just have to tighten the reins.

I filed my income tax early and received eight hundred dollars back from my small stint at Ford Motor Company before they shut down the plant. With that money I put a down payment a '02 Toyota Corolla from one of those buy-here, pay-here dealerships. For the record: yes, I owe more than the car is worth—but the end justifies the means.

With a car my ass can do a roll-by or drop-by any damn time I feel like it. I already had to put a few bitches on blast. However, Tyrik insists the girls were there for his cousin, Rufus.

Rufus. Four hundred plus-pound Rufus?

Nigga, please. Do I have "Boo-Boo the Fool" stamped on my forehead? So I had to check his ass, too. He takes the shit because I've discovered how to make Tyrik's dick gush like Niagara Falls whenever I deep-tongue his tight asshole.

Say what you want, but this bitch is gettin' the fuck up out of Bentley Manor one way or another.

Tyrik isn't complaining either. I'm sexing his ass so good I had that nigga sucking my motherfuckin' toes last night. My chomp change has been upgraded to my very own platinum card, and in addition to my Corolla, as of yesterday, Tyrik bought me a brand-new, shiny, silver Lexus. Of course, I'm not a dumb bitch like that Aisha Cummings and roll my tight ride in front of a bunch of crackheads and two-bit hustlers. I plan on keeping my shit. I keep the Lexus at Tyrik's and ride the Corolla to Bentley Manor.

Of course, I pulled a few down-low moves, too. I stole Tyrik's house key, made a copy and returned it before he even knew it was missing.

My one problem? Tyrik won't fuck me without a condom. Period. No matter how hot I get him or how inconvenient it is to stop and look for one. I've tried and said everything I can think of to get him to change his mind. "'Don't you want to feel every inch of my good pussy?' or 'Oh, Baby. It just doesn't feel the same.' "

He isn't having it.

Apparently the National Football League actually teaches players about the pitfalls of running into women like me. Which goes to show you there is always someone hatin' on your game.

"I swear you're one dumb-ass bitch, Devani," Momma says after stuffing the grand I just handed her down into her bra.

"Word." Koolay chuckles, flashing only one front tooth since Momma knocked the other one out his mouth.

"You're welcome," I say, more than a little annoyed that she acts like she's accustomed to getting a thousand dollars on the regular.

"I mean it," Momma says, setting up the card tables for their Saturday night Bid Whist tournament. Something tells me that my little donation is going to be funding the alcohol and hot wings. "If the nigga won't do it without a condom then give him a condom."

"Why in the hell would I give him a condom? He has an endless supply in the nightstand drawer."

This comment apparently warrants a pop upside the head because that's exactly what my momma gives me. "Ow. What the hell was that for?"

"Think," she barks. "Give him a special condom."

At this point I'm afraid to ask what the hell she means in fear that I'll loose a tooth as well. And that shit would really fuck up my game. "A special condom," I repeat, stalling for time, but then I finally hop aboard the same train. "A defective condom."

"The easiest thing to do is punch a tiny hole in that motherfucker. Do it tonight and you may still be able to get a Christmas baby."

I can't help but smile at that shit. As I walk out of my mother's apartment I'm still smiling and even agreeing that I am a dumb bitch for not having thought of this sooner.

As I march over to the Corolla, I see Smokey's ass looking as if he's been sucking on that glass dick again. He's twitchin' and eyeballin' Aisha's Benz. Word on the street is her man can get ten years or worse—which means no protection—which means she needs to watch her back *and* that motherfuckin' Benz.

"Hey, Smokey," I say, distracting him from fuckin' up—especially under the eagle eyes of Miz Cleo and Miz Osceola. "Whatcha know good?"

He jumps as if I'm a cop but then gives me a nervous smile when he recognizes me. "Oh, hey, Devani." He scratches his head as if he has a rash of fleas embedded in his dusty braids. "Ain't nothin' going on. You know—not since Keisha and the kids left."

"No shit? She left?" Well, there goes my old hairdresser. Now I get my hair whipped and buttered out in Buckhead.

"Fuck her." Smokey shrugs and waves the question off. "She'll be back. She always comes back after her sistah gets tired her of her big mouth."

The sad part about what he's saying is that it's true. Keisha has jumped ship before, but she always boomerangs back. "Well, all right, then." I say pulling out my car keys and walking toward my car. "Keep your head up."

"Fo' sho. Fo' sho," Smokey says, strolling up behind me. My hands instantly dive back into my purse and wrap around my 908S Smith & Wesson pistol in case some shit is about to go down. "When you gonna break my bro off a piece?"

The question surprises me and I jerk a glance over my shoulder. "What?"

"You know he likes your fine ass, girl. Have him spinnin' all that poetry shit."

"What?" I'm still stunned . . . and flattered. "Shakespeare has been writing poetry about me?"

"C'mon, girl. Don't front. Dat nigga gots tons of journals he keeps on lock about how he wants to git wit you. Lately, he keeps talkin' about some book dat's gonna get you and him up out of this joint, but his game must be whack if he ain't hittin' dat by now."

"Ain't none of these country Negroes hittin' this," I inform him, swinging open my door and nearly scraping the paint of Aisha's Benz.

"Ha. Careful. You don't want Aisha to beat that ass." Smokey chuckles, starting up another frenzy of scratching.

"I ain't stuttin' Aisha's ass." I slide behind the wheel and start up the car.

Smokey's persistent ass leans down into the car when I roll down the window. "Yo, Dee. You got twenty dollars? I'll hit ya back when my income tax check comes in."

Now I must really have "Boo-Boo the Fool" stamped on my forehead. Smokey ain't never had a job so how in the hell is he gettin' some refund? "Nah, man. You know I ain't working right now."

"C'mon now. Everybody knows you fuckin' Junior's cousin. That nigga got mad money. He got to be breakin' you off somethin'. Ain't those real diamonds in your ear?"

And I thought those two old birds across the street were bad. "I gotta go, Smokey." I hit the window's power button and Smokey jumps back.

"I know you got some money, gurl," he hollers, smiling and scratching as I pull out of my parking space. I just roll my eyes and jet down the cracked street to the security gate. At the corner, Shakespeare is strolling up from the Circle K and I take another good look at him.

He's fine, no doubt—but broke as a joke. And I ain't havin' that shit. "Writing a book, my ass." I hang a right and happily cruise out to the suburbs.

After a bomb meal at Ruth's Chris Steak House, Tyrik and I got our groove on at The Compound nightclub. I'm wearing the hell out this red silk dress with a neckline that plunges straight to my navel. My titties are taped in place but every nigga in here is waiting to see whether they fall out.

Being on the arm of a pro athlete, I'm given the star treatment. But it isn't long before these booty-poppin' chickenheads start crowding my man and I have to check them.

"Excuse you." I stab one girl with my acrylic French tips. "You want to back the fuck up?" The bitch turns and wouldn't you know it's that same Latino J-Ho wannabe I had to beat down at Tyrik's party. "What the fuck?"

I launch before thinking and take the first swing. When my fist connects against her jaw, it's like sweet music to my ears. But the bitch is quick and she manages to draw a long scratch across my jawbone.

"Yo le mataré, Puta!"

"Dee—Elsa. Break it up," Tyrik plants himself in between us. A few dudes from his entourage jump and pull Elsa out of the way.

"What the fuck she doing here, Tyrik?" I challenge him. "You two still got somethin' going on?"

"Calm down, Dee. Calm down."

"Answer me, goddamn it. How come every time I turn around there this bitch is, huh? What the fuck is going on?" I press my hand against his forehead and push his big watermelon head back, daring him to jump some shit off.

"Calm down, baby. You wanna get us thrown out of here?"

"Answer the damn question." I lean to the side and see Mamí being escorted out of VIP, but the heifa had the nerve to blow me a kiss. "I'm going to kick that bitch's ass." I start around Tyrik, but he quickly grabs my arm and pulls me back.

"Ain't nothin' going on, baby girl." Tyrik says, backing me toward a corner. "This is a public place. I can't control who they let in here."

Every pore in my body tells me this nigga's lying.

He licks his thick lips and his eyes travel down my body's curves as if he's ready to fuck me right here in the club. Actually that shit sounds kinda good. The place is big and crowded. We can probably get away with a quick freak without anyone noticing—well, not too many people noticing.

"I'm your girl?" I ask, suddenly flipping the script and becoming syrupy sweet.

"You know you are," he whispers thickly into my ear. "You got to do something about that temper. For real."

"Then stop trying to make me jealous," I purr. "You knew I'd go off if I saw her."

Something in his smirk tells me I'm right. Tyrik gets off on my jealous streak. Just like some women like a rough-neck, there are some men who want a ride-or-die chick. That's me to the fullest—if it gets me what I want.

I pull him the rest of the way to the back corner and hike a leg up over his hip. "C'mon. Let's do it right here."

He laughs and shakes his head, but there's a definite twinkle in his eyes.

"You scared?" I challenge again.

"I ain't scare of nothin', baby girl."

"Good." I open my clutch purse and pull out a condom. "How about we get this party started?"

Tyrik, still smiling, glances down at the condom and then shakes his head. "Thanks, but I, huh, have a rule about using my own."

No shit, my smile hits the floor and there's a different sparkle in his eyes as if he knows what the fuck I'm trying to do.

"C'mon." He pulls me along and the next thing I know he crams me into a small stall in the men's bathroom. I've never been fucked over a toilet before, but I perform like a porn star all the same. But even as I'm moaning and groaning, I realize I still have no guarantee of a one-way ticket to Pittsburgh. So I better think of something . . . and fast.

12

Molly

It's laundry day.

I need a drink and a joint before even considering spending the day in that damn overheated sauna this place calls a Laundromat. Not only does the place smell as bad as, if not worse than, my building's pissy hallway, the fuckin' women in the place are ready to cut you if you move their clothes from the machines so you can use them.

I learned that the hard way.

Some chick named Geneva was all set to give me a beat-down because she'd left her clothes in the washing machines for God knows how long and I took them out. Hell, I was even going to put them back in. Next thing I knew, I had this mad, black woman swiveling her neck, waving her finger, and screaming at the top of her voice.

Half the complex raced down into the basement and

was urging her on to kick my ass. That was the first time I realized how much these people hated me. We got into it, and yes, I got my ass beat, but I got a few good licks in, too, before it was all said and done.

That weekend I met my mom for lunch. The moment she saw my black eye, she bought me a gun for protection. If I lived in any other place, I'd say she overreacted. The only problem is I don't like guns—so it just sits on top of the bedroom closet, along with the bullets.

The second time Geneva pulled that shit, I moved her clothes again and got another face full of spittle—but I didn't get my ass beat. Now I have a reputation in Bentley Manor as "The Clothes Mover." It's not much, but it's something.

My buzz has finally settled in and I stuff my jeans with quarters before heading out the door with the clothes baskets. The sole Laundromat on the premises is in the center of the U-shaped complex where Miz Cleo and Miz Osceola keep vigil over the place like guardian angels. Truth be told, they are the only two who give me the time of day.

Only thing is: I got a feeling they don't care too much for my husband, which is unfortunate. I want them to like him.

The streets and sidewalks are littered with kids and they make no attempt whatsoever to move out of the way.

"Hey, lady," Some nappy-headed kid hollers out from his bike. "How come you so fat?"

His circle of snot-nosed friends bust out laughing.

I clench my jaw and keep walking like I don't hear him. However, I'm sure the entire complex heard him.

"Hey, lady. Hey, lady!" They all chant.

"Hey, gurl. You got twenty dollars?"

Smokey waddles up to me with his hand held out. Why the hell he bothers to beg money from broke people, I'll never know. "No, Smokey. You know I don't have any money."

"Then how in the hell are you gonna do your laundry? Ain't that your daddy selling dem Fords on dem commercials? Can't tell me he ain't got no money."

"He ain't me. I-I mean . . . isn't me." Lord, I swear you don't have to be here long before your English starts getting jacked up.

"Well, how about a dollar? You got to have a dollar if you about to do laundry."

As he's talking, he's scratching like he has the chicken pox or something. Plus, his eyes are wild and his lips are in desperate need of some ChapStick.

"C'mon now, bitch. Gimme a dollar." When he grabs my arm, no shit, my heart leaps into my throat. He's going to attack me right here in broad daylight.

I drop the baskets and try to pull away. "Let go of me!"

"Hey, get your hands off of her," Miz Cleo's liquid southern voice snaps like a whip.

"I ain't bothering her," he lies. "She just about to give me a dollar. I just need a dollar."

"Boy, we said let her go," Miz Osceola's rough voice adds to the mix.

Before I know it, the older ladies rush off their stoops, down the sidewalk and begin hitting Smokey with actual wooden baseball bats.

"We said leave her alone," Osceola barks, delivering a blow against his legs.

"Ow. Shit. Hold up." Smokey drops to the ground and covers his face.

An army of children race to see what's going on and when they witness Smokey getting his ass kicked by two elderly ladies in housedresses, tan knee-highs, and patent leather shoes, they burst into a chorus of laughter.

Frankly, I'm too stunned to move.

"Whoa. Whoa." Shakespeare, Smokey's younger brother, parts the crowd. "What happened? What's going on?"

Miz Cleo stops pummeling the poor bastard to turn her angry eyes on Shakespeare. "I'll tell you what's going on," she says, waving the bat in front of Shakespeare's face. "He attacked this poor girl for a damn dollar."

"That's not true," Smokey croaks from between his fingers. "She said she was going to lend me the dollar, ain't that right?"

Smokey looks to me with pleading eyes, but I shake my head and grab my baskets again. It's getting more than a little uncomfortable with the whole complex staring at me.

Shakespeare sighs. "I'm sorry if he scared you." His

kind, brown eyes settle on me and I suddenly feel guilty for the ruckus I caused.

Miz Cleo's anger, apparently, refuses to cool. "You need to get his dusty behind off the streets and into somebody's clinic before he seriously hurt somebody."

"Or in somebody's church," Osceola amends.

"Yes, ma'am." Shakespeare loops Smokey's arm around his shoulders and helps him up.

"I ain't going to no damn clinic," Smokey protests. "That white bitch is lying. She said she was gonna give me a damn dollar."

I just shake my head and trudge my way to the Laundromat.

Behind me, I hear Miz Osceola shooing and breaking up the crowd. Needless to say my buzz is gone and when I walk into the Laundromat my mood continues to drop at the sight of Geneva and her circle of friends.

They, on the other hand, clam up the moment they see me. Thrusting my chin up, I make a beeline to the row of old washing machines. As I pass Geneva, I hear her whisper, "Dumb-ass bitch."

I whip my head around and Geneva plants her hands on her hips. "What? You got something to say?"

My hands itch to pull out her Korean weave, mainly because it doesn't match her kinky roots, but there's no way I want to get into a four-on-one situation. So I do the only thing I can do: turn around and mind my own business.

However, it becomes painfully clear that Geneva have other plans.

"Yes, girl," she says loudly to one of her friends. "I rode that big, black cock until I got saddle sores."

The women giggle and glance over at me.

"I told him if he can't get what he needs from that fat-ass wife of his that he was welcome around my way any damn day of the week."

The hair on the back of my neck stands straight up. They're not talking about who I think they are.

"Of course I don't know where the hell she think he is all hours of the night. Surely, she doesn't think his ass is really going to be the next Jay-Z. Motherfucker can't rap for shit, but he sure knows how to get his stroke on." Geneva slaps hands with some bug-eye bitch who continues to sneer at me.

"I hear what you're saying, girl. I had a piece of that chocolate ass a couple of weeks back. Brother is a straight freak, but I just love how he calls me 'li'l ma'.'"

The quarters slip from my hands and scatter across the floor.

The women point and cackle like a group of hyenas. Tears sting the back of my eyes and I'm literally trembling with rage. *They're lying. They're just fuckin' with you.* Closing my eyes, I draw a deep breath and then kneel to pick up my quarters.

They're lying. They're just fuckin' with you. Am I reasoning or trying to convince myself?

When I stand up again, the women are now grouped around me.

"What the hell do you want?"

"Nothing, gurl." Geneva smiles as if we're fast friends. "We just came over to see how you're doing. How's Junior?"

"Just leave me alone," I say, cramming the money into the machine and then dumping my clothes inside.

"What?" Geneva asks. "We're just being friendly."

"I'm not looking for any new friends."

"See?" She tells her girls. "This just goes to show that opposites really do attract . . . because Junior is always looking for a new lady friend."

That's it. I have to beat this bitch's ass.

13

Aisha

I can't stop pacing.

I walk from the kitchen to the bedroom. The bedroom to the kitchen. The bathroom to the living room. From one end of the living room to the other to look out the window at my bullshit-ass neighbors. And all back again. And again. And again. And fucking again.

The whole time I pace I smoke a L and drink straight from a bottle of Dom that Maleek and me been saving for a special occasion. Pace. Puff-puff. Sip. Pace some more. Puff-puff some more. Sip some more. Until I am paced out, puffed out, and sipped the fuck out.

This small-ass apartment feels smaller but I'm not going outside because everything outside my front door costs. Be it money or time. I'm running out of both.

I sit on the edge of my bed nearly biting off the colorful

acrylic tip from my fingernail. I twist my hands. I cross my legs and then uncross them. I flop back on the bed. I roll over onto my stomach—a stomach filled with nerves and shit.

What the fuck am I gonna do?

Maleek promised to take care of me. To always treat me like a queen. Now I'm running out of money and his ass can't do a damn thing about it. On top of that, I think he's lying about his momma ain't got none of his money. What, he thinks I'm crazy? What is it, fuck me and my finances as long as his parents and fat-ass sistah sitting straight? Shit, his momma has her fucking husband. I ain't got shit. No husband. No money. No dick. And yes, I miss that dick. It's been five months since Maleek *and* my pussy was put on lock.

And Momma's stressing me the fuck out. I paid the bail for Nasir to get outta jail and that cost me a grip. I couldn't leave my baby brother in that motherfucker. Hell to the no. Now the little Altima we bought my momma last year is acting up and she might need a new motor. How can I tell Momma I ain't got it? She do the best she can with what she got. It wasn't her fault she couldn't get a good job. She works hard until she's tired to take care of my little brothers. She always put them first. She is a good momma. Fuck that. If Maleek can take care of his momma, my momma ain't going lacking. So if the motor cost a grand, then fuck it, she gonna ride.

My momma needs me.

My brothers need me.

Maleek needs me.

Funny thing. I'm so busy taking care of everybody else, who the fuck gone take care of me?

I ain't never had no fucking job and I'm not looking for none. Besides, what fucking job can I get that would keep me in the shit I love—the shit I'm used to, the shit I refuse to give up?

I think about leaving Bentley Manor but to move out of low-income housing when my income is low is just crazy.

I think about taking some of the money and getting some nigga to flip it but who can I trust? If they split with my shit I will really be ass-out.

I'm back pacing when someone knocks at my front door. I frown as I hold the blunt with my index finger and thumb to keep from burning my acrylic nails. "Who?" I ask, even as I look out the peephole.

"Kaseem."

What the fuck he wants? I open the door but I step out into the hall before he can step up in my shit—someplace he has no right to be. "Whaddup, Kas?" I ask, holding the blunt behind my back.

He makes a face like "Damn." I look down at myself remembering the snug baby tee I have on with sweat shorts that ride low on my hips, showing off my flat stomach and a print of my pussy. My nipples are hard and poking through the shirt.

I use my finger to first close his fucking mouth and second to raise his eyes from my titties to my face.

He laughs, wiping his hand with his mouth (a little undercover drool check?). "I just came thru to check up on you, but I see you looking fine as hell."

This nigga resembles that supa-dupa sexy Nelly. The platinum and diamond gleaming around his neck, wrist, and fingers. The fly-ass Tommy Hilfiger striped polo he has on with khaki shorts and colorful Nikes that matched the stripes in his shirts. Haircut freshly faded. The grills on the bottom of his teeth just the right touch. This nigga is pure balla status.

Damn. Kaseem is smelling good, looking good, and standing there looking at me like he wants to fuck me good.

"I been doin' a'ight. Just tryna hold my man down, ya know."

He crosses his arms over his chest. "Every man should have a female like you in their corner."

"Damn right," I tell him, my voice slurring a little bit. I pull the blunt from behind my back and take a long drag. Fuck it. The scent of it will kill that slight tinge of piss and God knows what else floating around this bitch.

"Can I come in?" he asks.

I laugh, letting out a stream of thick smoke from my nose. "Nah."

"You scared?" he asks, smiling a little bit.

I raise a brow. "Scared of what?"

"Nothin'," he says, raising his hand again to wipe his mouth.

This nigga is flirting with me and if I don't catch my-self—my horny and slightly-pissed-at-my-husband self—I'll be flirting right back. Not with my man's best friend. That's some shady shit and I'm not even gone be *that* kinda bitch. No, not my husband's homeboy. Shit, Maleek might be set-ting me up and asking Kaseem to come at me to make sure I have that pussy on lock. I ain't no dumb bitch.

"I'll let Maleek know you came by to check on him."

Kaseem nods and reaches in his pocket to pull out an-other wad. "Need something? Anything? Let me know."

"Nah, I'm straight," I lie, even as my mouth waters a little bit. "Thanks."

He peels off some hundred-dollar bills and pushes them in my free hand.

"For the commissary?"

Kaseem shakes his head. "Nah, that's for you and it's more where that came from. Just let a nigga know."

"Let a nigga know what?"

He nods his head in my direction. "You know what's up, Aisha."

Yeah. He's right. I do know. Kaseem—whether doing it for Maleek or whether he's being straight up—just put in his bid to be my man.

He gives me another long look with a shake of his head before he walks away.

I shoot off behind him, pushing the door to the stairwell open so hard that it echos. Kaseem turns at the door to look up at me but the rest of my words freeze at the sound of voices in the stairwell. I don't need nobody sniffing out my business so I just wave at Kaseem and walk back toward my apartment. *I'll get his ass straight later*, I'm thinking, walking back to my apartment.

I ain't even have time for nothing but money. It's time for a bitch to get on the grind.

But it's hard to think when I'm so fucked up. I lock my front door behind me and walk into my bedroom to sit on the bed. I feel a little dizzy, hot, and sweaty. This happens to me every time I smoke too much weed. Topping four blunts off with champagne didn't help it any. I yank my Baby Phat tee over my head and fling it away from me. I work my sweat shorts down my legs and use my foot to toss them over my head.

Brrrnnnggg.

I wince at the sound of the phone ringing like a damn fire alarm. Probably Maleek. It keeps on ringing but I ignore it. I'm not ready to talk to him right now. I have my mind on money and money on my mind. Plus I'm high and Maleek thinks I gave up smoking. "Yeah well, I thought he left me straight with money 'til his ass got home."

I guess we both were wrong.

I roll off the bed and make my way to the kitchen. I'm trying to get my mind right to make a ham and cheese sandwich when I hear loud voices outside in the parking lot. Holding my sandwich I walk to the window in the living room and pull back the silk jacquard curtains.

"Dayum!" Those two nosy, old ladies, Miz Cleo and Miz Osceola, are wearing out Smokey the Crackhead with bats. I start laughing my ass off.

I stand right there holding the curtain back with one hand and holding my sandwich with the other like that crazy shit is my personal fucking entertainment. Bunch of damn clowns, I think, as I shove the last bite of sandwich into my mouth just as somebody breaks up the beat-down. "Terrible damn situation," I mutter, mellow as hell as I head back to my bedroom.

I lay back on the waterbed and my body moves in a snakelike motion. I moan a little at the memory of the steamy nights Maleek and I spent in this bed. Long, steamy, sweaty, fuck-me-'til-I'm-funky, freaky nights.

I rub my hands down my belly and slide them beneath the rim of my low-cut panties to play in my curly hairs. I split the lips of my pussy, already slick and wet from feeling horny, and I hiss a little as my hips lift off the bed at the first feel of my swollen clit.

"Whoo," I say soft as hell.

I circle my clit with my fingers and spread my legs wider.

This is my release. Miss Palm and her five daughters is my lover for now. And I know my g-spot so good that I'm usually humming, cumming atcha in fifteen plucks of my clit.

My heart's beating fast as hell. My pussy is super wet. But I can't cum this time. My mind is somewhere else, I'm aggravated about my money, and plus I'm sleepy as hell in the middle of the day. The pressure of my fingers slacks up as my eyelids drift close.

Maybe a little nap will shake off this high so I can think straight.

Just before I feel myself falling to sleep, the words of a stranger float in my head.

"You look like you could use some company for the night."

14

Molly

I've been calling Junior's cell phone for the past two hours. Each time I get his voice mail I hang up. Here it is, one of the worst days of my life and my absentee husband is nowhere to be found.

"Are you ready to go, hon?"

I flip my cell phone closed and glance up at Miz Cleo. Not only did the old lady beat a crackhead off me today, she was also kind enough to drive me to the emergency room after Geneva and that bug-eyed bitch broke my arm.

"Yeah. I'm ready." I drop my gaze to avoid her piercing one.

"Don't fret," she says, sliding an arm around my waist and giving me a hug. "Ain't no shame in asking for help."

I try to smile but instead tears burn my eyes.

"I take it you weren't able to reach that husband of yours?"

I just shake my head in shame. "I'm sure he's still working at the studio," I lie.

"Uh-huh." Miz Cleo reaches over to inspect the cast on my right arm and then tugs me along. "C'mon, hon. Let's get you home."

Silence grows between us as we walk out the emergency room and to her old, burgundy Lincoln Town Car. I can feel Miz Cleo's pity pulsing off her and a part of me wants to shout that Junior is a good man. I love him. He loves me.

For some reason, the words are trapped in my throat.

If Junior loves me so much, why is he never home? Why doesn't he ever answer his phone?

"I told him if he can't get what he needs from that fat-ass wife of his that he was welcome around my way any damn day of the week."

Was Geneva fuckin' with my head or telling the truth?

I don't know anymore. I do know that I'm tired of being a prisoner of Bentley Manor where just trying to do laundry can turn into a matter of life and death, tired of taunting children and jealous, black bitches who hate me for no damn reason.

"Honey, are you all right?" Miz Cleo asks as I settle into the passenger's seat.

Until now I wasn't aware of the tears streaming down my face. I needed my man today and he wasn't here.

"Aw, now. Ain't no need for these." Miz Cleo reaches over to her glove compartment and pulls out a travel-size pack of Kleenex.

I accept the packet and quickly mop my face. "I'm sorry," I mumble.

"Whatcha sorry for, chile?"

"I don't know. Everything, I guess." How can I begin to explain how much I've fucked up my life? What am I doing? Where am I going? How much longer can I go through with this?

"Honey, where's your family at?"

I start to answer, but just thinking about them now tore at my heart. "Can you please just take me home now?"

Grady Memorial Hospital isn't far from Bentley Manor, but with Miz Cleo's unwillingness to get on the expressway or drive faster than thirty-five miles an hour, the short ride takes forty-five minutes.

"Thank you," I say as she finally parks the car in front of her building. I unsnap my seat belt with my good arm, turn and climb out. Though I want to race to my apartment and cry into my pillow, I force myself to be patient and walk Miz Cleo to her apartment. This seems silly to me since the seventy-plus-year-old woman can take better care of herself than I can.

"Good night," I say when she finally turns the key in her lock.

"Molly," she says kindly before I'm able to turn around good. "You know I don't make it a habit to butt in other people's business . . ."

Since when?

"But if you have a way to get out this place, even if it takes swallowing your pride with your family, take it."

"What? And leave my husband?" I shake my head.

"Honey chile," she says reaching over and cupping my right cheek in the palm of her hand. "Open your eyes and see what's in front of you."

More tears burn my eyes and blur my vision and I turn and race back to my own roach-infested prison cell. To my surprise Junior is home and toweling off from a shower.

"Where in the hell have you been? It's ten o'clock."

Numbly, I lift my cast and feel a bit foolish for jumping to the wrong conclusion.

"What the fuck happened?" He walks over to me and takes a look at my arm. "Don't tell me you broke it while running from another rat." He chuckles.

"Geneva broke it," I admit flatly. I feel his body stiffen as he holds my arm. "Are you fucking her?" My question stuns me and him, too, judging by the look on his face.

He drops my arm. "How the fuck you gonna ask me some shit like dat?"

That isn't an answer. "Are you?"

Junior turns his back. "I ain't answering dat bullshit." He storms to the bedroom.

"Her girlfriends claim you're fucking them, too," I say to his retreating back. I need an answer from him—any answer. I follow him to the bedroom scared of what he might say.

Junior whips the towel from around his hips and walks naked over to the tall chest of drawers in the corner of the room. "Why the fuck are you listening to a bunch of jealous-ass bitches for, huh?" His eyes darken venomously. "I'm stressed out to the max, tryna hold us down, tryna get my career to jump off, and you gonna toss a bunch of bull-shit in my face?"

"How can I not ask?" I shout back, feeling like I'm having a nervous breakdown. "You're never home. You never call. You never even answer your damn phone."

"Who the fuck you hollerin' at?" He roars back in a voice I've never heard before. "What? You think you're run-nin' shit in this motherfucker?"

Thump. Thump. Thump.

"Shut up down there!"

Junior moves to within inches of my face. "I'm the head nigga in this motherfucker. You got dat?"

I've lost my voice. He bumps me with his chest as if daring me to challenge him. To do so suddenly seems like suicide.

"I ain't got time for this shit." He turns and starts pulling out clothes and getting dressed.

Tears leap from my eyes.

"Where are you going?" I ask, struggling to keep my alarm to a reasonable panic.

"Somewhere where I'm appreciated. I finally finish my new demo and I come home to celebrate wit my wife and this is the bullshit I get? Naw. Naw. I don't think so, partner. I'm rollin' up out of here."

Fuck it. I'm in full panic mode now. "No. Don't go." I rush over to him. "I-I just didn't know what to think. They surrounded me and were laughing and teasing. They made me feel like a fool!"

Junior shakes his head. "Naw. Dudn't matter. You're my wife. You're supposed to believe in me and shit. After all we've been through? Those bitches don't know shit dat goes on in this crib. I can't stand a gossiping bitch. I swear I can't." He jams his long legs into a pair of jeans and then grabs his favorite t-shirt. "Yo, maybe it's time we just break this shit off."

"What? No!" I reach for him, but he quickly pushes me away. "Junior, don't do this. I'm sorry."

"Naw. I need a bitch dat's got my back, nahmean?"

"I do have your back. I swear," I cry. Oh God, please don't let him leave me. Where will I go? What will I do?

Junior ignores me and plops down on the edge of the bed to cram his feet into his sneakers.

I drop to my knees beside him and continue to plea, "Baby, please believe me. I'm sorry. You're right. I should have never stepped to you like that."

He stands up and heads toward the door. I grab hold of his leg and grunt through the pain of my broken arm. "No. No. You can't leave me. I'll die if you leave me."

Thump. Thump. Thump.

"Goddamn it!" the upstairs neighbor shouts. "Shut the fuck up down there!"

"Mind your own goddamn business!" Junior roars up at the ceiling.

Junior stops and draws an impatient breath. "Molly, let go of my leg."

"No. Oh God, Junior. Please. I swear I'll do whatever you say." I'm sobbing and struggling for breath. Why did I ever doubt him? Why did I let those jealous women fuck with my head?

"Molly, get the fuck off me. I ain't playin'."

I can't let go. I won't let go. Somehow I got to make him see how much I love him. No other woman can ever love him as much I do. To my surprise, Junior reaches down and grabs a good chunk of my hair and snaps my head back.

"I said get the fuck off," he growls. "You had a good thing and now you done fucked it up."

He jerks me back and smacks the shit out my head against the closet door. Still sobbing, I wobble onto my feet and race after him into the living room.

While Junior leans down to snap up the car keys from the coffee table, I race around him and block the front door.

He looks at me as though he's ready to bounce me off every wall in the apartment. "Goddamn it, Molly. Get the fuck out the way."

"No. Not until you forgive me," I croak determinedly. "You know how I feel about you. I couldn't stand it if you left me. I swear." I can't stop crying. "Please, Junior. Please give me another chance." I don't know what else to say or do to make him change his mind. "You got to forgive me." Finally, I just bury my face in my hands and let my hysteria sweep through me.

It's a long time before I feel the gentle kisses my husband trails across my forehead, temples and even my closed eyelids.

"Shh, baby gurl," he whispers. "It's a'ight." He now kisses my tears. "Shh. Calm down."

"I-I can't," I pant as my chest continues to heave. "D-don't leave me," I beg.

"A'ight." Another kiss. "I ain't goin' nowhere, li'l ma."

Our lips finally connect and again I push all pain aside and throw my arms around his neck. As our mouths part and our tongues duel, I try to pour all my emotions into him—drown him with my love.

I swear he's trying to do the same thing to me because his love overwhelms me.

Our clothes hit the floor in a frenzy and my baby picks me up and rams me against the door as if I weigh nothing. With each smooth thrust his beautiful cock feels as if it's bouncing off my tonsils and ripping me in half. That's all right though; I love how my baby makes me feel. I love the way his face twists and how nasty he talks.

"You love this good dick, don't you, li'l ma?"

"Yes, baby. Yes."

"You'd do anything for this shit, won't you?"

"Oh God, yes."

"Don't you ever fuckin' question me again like dat. Ya hear me? I own this shit. I own this pussy. Tell me whose pussy this is."

"Y-yours."

"Huh? Whatcha say?"

"It's yours."

"Say this pussy is mine."

"This p-pussy is yours."

He fucking me so hard some of the pleasure turns into pain.

"I want to stuff this shit in dat tight white ass."

I tense as he bites at my neck. We've only done anal a few times. He's so big that I can't take it. He apparently senses my hesitation because he's suddenly angry again.

"What? You said this shit is mine, so I can do what the fuck I want, right?"

"Yes, baby. Yes." I kiss him to reassure him that I'm not trippin'. "Fuck me any way you want." I want him to feel good.

"Damn right." He pulls out of my pussy and jams into

my ass with nothing more than my pussy juice as lubricant. The scream is out of my mouth before I can think straight.

Thump. Thump. Thump.

"Motherfuckers, don't make me come down there!"

Tears are streaming down my face and Junior kisses them away while he moans out his pleasure.

"Ooh. Goddamn, baby. Goddamn."

He kisses me again and thrusts his tongue down so deep it feels as if he licking my clit. That part does feel good. With his dick in my ass and his hand in my pussy, my orgasm pops off like the Fourth of July. Soon after, Junior growls and cream fills my ass.

We're both a sweaty mess and panting like we just hiked Stone Mountain.

I finally slide down the door until my feet touch the floor, but even then my legs tremble so bad I have a hard time standing.

"Thank you, baby." Junior grabs my hair and forces my head up. "I love ya, gurl."

Our eyes lock.

"No matter what," he adds. "Don't you ever forget dat shit."

"I won't." I hug the man that is my world and I vow to be a better wife. Next time Geneva start some shit, I'm going to be ready for her ass.

15

Devani

I'm worried.

Ever since the freak episode in the men's bathroom at The Compound, Tyrik has been acting funny. Was it too much? Had I just pigeonholed myself into the "good fuck" category as opposed to the "marriage material"? Even worse, in one week's time, I've been delegated back to Bentley Manor with phrases like: "I think we should slow down" and "Baby, I need a little more space," and last but not least "Call before you come over."

Everything is changing, but I still have my platinum card. And I'm not giving that shit up. Nigga will have to pry that motherfucker out my cold dead hands.

Still, no word about Pittsburgh.

I'm not dumb. He's tryna dump me—and I can't have that shit.

It's Easter Sunday and Tyrik is getting his praise on at Creflo Dollar's World Changers Church Ministries at the World Dome. I may do a lot of things but I don't do church.

And I don't believe in fakin' the funk—unlike a lot of these heathens running around in the Bible Belt. Drinkin', smokin', sexin' and cursin' Monday through Saturday and then jumpin' and filled with the Holy Ghost on Sunday—Negroes kill me with that shit.

Tyrik included.

Of course, Tyrik's father used to be a minister at some fancy-smancy church in Birmingham, Alabama—until there was some big hoopla about him laying "hands" on a lot of the single women in his congregation.

Typical. Like Momma says: a nigga is a nigga is a nigga. So church niggas ain't no different.

Since black folks like to stay up in service all day, I figure I have more than enough time to do my specialty roll-by. See, I have a date tonight with Tyrik and no doubt the night is gonna end with a pussy nightcap.

Tyrik made it clear he only uses his own condoms, then I think it's time I take my little sewing needle and visit his stash in the nightstand by his bed for extra insurance. After a little online research at the library yesterday, I discovered oil-based lubricants could weaken a latex condom. So I made a trip to Starship novelty shop and got hooked up on some Kama Sutra body lubricants that were oil-based.

Now I'm in serious business.

I park in the center of the circular drive and hop out, wearing my pink, low-cut sweatpants, short tee, and an open light jacket. I figure I'll go work out after this quick job.

I slip my copy of the house key into the lock and turn it. My heart is absolutely racing as I creep into the house and over to the security keypad to enter Tyrik's birthday. After two beeps the password is accepted.

I'm in.

Turning around, I take in the house's wide-open space and I swear I feel like a queen entering her palace. This shit is a long way from Bentley Manor. Cathedral ceiling, Italian marble floors, seven bedrooms, nine bathrooms, and two kitchens.

Why in the hell would anyone need two kitchens?

"All this shit for just throwin' a damn ball across the field." I shake my head and climb the stairs to Tyrik's bedroom. As I walk, I continue to imagine that all this shit belongs to me. Of course, I would fill the place with servants so I could be waited on hand and foot.

My mornings would begin with either breakfast in bed or a few laps in the pool—after I learn how to swim, of course.

I'd shop all day and show up at every hot party and turn every bitch there green with envy, including Aisha Cummings.

I'd show her how a real balla rolls.

The day I move out of Bentley Manor, I'm blastin' Tupac's "All Eyez on Me" so the whole joint will know what time it is or maybe I'll throw one of those old block parties.

That would be a lot of fun.

I slip into Tyrik's room and inhale the woodsy cologne that still hangs in the air. On top of getting paid and looking good, Tyrik smells like a man's man—not one of those fruity metrosexuals in suits running around downtown.

The bedroom is decorated in handsome, dark mahogany that undoubtedly cost a fortune. The carpet is so plush I can literally feel myself sinking into it. A baby would be nice—but a ring would be better.

"Mrs. Tyrik Jefferson." I like the sound of that shit.

I want a house like this. I deserve a house like this.

Finally I pull my big head out of the clouds and get back to my plan of action. I stroll over to the nightstand and open the top drawer. But there's only two condoms left in the box. There was definitely more than this left in here the other night.

"That motherfucker!" I clench my jaw, wishing Tyrik was here right now so I could sock him in his lying mouth. I bet it's that damn fake-ass J-Ho I keep seeing everywhere. Yeah, I may be after the nigga's money and all, but at least my ass has been faithful these last few months. Why do niggas always try to nail everything with a hole?

I sit down on the edge of the bed stunned by how much this bullshit hurts. Do I love Tyrik? I don't know—but I do care about his ass. How can I not?

Shit.

I wipe my eyes before the tears fall and then punch the sewing needle through the center of the condoms. At a casual glance, the punctures are hardly noticeable in the gold wrappers.

In the distance, I hear a loud rumbling coming up the driveway. I jump up from the bed and race to the window. What the fuck am I gonna say if I'm caught?

Shit. This is what I get for daydreamin'.

At the sight of Junior's ugly-ass hoopty rolling up the drive, I relax and thank my lucky stars. It'll be a lot easier lying to Junior than Tyrik. I turn around and rush out the bedroom. By the time I reach the top of the stairs, Junior is coming through the door and flashing me a smile.

"If it ain't my favorite ghetto princess."

"What the fuck you doing here, Junior?"

"Told cuz I'd drop off my new demo in the mailbox. What are you doing here? Don't tell me you've pussy-whipped my cuz into lettin' you hang in his crib while he's gone." His annoying smirk irritates me, but then I notice how his dark gaze roams over my body.

"What's going on between me and your cousin ain't none of your business." I start down the stairs and try to brush pass Junior on his way up.

He grabs my arm. "Wait now, li'l ma. Where you run-nin' off to?"

This nigga's moves are so tired. "Let go. It ain't gonna happen."

His lips curve like he knows something I don't. "There you go, acting all bougie and shit. I'm just tryna be friendly and get to know ya, li'l ma." He moves closer and is even bold enough to put his hand against the curve of my ass. "How come we ain't never hooked up?"

"Because you ain't got shit I want."

This stupid nigga just laughs. "Is dat right?"

"Yeah. That's right."

Junior jams me up against his lean body and slow grinds his big-ass dick against my pussy. "What if I tell you dat you have something I want?"

I swear I can't think straight. How in the hell did I for-get the anaconda this motherfucker is packin'?

"C'mon. I want to see dat pretty li'l kitty you showed me a while back. You still got dat Mohawk?"

As he's talking my eyes lock on his thick, juicy lips. I swear his slow grind is gonna make me cum even though we're both fully dressed.

"Ooh, yeah. I bet you still got it." He leans forward and whispers. "I bet dat motherfucker taste good, too." His wet, warm tongue suddenly traces the shell of my ear and I shiver.

My voice trembles like a motherfucker, "I-I gotta go."

"Ain't nobody here but us. Cuz ain't getting out of service fo' a while. Dat's plenty of time for me to pop dat pussy."

"What about your wife?" The question surprises me. Why the fuck should I care about his wife?

"My wife ain't here. It's just you, me, and opportunity." Why the fuck am I considering this shit?

"C'mon now. You don't need to put your shit on lock. I love my cuz and all but you know he fuckin' plenty of bitches."

And there it is.

"C'mon," he begs softly, taking my hand and slipping it through his open zipper.

His big dick is still as hard and smooth as marble, just as I remembered. As I begin to stroke him, my clit begins to ache. My brain is screaming "no" but my body has a mind of its own.

"C'mon," he begs again. "I ain't gonna tell nobody."

This time he slips his hand between the band of my sweatpants and then dives into my panties. "Aw, shit. This pussy is sloppy wet, too."

He easily glides two fingers inside of me. I nearly come unglued while he pumps his finger for a few strokes. He removes his fingers when they're good and covered with pussy juice and then put them in his mouth.

"Hmm. Hmm. Hmm. Finger-lickin' good."

Our eyes meet and I know right then and there: I'm fucking this nigga.

He knows it, too.

16

Lexi

April in Atlanta is almost like summer anywhere else. The weather's nice. Hot but not too hot. Mid-seventies. But it's enough to draw people out their houses like they're thawing out from winter.

And Bentley Manor is no exception.

You never really know how many people live in the complex until it gets warm outside. And what a sight some of my neighbors make.

After work, I make baked spaghetti for dinner and change into a pair of jean capris and a tank top. WooWoo didn't get off work until five so I take myself right out there with Miz Cleo and Miz Osceola.

I like hanging out with the ladies. They know any and everything that goes on in Bentley Manor. Plus they're funny and wise. They remind me of my nana.

"This place sure has changed over the years, ain't it, Cleo?" Osceola asks, her light-complexion skin speckled with flat moles and freckles across the bridge of her nose. Her t-shirt reads: BUSH—No More Years, and she smokes a Marlboro cigarette with one hand and cracks the shells of boiled peanuts with the other.

"You ain't never lied, Osceola." Cleo's skin is smooth, dark, and tight like she's straight from the motherland.

"And these men. I ain't never seen so many during the day. In between nine to five I don't want to look in no man face 'cause that mean he ain't working." Osceola pitches the emptied shells into a plastic bag by her feet before tossing a few peanuts into her mouth on that one.

I wince from the sun as I look around at the parking lot. There are a lot of men loitering about to say it's just after three in the afternoon. I didn't say anything, though. When you sat with these ladies you usually didn't have to. They have enough conversation for anybody.

I reach down beside me for the big glass of sweet tea I brought downstairs with me.

"Especially all these men running 'round here hooked on that stuff," Osceola adds. "That dang-on Smokey make me sick, always 'round here begging people for money."

Cleo shifts in her seat. "Yeah, and looking like he'll snatch your bag in a hot second."

Osceola drops her bag of peanuts into her lap and

reaches down beside her to pick up her bat. "I triple dog-dare him to snatch mine."

Cleo laughs as she holds up her own bat. "I think he got enough of these," she jokes.

The ladies tap their bats together and it reminds me of the Wonder Twins' powers activating. We all just laugh and laugh.

"A lot of these no good men 'round here could use a good whack in the head and on the behind." The ice in Osceola's jelly jar of water rattles as she takes a deep drink of it.

These women sat in these chairs at the end of the U-shaped complex from early morning until just before the sun starts to set. It's the best position to see every car that turns into the lot, everybody coming and going from building to building, every dang-on thing going down in Bentley Manor. From a secret look between two people creeping, who got new furniture, whose furniture got re-possessed, who got served papers by the police, who got thrown out of Bentley Manor, who moved in, who bought drugs and who sold drugs to even who farted and which way the wind sent it floating.

They are the living and breathing *Atlanta Journal-Constitution*s. I have no doubt that when they speak they have a story or two to back up what they saying.

I hear the school bus pull up outside the front of the

complex. Just moments later about twenty kids noisily come around the curve from the gate. My eyes scan the crowd counting the heads of mine. I frown when I see all but two.

My littlest one, six-year-old Imani, comes flying at me first. "Mommy. Mommy."

"Ooh, Momma, Monique carried her hot self to the store," Danina, my ten-year-old, says, ever the tattle-tell.

"Trey went to get her." That's from Imani as she squints through her round glasses.

"Did ya'll speak?" I ask, even as I gather up my keys and cup.

"Hello, Miz Cleo and Miz Osceola."

"Hi, babies," they respond.

Montel, my seven-year-old, finally walks up dragging his book bag behind him and looking like he touched everything dirty in school with his shirt and jeans.

"Ya'll sit here with the ladies 'til I come right back."

"I wanna go, Momma," one of them whines. I look over my shoulder with the momma stare and keep on walking.

Molly steps out the building just as I near it. She frowns as soon as she sees me. I just roll my eyes heavenward.

I've always felt the tension from her. If she wants a reason not to like me I can give her one. Like the nasty picture her husband sent me of his dick, or him trying to jack off in front me on Valentine's Day, or the fact Junior

bragged to me he didn't get her nothing for Valentine's Day
but two forties of malt liquor.

I have my own memories of a Junior Valentine's Day, so
even though I don't like her ass I did feel sorry for her. I
know firsthand that a man's betrayal hurt extra worse on
Valentine's Day.

Hell, even though Luther got off late from work he
came right on through with a new bracelet for me.

"Molly," I say kind of short.

"Lexi," she answers even shorter.

Whatever. I keep on moving. Usually I didn't have no
problems out my kids, but Monique know I don't allow
them to go to the store alone. So I'm on my way to show
her just who the boss is, since she obviously had a lapse in
memory. I can't let go of my kids to the streets, especially
Monique. Every so often I see that same wildness that reminds me of her father. A wildness that scares me.

*Nineteen ninety-seven. I was on the grind working in house-
keeping at a hotel and trying my best to raise my two children. After the way he played me Valentine's Day I finally
had Junior out of my system. That was partly due to Evan
Wiggins.*

*I met him when he came to my apartment to hook up
my cable. And I do mean hook up, since he immediately
tried to holler at me and gave me all the premium chan-*

nels for the price of basic. He was just my style. Tall and slim with that deep-set eyes and high-cheekbone look. And I liked that he was an older guy—thirty-seven. He had seventeen years on me and after dealing with Junior's immature self I got to thinking an older man was just the thing I needed.

We started out talking on the phone. Two weeks after that I was sending my kids to my nana so he can spend the night. Three months later he was living with me. Life was good. When I found out I was pregnant I was stressed out a little bit. Did all the coulda, woulda, shouldas but Evan had been happy as all get-out to have a child.

I was about six months pregnant when things started to change. He started to change. He got home from work later and later every night. The money he used to give me every Friday got shorter and shorter until he had nothing but excuses of why his check was short. We began to argue more and more. Hell, I had two kids, was pregnant with my third, and wasn't looking for a fourth in the shape of a grown man. Soon his late nights out on the weekends became him disappearing completely from Friday until Sunday.

Life around apartment 4C became hectic as hell. I spent many a night crying over the mess I got myself into. But that wasn't even the half.

I came home from work early one day. This pregnancy was the worst ever. I was always sick. My legs were beginning to swell and my back was always aching like crazy. I *just wanted to take a hot bath and lay across my bed to rest before I had to get my kids from the babysitter. I didn't even care if Evan didn't show his face.*

As soon as I opened the door the smoke escaped and swirled out into the hallway like it was just waiting to be freed. The smell was like burning rubber and it stung my eyes. "Evan, what the hell is burn—"

The sight of my man—my man—sitting there hitting the pipe shocked the rest of the words from my mouth. He looked up at me with his lips still wrapped around the pipe and I didn't know this man. The ashen and sweaty face. The red and glassy eyes. His lips white and chapped. I was having a baby for damn Pookie from New Jack City.

"Get the fuck out!" I started yelling, dropping my purse to the floor as I stormed over and knocked the pipe out his mouth. It flung and hit the wall, shattering to pieces.

He jumped to his feet and whirled on me. His eyes were crazed and I backed up from him. For a moment I thought of the headline: "Pregnant Woman Killed by Drug Addict Boyfriend."

I put one hand on my round belly and stretched the other out to him. "Just leave, Evan. Just get your shit and go," I told him, my voice low because I didn't have the strength or the will to yell and argue. I was tired. I was sick and tired of being sick and tired.

The look on his face changed. It softened. He reached for me. "I'm sorry, Lexi."

I stepped back. "You damn right you sorry. You smoking dope. You got to go. I'm not gone have that around my kids."

He reached for me again and I moved past him to pick up the crack rocks on the glass coffee table. I headed toward the bathroom and suddenly felt his arm around my neck. I gagged for air as he wrestled the tiny Ziploc from my hand. When he released me I slipped down to the floor crying, "Get out, Evan. I'll swear to God I'll call the police. Get your shit and get the fuck out!"

I didn't look at him. I couldn't.

I sat on the floor for a long time. Long after he begged me to forgive him. Long after I begged him to leave. Long after he finally did.

It was hours later when I made myself get up. I cleaned every inch of that apartment with bleach. I couldn't have my kids touching on crack residue. So I cried and I cleaned until my hands and my insides were raw.

I packed his clothes, shoving them into garbage bags. Him leaving them let me know he thought he was coming back. Wasn't no coming back. And I meant that. I would drop his shit to his momma's house.

I wasn't putting up with no damn crackhead.

I didn't realize until I was about to leave to pick up my kids that the junkie bastard took my pocketbook when he left.

❖　　❖　　❖

After I make sure the kids and Luther are all fed, washed and in bed, I take a long hot bath scented with the Brown Sugar & Fig bubble bath from a Bath & Body Works gift set I got from a booster today. After I had to snatch up Monique's behind and remind her with a switch who laid down the law, I need a little me time. I don't really like to spank my kids but my nana always told me you whup them now and you don't have to worry about the police whupping them later.

So I do what I have to do to make sure the environment we live in doesn't snatch up my kids. "I did what I had to do," I repeat out loud to myself like I'm getting it straight in my own head.

After my bath I take my time cleaning up the bathroom and wrap a towel around my body to walk to our bedroom. Luther's in his boxers propped up on pillows in the middle of our full-sized bed watching television. "I didn't think you was ever coming out there," he said, sounding distracted as his eyes stay on the TV screen.

In the mood for a stress reliever I lock the door. ESPN just isn't going to do it. I step in front of the TV.

"Move, Bay, I—"

I drop my towel.

His eyes start from my toes up to the smile on my face and he doesn't miss a thing in between. His dick gets hard and tents his boxers. I try not to notice that, even hard, his dick is just six inches strong.

I walk to the bed and straddle his face. "Damn this pussy smells good." His words brush against my exposed flesh.

"Hungry?" I ask.

Luther strokes the tip of his tongue against each of my lips before he circles my clit.

My ass jiggles as my body jerks and I bite my mouth to keep from hollering out.

Yes, my man can eat my pussy until I pass out and that's why I climbed in his face before he can try to climb in me. Sure, I'm gonna give him some, but first I want to make sure *I* cum. I'm not in the mood to instruct him how to sex me right. I just want to enjoy him pleasing me.

I circle my hips on his face as he sucks my clit and sends a jolt through my body.

He will cum in this pussy before the night is over but first I'm going for mine.

17

Aisha

Desperate times. Desperate fucking measures, right?

I take another long drag of my blunt—a nice Hawaiian blend wrapped in the peach-flavored skin of a Philly. "No big deal," I say to myself. "Boom. Bam. Fifteen . . . twenty minutes tops and it's a wrap."

"Are you okay in there?" he asks through the solid door.

I roll my eyes. "Be right out," I call back in this fake saddity voice as I sit down on the commode.

I stand up and drop the end of the blunt into the toilet. It hits the water with a *hiss*. I avoid my reflection in the mirror. Not that I'd recognize myself.

I want to fit in—or at least look like I fit in—with the classy bitches strolling through or chilling in the lobby of the Ritz-Carlton. The Chetta B print silk-jersey dress, Ferragamo peep-toe pumps, Gucci tote, and my hair long and pressed straight with light makeup all said this is a rich black bitch that belongs.

The whole getup had drew him to me just like I wanted. Now here we are.

I undress until I'm standing among the luxury of the suite's bathroom in not a damn thing but a silk teddy that showed everything I have—especially my wide hips and make-a-nigga-moan ass.

"A'ight. Let's make this money," I tell myself as I open the bathroom door.

The bedroom of the suite I insisted he purchase (nothing but the best, fuck dat) is lit the hell up. Guess he doesn't want to miss a thing. My eyes dart around the room. A bottle of champagne and two flutes on a tray. The fireplace lit and popping although it's damn near seventy outside. And him laying his white ass in the middle of the plush bed naked as the day he was born. His condom-covered dick is already hard and he licks his lips like he's damn starving as he peeps the tits-and-pussy print in my teddy.

I force a smile as I walk to the foot of the bed and crawl my way up between his open legs. I try to ignore the way his hairy-ass balls are reddish and laying against the bed like they will drop to his knees when he stands up. This motherfucker has to be about sixty, but who cares? The room can look as romantic as it fucking please but this is straight business.

I straddle his hips and grind my dry pussy against his

erection. Not bad for a old white dude, I'm thinking. Motherfucka probably on Viagra or some shit.

"May I touch you?" he asks, his voice nervous as his hands stop just before my body.

I swallow back my irritation and pull his hands to my titties. They are cold and his fingers squeeze my nipples too tight.

I see the five one-hundred dollar bills laying on the night stand. The sooner this shit starts the sooner it will be over.

"You ready for some of this good pussy?" I ask him with a hot lick of my glossy lips.

My first trick ever shifts one hand down to slap my ass.

I think about Maleek. My marriage. My loyalty.

Now is not the time. Loyalty from him would've meant my ass is taken care of. He should of made sure I wasn't pushed to this shit.

Long after he's gone back to meet his wife in their own penthouse suite—I douche twice and take the longest, hottest shower ever—I drink the whole bottle of champagne and smoke another blunt, and throw the fuck up, and decide to go home before them nosy hawkeyed motherfuckers at Bentley Manor spread the word that I stayed out all night. I finally look at my reflection in the steam-coated mirror of the bathroom. For the longest time I stand there naked and exposed inside and fucking out.

18

Lexi

"Damn, can she go any slower?"

I hold my temper in check and keep right on scanning and bagging the items of these two wannabe ghetto princesses. I eye the one that made the smart-ass comment. Bright, multicolored hair stacked to the sky, manlike gold jewelry (probably her man's), gold tooth, neon acrylic nails about a good three inches long (how she wash? Her butt probably funky), and a jean dress short enough and low-cut enough to barely cover everything.

Her and her buddy look like a couple of rejects from that stupid-ass movie *BAPS*.

I'm on my job and here it is midmorning and neither one them look like they rushing to go anywhere and they stressing me about I'm going slow. Whatever. They start gossiping about this one sleeping with that one.

"Nothing but a no-good bitch would fuck somebody husband." Funky Butt says this around a piece of gum she is making sing.

"Damn right. I'll do many things but I ain't tryna fuck up nobody home 'cause I ain't want nobody fucking up mines," Silly Sidekick adds.

I roll my eyes heavenward. These chicks don't know the half. Life isn't always black-and-white.

Two thousand. Three kids. Upgraded—if you can call it that—to a two-bedroom apartment in Bentley Manor. Working my ass off as a waitress in Waffle House. Deeply in love with Klinton Jackson. Seven months pregnant with his child. Happier than I'd ever been in my life.

Oh, it took a minute to get happy about being pregnant with my fourth child. I was barely into my twenties and struggling like crazy. My nana stopped speaking to me for a whole month and even WooWoo told me "you a crazy shot-out bitch." I didn't miss the looks people gave me when I started to show.

But I did eventually get happy.

This time was different. This pregnancy was different. My Klinton was different.

I met him a year ago when WooWoo and I went to Florida for one of our cousins' wedding. Klint was driving the Greyhound bus and we eyed each other as soon as I stepped aboard. He was tall, muscular, and that high-

yellow fine like The Rock. Suddenly that seat in the front of the bus was looking too appealing to pass up. After a few long glances we started talking as best we could as he focused on the road. As WooWoo slept through the night, I stayed up talking to this man about any and everything. Almost nine hours later, we arrived in Jacksonville and I left the bus with his cell phone number.

He worked on the road a lot and there were times we had to miss all the "couple" times (Christmas, New Year's Eve, and Valentine's), but the time we did spend together was good. I even hinted at marriage but his idea was that we wait until he got a job that let him be closer to home on the regular. That made sense to me.

I was sitting in the living room with my kids, talking on the phone with Klinton one day, when WooWoo breezed into my apartment. I watched as she picked chubby Monique up from the floor to spin in the air.

"What's that noise?"

"That's WooWoo playing with the kids," I said, shaking my head as my sister moved to snatch up an even chubbier Danina. "She came over to braid my hair so I don't scare you in the delivery room looking like Buckwheat."

"I'm not going to miss the birth of my first child for shit. Even if I have to quit this damn job if they don't give me time off."

I smiled, rubbing my hand over my belly. "I know I want you there."

"Ain't a damn thing gone keep me from being there."

"Good."

"Well, let me go, baby. I gotta get this bus to Columbia before five."

"I love you, Klint."

"Love you, too."

I dropped the cordless phone onto the sofa.

"Lexi, get that roach," WooWoo said.

I saw Monique waddling past. "WooWoo, I know you didn't just call my baby a roach."

"No, I'm talking 'bout the one 'bout to crawl up your damn leg."

I flew off the chair and the roach dropped to the floor. I stomped his ass and put us both out of misery. No matter how much I kept my place clean, put down boric acid, and sprayed a ton of Raid, them things were a part of Bentley Manor just like the bricks.

"Want me to watch these little buggers while Klint comes over?" she asked, walking into the kitchen to open my fridge.

"Klint's in South Carolina."

"No he ain't," WooWoo said simply, as she opened a bottle of Pepsi.

"Yes, he is. I just talked to him."

"Well, I just saw him so that trumps your phone call any day."

I opened my mouth to protest.

WooWoo held up her hand. "Don't tell me I didn't just see Klinton coming out the flower shop over on Spring Street. I know that big-head motherfucker when I see him and I saw him."

Me and WooWoo looked at each other for a long time. If Klinton was lying about his whereabouts, the question was why. When else did he lie? Who were the flowers for?

"Time to do a late-night drive-by," WooWoo said, twisting her waist-long braids around her finger.

"I don't know where he lives," I admitted softly.

"What?" WooWoo gasped in that mixture of shock and disbelief—that kind of are-you-stupid? disbelief.

"He always comes here and he ain't hardly ever home." I tried to explain but WooWoo's face said it all.

I picked up the phone.

"What are you doing?" WooWoo asked, snatching the phone from me.

"I'm calling Klint to ask his ass what the hell is going on?"

"Lord have mercy. Lexi, you never tip your hand to a man. Play it cool or you'll never catch his ass." WooWoo held on to the phone and started pacing in full plotting mode. The girl knew she could scheme up on some shit.

The rest of the day was a blur, but let's just say I found a ticket I got in Klinton's car and WooWoo made a call to this sheriff she knew and boom-bam we were in our nana's Lincoln pulling up to a nice two-story brick house in Alpharetta. Sure enough, his black Ford Explorer truck sat in the driveway beside a 2000 Toyota Camry. The yard was pretty like a picture with the flowers and green lawn.

"I thought he lived in an apartment downtown," was all I could say.

Lies on top of lies on top of lies.

"What you want to do, Lexi?" WooWoo asked, biting the tip of her acrylic fingernails.

I didn't even answer her. I hopped out the car, big belly and all, and walked right up to the door. I rang the bell before I could think to do otherwise.

The door opened just moments later and I looked up into the face of the man I loved. He was just as shocked as I was. Deep down a piece of me was still hoping I was wrong. Stupid me.

"Who is it, Klint honey?" a female voice called out just as my eyes dropped and saw the gold wedding band on his left hand.

"That's fucked up, Klinton," I whispered to him, hating the tears that filled my eyes.

"Klint?" the faceless woman called again.

"Daddy, Momma said come and cut the cake."

My mouth fell open to see the little boy tugging at Klinton's pants leg. He was no more than four or five and the spitting image of Klinton.

I thought mine would be his firstborn.

Lies on top of lies.

"Go home, Lexi." That's all he said to me before he picked up his son, stepped back, and closed the door in my face.

I didn't even know WooWoo was standing behind me until I turned around. "Take me home."

"Oh hell to the no. It ain't even going down like that," she said, stepping up to ring the doorbell and knock like she was the police.

I felt weak and dropped down to sit on the top step. "Just take me home, WooWoo. Please."

I could hear tussling on the other side of the door and I knew Klinton was keeping his wife from opening it. Their words were muffled but definitely heated.

"Oh fuck no. These motherfuckas done call the po-po."

As if I wasn't embarrassed enough. "Just take me the fuck home, WooWoo!" I screamed, my hand pressed to my belly.

I was angry. At Klinton. At his beautiful house and family. At his wife, who was innocent in this shit. At WooWoo. But mostly at myself.

I never saw Klinton again. He never kept his promise to be there when I had my seven-year-old, Montel. Once a month he sent a check from his joint account with his wife but he acted like me or our son never existed.

So these chicks didn't know the half. Sometimes life isn't black-and-white. There are shades of gray filled with the lies and deceit of a married man.

I'm more than happy to finish checking them out so they can carry their gossip with them.

My shift is over and ten minutes later I'm in my Lincoln headed home. Luther had a doctor's appointment this morning so he took a sick day from work. When he called me earlier he was already back home and frying chicken wings for dinner. I just hope his version of frying didn't mean cooking on high until the grease and the chicken are black as tires.

I was so busy hightailing it from work that I forgot to walk over to the supermarket side of the superstore to get sugar. I stop by the gas station on the corner. The kids go through Kool-Aid like it's water. I'm standing in line when I get a message alert on my phone. I see it's from Junior's number and I delete it.

I'm used to Junior begging for ass, but ever since Valentine's Day that fool has been putting the pressure on hard like he can just taste my pussy. Even down to coming to get the kids more often than he used to. Not much but more than before.

Luther didn't like that we live in the same projects as Junior but he's real cool about not interfering on those rare moments Junior's sorry ass did more than just wave to his kids in passing. Deep down I know Junior was another reason Luther wants to move. Shit, if I ever admit that Junior's dick used to have me whipped Luther would really freak out. No need to share.

Luther is lounging on the couch sipping on a can of Budweiser and reading some brochures when I walk into the apartment. He looks up and smiles.

My heart kinda leaps in my chest as I sit my purse, keys, and bag with the sugar in it on the kitchen table. I smile as I move over toward him. "Whatcha reading?" I ask.

"I got these brochures about a program that helps with down-payment assistance on your first home."

"Really?" I ask, sitting down in front of where he lay. His arm came around my waist as we both look down at the colorful brochures of smiling faces—most of them black—in front of nice homes with yards and fences. A vision of me and Luther and the kids grinning and chinning just like these folks makes me smile. "What's the catch?"

"Some kind of classes. They'll even help repair credit." His hand shifts up to massage my breasts beneath my t-shirt and Wal-Mart vest. "This might be our ticket out of here a little sooner. What you think?"

I shift so that I lay in his arms beside him on the couch.

I almost fall off but he holds me close. "I think I love you," I whisper against his lips as I look into his eyes. "I love you. I love you. I love you."

The rest of my loving words get swept up in our kisses and I thank the Lord that for once I made the right choice. There is no way my undying desire for a jackass like Junior is going to ruin this.

No way in hell.

19

Devani

Let's face it. Memorial Day is just an excuse for niggas to get together and have a big-ass barbeque. Bentley Manor is no different. Way before noon (which is amazing in itself because most of us don't get up before lunchtime) the air is filled with spicy, smoky, and honey barbeque sauces.

The heat in everyone's apartment nearly triples because of all the cooking going on in the kitchens, and we're forced to keep the front doors open. The piss and mildew growing out in the halls are quickly overpowered with the scent of chitlin's, hog mogs, and baked beans. Even Momma is in the kitchen cookin' up collards and stirrin' up a thick-ass batch of macaroni that has so many different cheeses in it, it's amazing you don't drop on the spot from a heart attack after eating it.

Niggas don't care. Despite the genetic disposition to high blood pressure, heart disease, and strokes, they won't give up the sacred hog.

Me? All this shit is making me sick to my stomach. Literally.

Koolay ducks his head into my room without knocking and looks disappointed to see I'm already up and dressed. "Yo momma wants you."

I run the brush through my hair a final time as I glare at him. "How many times have I told you about walkin' in here without knockin'?"

"If you really wanted me out of here you'd lock the door." Koolay chuckles and takes another long look at my thick frame. You'd think his ass would learn his lesson.

"Momma!" I shout out as a threat.

"Shh, gurl." Koolay jerks a glance over his shoulder to make sure he wasn't about to loose another tooth.

I just laugh at his retarded ass.

"You bitches play too much," he complains and finally shuts my door.

I glance in the mirror and pose prettily in my white capris and white baby-doll top. It's scary how innocent and virginal I look. I just hope Tyrik's parents buy my act.

Yes. Today I meet the parents. A clear sign that this relationship is back on track and moving in the right direction. It's also the day my life will change for the better.

My door jerks open again and before I can react my

mother snaps, "What's takin' you so long? Didn't Koolay tell you I wanted to see you?" She crosses one arm and takes a sip from her afternoon drink.

"Yeah, but I was busy." I'm giving her as much attitude as she's dishing out. "Whadda you want?"

"Watch it, missy. You're still living under my roof."

"Not for long," I assure her.

"What? You gonna pull a miracle out your ass in the next five weeks? That is when he's leavin', right?"

"It's hardly a miracle, Momma," I say, patting my belly. "It's talent, hard work, and manipulation."

"That's my baby girl." Her eyes twinkle with pride. "You want me to fix you a plate?"

"Momma, I'm going to a barbeque." I slip my feet into my sandals. "I don't need to eat before I go eat."

"A'ight. But I need you to run to the store before you head out to dat nigga's place."

"Momma! Why can't you send Koolay?"

"Be back!" Koolay shouts on cue from the living room.

"He's making a run to see M. Dawg."

"Of course he is," I sigh. "Let me guess: pack of Philly blunts and tampons?"

"Just the blunts. Spot me and I'll hit ya back later."

I don't even know why she bothers lying. She never pays me back. "Momma, I'm supposed to be at Tyrik's at one thirty."

"What you bitchin' for? You got a car."

No sense in arguing.

I hurry out the apartment and barely get two feet before someone else is offering to fix me a plate. Despite the aromatic scent of my mother's collards, everybody knows her ass can't cook and likely the collards are tough and gritty.

"No thanks," I tell Miz Duncan across the hall. "I'm going to my boyfriend's barbeque this afternoon."

Miz Duncan holds the record of the most children in Bentley Manor with nine kids, beating out Lexi Mitchell across the way—at least Miz Duncan's all had the same daddy. "I bet your boyfriend don't make potato salad like I do. Everybody knows I put my foot in it, girl."

She does make a mean potato salad. "I'll let you know tomorrow."

I jump into my ride and drive down to the Circle K. The usual suspects are lined up outside the store. I ignore both the jobless brothers and the eager-to-work Mexicans as they hoot and whisper about my round booty.

They can look, but they can't touch.

When I walk up to the counter, I'm surprised to see Shakespeare behind the cash register. "What the fuck? Where's Osama at?"

"The owner's name is Manmohan and he's from India, not Afghanistan."

"Hell, they all look alike if you ask me."

Shakespeare laughs. "That's the problem with all you ig'nant black folks. Can't see the world outside your hood."

"Last time I checked you were living in the same hood I do. What—gettin' a minimum-wage job suddenly makes you better than everybody else?"

He crosses his arms. "I didn't say that."

"Uh-huh. Where's your crackhead brother at? I ain't seen him around in a while."

"Rehab." Shakespeare drops his gaze. "I'm prayin' it works this time."

I nod and shift uncomfortably at the sight of his vulnerability. "I need a pack of Phillies."

He nods and snaps back to his normal self as he reaches for my box.

"So what's all this shit about? Why you working here? Can't be no real money in it."

Shakespeare shrugs. "It's *honest* money. Figure I save up, finish my degree and maybe get one of those HUD homes out in Alpharetta."

"Oh, you tryna be a big balla," I tease.

"What can I say? I got dreams." He leans toward me over the counter. "You know, I'm always looking for someone to share those dreams with."

He might be cute as a puppy and maybe if I was more the romantic type where love outweighed common sense I might've kicked it with him, but dreams don't put food on the table or clothes on my back. Plus, I ain't got years to be waitin' on some nigga to finish school. I'm rollin' up out Bentley Manor quick, fast, and in a hurry.

"Sorry, Charlie, but I'm already taken."

Disappointment flashes across Shakespeare's face as he finally rings me up. "Still with Tyrik?"

" 'Til death do we part."

An hour later, I park my butt-ugly car behind a line of luxury vehicles on Tyrik's circular driveway. This is the first time I hate that my "nice" car is already here. It fucks up my dramatic arrival on the property. As I step out the car, I can hear the music bumping in the backyard.

I follow the sound and the scent of barbeque.

Tyrik described this get-together as a small affair with a few friends and family members. He'd even said I could bring my mother and Koolay along; but I'm not that goddamn crazy. The turnout looks to be about sixty people.

"Ah, look who's here. My baby." Tyrik's smile stretches wide across his face before he steps out from behind his mega-size gas grill. "You're late," he whispers and then kisses me. "Where's your mom?"

"She's not feeling too good today," I lie effortlessly.

"Oh." His brows dip together. "I'm sorry to hear that." He rewards me with another kiss. "C'mon. I want you to meet my parents."

For the first time in my life I'm nervous.

"Mom. Dad. I'd like for you to meet my friend, Devani Rodgers."

Friend? What's this friend shit?

"Devani, this is my father, Reverend Donald Jefferson, and my beautiful mother, Pauline."

Why the fuck did he just introduce me as his friend? "It's a pleasure to meet you," I say with a plastic smile.

"Yo, Devani!"

Still sort of shell-shocked by Tyrik's introduction, I don't immediately realize someone's calling me.

"Gurl, don't act like you don't know nobody." Junior says. "Hey, Uncle Donald—Aunt Pauline."

Finally everyone turns toward Junior and his brick house of a wife, Molly.

"Hello, nephew," Rev. Jefferson says.

I note that the haughty-taughty Pauline doesn't say jack shit. In fact, she looks Molly over like the girl had just crawled out of a Dumpster or something; seconds later, she's giving me the same look.

"See, Moll. And you didn't think you'd know anybody here. You know we all could've rode here together."

My gaze dances around the couple—primarily out of guilt for having fucked this woman's husband inside Tyrik's home, or rather, his bed.

"I see you got your cast off." I'm tryna make casual conversation.

"Yeah. It came off Friday."

"You also live in the projects?" Pauline asks.

The direct question stuns me and I have no choice but to

answer with the truth. I glance around at the multimillion-dollar players and their wives and feel as though I've been demoted to the maid or something.

"So," Pauline continues. "How long have you and my son been friends?"

"Oh, for about six months," I say, mimicking her soft southern voice.

Her brows arch high into her forehead. "And this is the first I've heard of you?"

It's funny. Her voice remains sweet but her words pack venom.

"Well." Pauline smiles. "I guess there's nothing wrong with a little summer fun before he ships off to Pittsburgh."

Oh, this bitch is good.

"I'm sure we'll be having fun for a lot longer than that."

"Yes, yes. That's what they all say." She turns toward her son as if she'd grown bored with my ass. "Tyrik, baby. Whatever happened to that one girl I liked—Ellie-Elle—"

"Elsa?" I snap and then turn toward Tyrik, ready to whup his country ass in front of his own damn momma. "Elsa met your mother, too?"

"Met me? Why, she was just months away from becoming my daughter-in-law before Tyrik called off the wedding last year. Cold feet."

What the fuck? "You were engaged to that Latino bitch?"

"Oops," Pauline says. "Did I let the cat out of the bag?"

Fuck it. I'm ready to beat his momma's ass.

"Pauline, honey." Rev. Jefferson wisely steps in between us. "You're upsetting the girl."

"Me?" Pauline sounds indignant. "It's not my fault I can't keep up with the women revolving around here. Tyrik needs to settle down and stop all this foolishness. We raised him better than this."

"Momma," Tyrik hisses under his breath. "You're causing a scene."

"I'm doing no such thing." She turns toward me again. "If anything, I'm merely warning the poor girl not to get her hopes up and think there's some sort of future with you."

"Momma," he hisses again.

"What?"

"I'm sorry to disappoint you, Mrs. Jefferson." I sneer. "But I'm not just 'summer fun,' I'm having your damn grandchild."

20

Devani

Oh, shit.

That is not how I wanted to drop the baby news on Tyrik. But at least I finally shut his bitchy mother the fuck up. Actually, I did more than shut her up; the woman now looks as though she's having a heart attack.

Reverend Jefferson, too.

Tyrik, on the other hand, is pissed.

The only one that lights up like a goddamn Christmas tree is that dumb bitch, Molly.

"You're pregnant?" she gasps, clasping her hands together. "Congratulations!"

I flash her a weak smile, still careful to avoid Junior's heavy gaze. "Thank you."

"I'm so jealous," Molly went on. "I so badly want to have little brown babies."

Now everyone in the small circle shifts their astonished gazes to this white bitch. Where the fuck did Junior find this heifa at?

"I told ya, li'l ma. I ain't tryna have no more kids."

My gaze drops.

"Moving on," Rev. Jefferson says, clearing his throat and shifting his hard glare back to his son. "I guess that means we're about to have ourselves a wedding?"

Fuck yes. I like how Papa Jefferson thinks.

"Over my dead body," Pauline croaks.

Here this bitch goes again. Before I can check her ass, Tyrik grabs me by the arm and hauls my butt toward the house.

"Excuse us," he growls over his shoulder. "I need to talk to Devani for a sec."

"Ow. Whatcha doin'? Ow. You hurtin' my arm." This nigga don't give a damn 'cause I nearly trip out of my sandals and start to tumble, but Tyrik lifts me up before I hit the ground and keeps moving without breaking his stride.

When we enter the house through the glass doors, there are more people dancing, laughing, and just milling about. Of course, one glance at Tyrik and people part like the Red Sea and allow him to snatch my ass across the house and up the stairs.

"What kind of bullshit you tryna pull?" he snaps the minute the bedroom door slams behind us. "There's no goddamn way your ass is pregnant. We've always used protection!" He throws me across the room.

I'm unable to catch my balance and hit the floor. "Shit, Tyrik. What the fuck you doin'?"

When the nigga comes at me, I think he's about to pull an O.J. My ass is slippin' because I ain't got shit to protect myself with. Who the fuck woulda thought my ass needed my razors out in the suburbs?

I jump off the floor ready to claw, bite, and scratch his ass into the middle of next week if that's what's going down. This baby is my ticket out the projects and I'm not givin' it up without a fight and makin' a whole lot of noise.

But Tyrik stops, balls his hands and backs away. "Yo ass is tryna play me."

Is this nigga tryna turn ghetto on me? "Don't be ridiculous." I force myself to relax and calmly hand-iron my clothes and hair in place before I turn the charm on full blast. "C'mon, baby. I thought you'd be happy."

He shakes his head and mumbles under his breath, "This isn't happening. I got a fuckin' reputation."

Now this Negro is worried about his reputation? Not when he's throwin' orgy parties and fuckin' me in men's bathrooms?

"Tyrik—"

"Shut the fuck up!"

I simply hold up my hands in surrender while he paces

the hell out of the carpet. "What the fuck were you thinking droppin' that shit on me in front of my parents?"

"I wasn't," I admit and cross my arms. "But your mother was being a—"

"Watch yourself!"

My hands fly up again. I guess I'll just watch him sweat this shit out.

"Are you sure about this?" He asks after a couple of minutes of pacing.

"Yes, I'm sure," I say, casting a bored glance at my nails.

"Well . . . well . . . are you sure it's mine?"

That I wasn't sure of. The day I fucked Junior in Tyrik's bed, the one safe condom I had in my purse broke over Junior's big-ass dick while he was ramming like he hadn't had pussy all year.

"What kind of fuckin' question is that?" I ask defensively. "Of course it's yours. We've been fuckin' like rabbits for the past three months. You didn't like it when I kept my legs closed and now you're gonna to bitch because you knocked me up?"

"Shh. Shh." He glances around like there was somebody else in the room. "Keep your voice down. You want everybody to hear you?"

"I don't give a fuck who hears me," I shout, real tired of his bullshit. "I'm pregnant and I'm having this baby—your baby. Deal with it."

Tyrik turns and straight punches a hole in the wall.

That shut my ass up.

"Rufus!" he roars and snatches open the bedroom door. "Rufus! Somebody get Rufus's ass up here."

What the fuck? Does he plan on having his four-hundred-pound cousin snap me in half?

Seconds later, Rufus charges into the room. "What's going on?"

"I need you to run an errand," Tyrik hisses while reaching to his back pocket for his wallet. "Go to the pharmacy and buy a pregnancy test."

"Come again?" Rufus blinks.

"Run to the pharmacy and buy a pregnancy test," Tyrik repeats and presses a twenty-dollar bill into his hand.

Rufus just stares. First at Tyrik and then at me. "I don't know nuthin' about buying no pregnancy test."

"Then ask for a salesperson to help you," Tyrik barks. "Just hurry up about it."

Rufus stutters some more but Tyrik pushes him toward the door. "Goddamn it, go!"

"You're wasting your money," I tell him, shaking my head and popping a squat on the bed.

Tyrik starts pacing again. "Well, if you are pregnant—there are options."

So much for a ring.

"I mean . . . I'll take care of everything. I-I'll be there for you."

"I'm not killing our baby."

This nigga looks as if he wants to cry. "Shit. Shit," he mumbles. "We were so fuckin' careful."

A knock sounds at the door. It's too soon for it to be Rufus so Tyrik barks, "Leave us alone."

"Son, open the door."

Tyrik mumbles another "Shit," and opens the door.

Rev. Jefferson enters the room and seems relieved to find me composed on the edge of the bed.

"Now is not a good time, Pop."

"I just came to make sure everything is all right." He puffs up his chest and closes the door behind him.

Tyrik and his father are strikingly handsome men with the same facial features, broad shoulders, and muscular chest. I see why women in his old church would risk a little fire and brimstone to get into his bed.

"Now son, I can tell this little lady's baby news comes as a shock to you . . . as well as to me and your mother. But I want to urge you . . . after all the appropriate tests . . . to do what's right."

I'm lovin' Rev. Jefferson more by the minute. Hell, if he gets me married off, I just might take my black ass up in somebody's church every Sunday.

Tyrik, however, still looks like he wants to cry.

"Your mother and I have worked real hard to get another church started and we can't afford for our congregation to learn about our son fathering babies outside of marriage."

You tell him, Papa Jefferson.

While Tyrik's father continues to preach, I become the pink elephant in the room. But it's all right, I'm day-dreamin' about my new house in Pittsburgh.

Rufus finally returns and Tyrik snatches the brown bag from his hands and then kicks him and his father out of the bedroom.

"Get up," he snaps.

The moment I stand, he grabs my arm and jerks me toward the adjoining bathroom. "You're taking this test."

"All right, all right. Let go." I snatch my arm back before he pulls the damn thing out of its socket. "Give it here." He hands me the bag and I level him with an evil glare before marching the rest of the way to the bathroom. I go to shut the door, but Tyrik pushes it back open.

"Hell no. You're going to piss on that stick in front of me."

I blink. "What?"

"You heard me. Drop your panties. I'm going to watch you piss on that thing."

I don't believe this shit. It's just on the edge of my tongue to protest, but one look in Tyrik's hard expression and I know it's a waste of time to argue.

"Fine," I say and unsnap my pants. In my time I've done a lot of kinky stuff and somehow squatting over a toilet and pissing on a stick in front of my man takes me to a level of shame I didn't know existed.

Of course these digital tests are easy as shit and the

reading in the oval window reads PREGNANT before I finish wiping and flushing the toilet.

Tyrik is back to looking like he wants to cry.

"Baby, this is a good thing," I tell him as I move over to the sink and wash my hands.

He's pacing again.

"You'll see." I dry my hands and turn toward him with a smile. "We're going to make great parents."

"Devani, it's—it's just not a good time. I mean, we still have other options."

My smile melts off my face. "I said I'm not killing our baby. I can't believe you would even suggest such a thing."

Our gazes crash, but this Tyrk has another thing comin' if he thinks he can intimidate me.

"I'm going for a drive," he announces and bolts from the bathroom.

"But you have guests," I remind him as I follow.

"I-I gotta go. I gotta clear my head."

He's out the door before I can stop him. "Let him go," I tell myself. Me and the baby will still be here when he gets back. I chuckle and head down the hall toward the staircase when a hand lands on my shoulder. I turn and my amusement disappears.

"Wit all the excitement, I forgot to say congrats," Junior says.

"Thanks." I turn, but Junior's heavy hand returns to my shoulder.

"I'm wondering how my cuz will react when I tell him you might be carrying my child and not his."

I pivot back around and give Junior my best DFWM glare while I stab his chest with an acrylic nail. "You keep your mouth shut," I hiss.

"Well, the condom did break—"

"You wouldn't dare. What about your wife?"

"This doesn't have anything to do wit her—plus, Molly will forgive me of anything. Can you say the same about Tyrik?"

He knows damn well I can't. "What the fuck do you want?"

His sly smirk returns. "Do you even have to ask?"

This nigga is a straight-up sex addict. "When?"

He eases up close. "Right now."

"Now?"

"I never put off tomorrow who I can fuck today."

"But the party . . . your wife . . . the baby."

He's already grinding against my hip. "It's just a quick nut, li'l ma. Ain't nobody got to know shit."

I don't fuckin' believe this.

"If not," he threatens, "I guess I'll have to wait here 'til cuz get back."

This sex-crazed motherfucker is not blowin' my chances to get out of Bentley Manor. "Fine," I snap, hoping this would be the last time and not the beginning of a lifetime of pussy payments.

The next thing I know this nigga crams me into some hall closet and jacks my legs over his hips while he pounds me against coats and jackets. What is it with these Jefferson men liking small confined spaces?

"Junior? Junior?" Molly's voice floats somewhere near the closet. "Has anyone seen Junior?"

Junior clamps a hand over my mouth and we both go still.

After a while it becomes hard to tell over the music if she is still by the door or has returned downstairs. Junior grows tired of waiting and begins to move inside of me again. I try to remain quiet, but goddamn Junior is a big motherfucker. Thank goodness he's true to his word. Soon after he busts a nut, we're out of the closet with a quickness.

Despite not being a religious woman, I'm praying I'm carrying Tyrik's child and not Junior's.

That shit will really fuck me up.

21

Lexi

It's late when we get back from Dixieland. The kids enjoyed the amusement park and Luther and I both agree that a day away from Bentley Manor is a good thing. Especially since Junior's lying behind promised Trey and Danina he would take them with him to Tyrik's barbeque. Like always he dropped the ball and left my kids with the sad face.

On top of that he gone have the nerve to call me while he's there talking about he wish I was there with him. I don't cuss too often but I blessed his behind out for 1) not even asking to speak to his kids and 2) still begging for pussy after he clearly disrespected me and my kids.

The kids pile out the car while Luther grabs Imani. Just the thirty-minute drive from Fayetteville has her sticky self knocked out.

"Daddy, I had fun," Imani says, stirring from her sleep as we all walk into the building.

"You did?" Luther asks, kissing her cheek softly.

"I did too, Luther," Trey adds, as he uses his key to unlock the door of the apartment. He switches on the lights before we all walk in.

Luther reaches forward with his free hand to playfully shake Trey's head. "I'm glad we was able to get a smile on your face after your daddy pulled another one of his disappearing acts today."

I see the sadness all of a sudden on Trey's face and I get pissed. "Trey, put Imani to bed. Luther, can I holla at you for a sec?"

I don't even look back to see if he is following me into the bedroom. By the time he does step in and close the door I'm already pacing. I whirl on him and step right in his face. "Don't you ever do that again," I tell him.

He looks confused and frowns as he starts to undress. "Do what?"

"Throw it in my kids' face that they Daddy ain't shit. They know that and they don't need you or anybody else—"

"Hold up. Hold up." Luther looks at me like I'm crazy. "If you're mad at your sorry-ass baby daddy then you need to save this bullshit for him. Don't fly up in my face like I'm gone cover for his ass when I'm here doing the job he ain't doing."

"I don't care if any of my kids' fathers are the worst ever—"

"Which they all are," Luther mumbles, walking away from me to toss his jeans into the hamper with anger.

"I don't talk shit about my kids' father in front of them." I point my finger in my heaving chest as I storm right back in his face. "And you not gone do it either."

"So you defending these deadbeats to me? Huh? You telling me Junior is too precious for me to talk about him? That's what you saying, Lexi? Huh? Is that what you saying?"

"I'm saying my kids don't understand shit like we do so all they know is what they feel. Me telling them that they daddy ain't good for a damn thing but a good fuck is hurting them, not him."

Luther gets quiet and tilts his head a bit to the side to look at me for a long time. A really long time. So long that it makes me pause.

"What?" I snap.

"You still fuckin' that nigga?" he asks me, his voice so low that I barely hear him.

Now I look confused. "What?"

"Since he such a good fuck maybe you still giving up the ass to that nigga."

I replay my own words in my head. *Ain't good for a damn thing but a good fuck.* Damn. In my anger I didn't even realize what I said. "Don't be stupid, Luther," I say, a piece of me feeling guilty at the times I imagined sex with Junior while Luther tries his best between my thighs to make me cum.

"Maybe if you wasn't stupid enough to have kids for motherfuckers who ain't worth nothing but a good fuck we wouldn't be having this conversation." Luther snatches a pillow and blanket from the bed before he slams out the room.

A long time later I walk out the bedroom and see the TV light flashing in the darkness of the living room. I peek my head into Danina and Monique's room. They both are knocked out in their bunk beds. I check on Imani in her room next. I think she's sleeping too until she calls out to me.

"Momma."

Imani. My baby girl.

"Why you still up?" I whisper.

"You and Daddy mad?" she asks. A little light shows on her face from the Dora the Explorer nightlight by her bed.

I walk into the room to sit on the edge of the bed and pull her into my arms. Her room is closest to our bedroom and I should have known she wouldn't rest easy. She hates for people to fight and argue.

"No, girl, please. We just fine," I tell her, kissing her forehead.

"Good," she says, her voice already getting heavy with sleep.

I sit there and rock her like I can take back the reason for her fears.

Two-thousand two. I was just twenty-four and life was good—at least financially. Raq, my boyfriend and the father of my one-year-old Imani, made my life pretty good. I didn't work. I was the good little housewife home all day cooking and cleaning while my older kids went to school, the babies went to day care, and my man left every day like clockwork to sling dope.

Raq had come into my life at just the right time. My nana had just passed away and I was feeling low. WooWoo actually introduced us after the funeral. He was shorter than I usually liked my men and had the hard face of a thug, but something about him turned me on. Maybe because he was different from any other man I messed with. Maybe a little thug love was what I needed.

He asked me to give up my apartment for good and move in with him, but Nana didn't raise that kind of fool. With my luck with men a part of me was waiting for the other shoe to fall. So we split our time either at my apartment or in the sparsely furnished double-wide trailer he owned in Decatur.

He came home at nights. I didn't hear anything in the streets about him running around on me. He didn't have a wife (I was his wifey) or a separate life. He sold dope and he didn't smoke it. Sex wasn't half bad. Money was flowing all right. So I was good to go.

I had packed the kids up and came down to Raq's place for the weekend like he asked. We were grilling the next day and filled this big-ass pool he bought for the kids. After I put the kids down for the night I took a long bath and waited for him to get home. Fridays was his busiest night because he would collect from all his customers who got paid and owed him money.

It was about one when I finally heard his key in the door. My cycle had just passed a few days ago and I was more than ready for some of that thug love. I just loved the way he would climb his little self damn near on my back as we did it doggy-style like he was trying to win a race or something.

"Lexi, you up?" he asked in the darkness. I could hear him removing his jewelry and setting it on the dresser.

I reached over and turned on the lamp. "Is that dick up?"

He looked over his shoulder and dropped his link bracelet to the floor when he saw me lying there in nothing but a pair of stilettos with my legs bent and open and oh so ready.

I moved to sit on the foot of the bed teasing my clit as he yanked his wifebeater over his head and flexed his muscles. I circled my hips and slipped my middle finger inside my throbbing walls as he dropped his jeans and boxers. He walked over to the bed with his hard dick swing-

ing before him. The words PLEASURE and PAIN were tat-
tooed on his hands. Raq said the choice was also yours if
his hands pleased you or fucked you up. I was ready to be
pleased.

He stood between my thighs and took my fingers from my
clit to suck the juices. I shivered with a moan. I loved a
freaky fuck. I leaned forward and took the tip of his dick in
my mouth. He smelled faintly of cologne and sweat but I
didn't care. I slowly sucked the tip before tracing the smooth-
ness with my tongue. His knees buckled.

"You know just how to welcome a motherfucka home,"
he said, flinging his head back as he twisted his fingers in
my microbraids.

I reached up to grasp his hard ass with both my hands as
I took nearly all of him into my mouth. "Mmmmmmmm-
mmm," I moaned as I felt the pulse of his dick against my
tongue.

"Damn," he swore, pumping his hips a little.

"Good?" I asked, looking up at him as my lips surrounded
his dick like a vice grip.

"Damn right," he said, his eyes meeting mine.

My whole body was hot. My nipples were taut and
aching. My pussy was wet and sticky. My clit was throbbing.

I sucked harder. Faster. Deeper.

He twisted my hair harder and pumped his hips faster
and deeper.

Sweat started to coat both our bodies.

"FREEZE! PUT YOUR HANDS UP!"

I opened my eyes and looked right into the barrels of about twenty guns as the police came busting into the bedroom. I froze. My naked body was exposed to their eyes. My lips still surrounded Raq's dick.

Seconds later more cops than I could count tackled Raq to the floor. Another one grabbed me and made me sit on the floor. I hollered out as they began tossing the mattresses and pulling the drawers from the dressers. They had Raq lying on his stomach with his hands cuffed behind his back.

I heard the kids holler out and I jumped to my feet. A beefy hand pressed down roughly on my shoulder to sit me right back down. I tried again to get up. "I wanna see my kids."

"Sit your ass down before I arrest you," was the gruff reply of the Fed who was faceless to me.

I couldn't stop my tears as I tried my best to hide my naked body with my arms and legs. I don't know how long I sat there because my fears and my questions kept me occupied.

Was I going to jail?

What was going to happen to my kids?

Would they let me call WooWoo to come get the kids if they did take me in?

Did Raq have the drugs they were looking for in the house?

What the fuck was I gone do?

No matter how much I pleaded no one let me at least go to my kids. They asked me questions about Raq and I played stupid. It seemed like forever before the police hauled Raq's naked body to his feet. They threw a blanket around him and shuffled him out the room before he could even say anything to me.

"She's clear."

Those were the sweetest damn words I ever heard. Moments later someone handed me a sheet and I hurried to wrap it around my body. When they led me into the living room I found more police. My kids were huddled on the lone leather sofa in the living room. I rushed to them and they all surrounded me as I took Imani in my arms to soothe her crying.

"Momma, why the police look in Imani's Pamper?" Monique asked.

"Sshh." I sat on the couch and tried to hug them all as Imani continued to cry.

Me nor Imani seen him since that night. They shipped him to Pennsylvania after his trial and soon the collect calls from him just stopped. I heard he got out like two years ago and moved to New York. Luther been in her life since she was two so he was the only daddy she knew. She's the only one who calls him Daddy and I don't stop her.

I hear her little snores and hold her just a little while longer before I ease her back into her bed.

Sighing at my life and my own jacked-up choice in men, I checked on Trey last. I open the door and peep my head inside his room. He's lying across his bed playing the Gameboy he got for Christmas. I clear my throat and he looks up with a sheepish smile. "Go to bed, right?"

"Right. 'Night," I say, smiling as I close the door.

"Ma."

I open the door and stick my head back in. "What, Trey?"

"I ain't mad at Luther for what he said about Junior."

I step into the room and lean back against the wall. "What I tell you about calling your daddy by his first name?"

"Then maybe he should act like a daddy, Ma."

What can I say?

"Me and Danina gettin' older. We see stuff for ourselves, ya know?"

"I'm sorry for that," I tell him, tears already building up in my throat. I could just beat Junior's ass.

Trey gets up out of bed, wraps his arm around me and kisses my cheek. "You ain't got nothing to be sorry for, Ma."

My little man. He doesn't know the half and I guess I'm lucky with all the men that came in and out of their lives that they still respected me, because time after time I put a man before my kids and even though it's in my past I am sorry as hell for that.

I leave his room and fight the urge to go to Luther. I go into the bathroom and take a quick shower, wrapping a towel around my damp body before I dash back into our bedroom.

I paused at the door to see Luther sitting on the edge of the bed. We never spent one night apart since we were married. I'm happy to see him but I pretend to ignore him as he flips through the TV channels. I dry off with the towel and climb between the sheets naked.

Luther turns around and looks at me with those sexy brown eyes.

I pat his side of the bed and pull back the covers. He climbs into bed and pulls me right against his warm body.

"I love you, Lexi."

"I know. And I love you, too."

Yeah, our marriage is worth swallowing pride.

22

Aisha

Life is good as hell.

My money is stacked like hell.

My clothes are bossy as hell.

Sometimes I get naked and finger-fuck myself on top of all my money spread across my thousand-count cashmere sheets.

It's going on six months since Maleek got locked up. His trial's scheduled for July and although my husband and I speak of nothing but the best I am not stupid. The most I can hope for is him getting a reduced sentence. The lawyers are hoping for no more than a couple of years. Fucking hoping.

I love my husband. I do. But some of that undying love and devotion died when I was about two weeks away from working at McDonald's to pay my bills while he's enjoying three hots and a fucking cot. Having a man is cool; but in the end, a bitch has to take care of her damn self.

So I accept my nightly collect calls—another fucking bill he running up—before I head to the Ritz to make my money.

I ain't no street ho looking to give some man an "around the world" for a ten-dollar crack hit. My rules are clear. Only at the Ritz-Carlton (the lobby bar is swimming with marks whose ass is looking for a little evening diversion). Only one trick a night (I'm not tearing up my pussy)—$500 minimum. Cash only. No more than thirty minutes. No weird shit. No dick sucking. No kissing. No raw dog. Only corporate suit-wearing motherfuckers (I'm trying to keep this shit on the lowest low). Junior suites or better with a bottle of Dom chilling on ice.

In the last couple of months I even have a few regulars who make it their business to meet me at the Ritz for a Diamond special (Diamond is the name I use. I am these men's best friend. Hey!).

There's Roger. Every Monday while his sweet little wife is in East Cobb doing whatever suburban housewives do he's paying me to lamp up in the suite with his ass. I like Roger because he's the quickest fuck ever. Sometimes I blink and it's over.

And Stuart is my Wednesday nights. He actually gets the executive suite and has room service bring up dinner. The majority of his thirty minutes is spent playing like we on a date or some shit. Sometimes he even brings me gifts. Whateva.

I recognized Reverend Arnez from his Sunday morning televangelist show and was surprised when he pushed up on me. He was just as surprised when I laid my price on the line without blinking an eye. After his church service he likes for me to spank him while he jacks off and at twenty dollars a lick I'm more than willing to whup dat ass.

And business is good. Damn good. I'm clearing at least three to four grand a week by my damn self. Imagine if I get some more hos working for me. Just two or three girls to pick up my slack. Give them half and I'll be clearing much more without so much as a sore ass. But for now I'm handling mine and nobody in the hood is hip to my shit.

"Aisha, this feels so good. Thank you."

I look over at my mother lying on her stomach as the masseuse works her magic. I'm treating her to a full spa day at N'Seya Salon & Spa. These ladies know how to keep my hair laid, my body massaged, my senses relaxed, and my mani-pedi on point. It's gonna cost me close to seven hundred dollars to get the works but it's worth it. We'll be here all day so as a part of the package the salon even provided a continental breakfast and a catered lunch.

My momma needs this. She's so worried about Nasir. Shit, so am I. White folks plus the South plus a black boy equals jail time for a nigga every time. Nasir been fucking with some white chick and little Nancy, Elizabeth, or

Becky Sue or whatever the hell her name is put all the details in her diary—the same diary her momma snuck and read. Police were called. Rape was accused.

Nasir is in some deep shit.

The lawyer says he can probably get Nasir off but that set me back another couple of grand. That plus his bail money and my brother's in my pockets deep. Needless to say I done schooled him on them white girls and since his choice in vanilla pussy was costing me that had better be a wrap on his love of the swirl. "You're welcome, Momma," I tell her, resting my face back on the table.

One thing my momma always teaches us. Family looks out for family all the time.

I reach for my new limited edition crocodile Gucci hobo as I climb out my Benz. I'm looking good and feeling good in a fitted Applebottom jumpsuit and sexy stilettos. Fat ass. Thick thighs. Flat waist. Oh the body is banging. Trust.

I already dropped Momma home and I'm stopping by Wal-Mart to get a supply of blunts for me and magazines to send to Maleek: *Vibe, Source, XXL,* and of course, *Grip,* based right in Atlanta. I'll throw in the newest *Vibe Vixen* for good measure.

My bikini wax has the pussy as bald as Michael Jordan and just walking in and out of Wal-Mart makes my lips rub together. That shit makes me horny as hell.

Six months is a long time to go without dick. I'm not talking about them tricks of mine where I lie there faking the funk with "Fuck me, Daddy," "It's so good, sugar," and "I'm cummin', honey" lies.

Fucking for money and fucking for fun is two different things. And ain't but so many times I can masturbate. Miss Palm and her five fingers is getting old.

I need to be fucked. Ain't like I'm not giving up the ass anyway so I might as well find me something to knock the edge off. A live body. A hard body. A nigga who know how to work it.

No ties. No phone calls. No conversations. No relationships. None of that.

I'm pulling out my spot in the crowded parking lot when I see a familiar face walking out of Wal-Mart. I pull up next to him after a quick look around the lot for any more familiar faces. He bends down and looks through the open passenger window.

Junior the jump-off.

"Get in," I say, before he can open his mouth and disturb my groove as I open my legs to ease the pressure of my thighs against my pussy.

"My car right up—"

"Just get the fuck in," I tell him, my voice hard. I look straight ahead. "And don't say one word."

He hops in and I speed out the parking lot.

✧　　✧　　✧

As soon as we walk into the hotel room at Knight Inns in midtown I drop the condoms I just bought at the gas station on the chipped wooden table and start to undress.

"Dayum, girl," he says, nearly tripping over himself as he rushes out of his clothes.

His dick is already hard and curving away from his body. I check him out. So that's the dick all the girls be talkin' 'bout. Well, the Lord blesses everybody with something and it's obvious Junior got all his blessings below the belt.

"Damn, your body is sick," he says, massaging his hardness as he eyes my hourglass frame.

I snatch a magnum from the box and toss it to him before I move to the bed to snatch the covers back. "Don't talk, Junior, just fuck me," I tell him, already feeling nervous and anxious as my pussy throbs and aches. I'm wet and ready.

He shakes his head as he stretches the condom down on his dick. "Fuck that. I been begging you for that pussy for the longest. I'm gone enjoy that motherfucka fo' sho.'"

Junior climbs on the bed and spreads my legs to lie between them. He grabs my titties with both his hands and holds them up as he starts to lick my nipples like they're candy. I shiver and my hands shoot out to grab the sheets to keep from grabbing him. When he presses my titties together and sucks both of the long and thick nipples at once I close my eyes and arch my back. "Aaah," I cry out as he licks and sucks, bites and plucks them with his tongue.

He moves down to lick from my deep cleavage down my flat stomach to suck my navel even as he stretches his arms to keep teasing my nipples with his fingers.

"Yes," I cry out, squirming on the bed as my breathing gets harsh as hell.

Junior takes the whole of my bald pussy in his mouth. My legs shake. I look down at him. He looks up at me and winks just as his tongue splits my lips to circle my clit. I feel my juices dripping as I buck my hips off the bed and spread my legs wide.

"That's right, give me this good-ass pussy," he says, shifting his hand down my body to slip first one and then two fingers deep inside me as he moves his tongue like a snake over my clit.

"Good, ain't it?" I ask, letting go of the sheet (and my control) to put one hand on his shoulder and the other on the back of his head.

When his hands shift down to massage my ass before working up my legs to jerk them in the air I play with my own nipples. Junior rises up a little to push my legs until my ass is open wide in his face. He looks me dead in my half-closed eyes as he licks from my clit down between my wet lips to circle my asshole before he sucks it.

"Ooooh, Junior," I cry out as my pussy throbs.

I feel his laughter as he goes from my ass to my clit and back again. Ass. Clit. Ass. Clit. Ass. Clit. Ass. Clit.

"Shit, I'm cumming!"

Junior drops my legs and they land on his shoulders with a jiggle as he locks his lips down on my clit and sucks away like crazy.

I holler out and try to squirm away from him but he just locks my legs down and holds on as I cum in his mouth. My body jerks and thrashes, my throat gets dry, my heart is pounding. I'm shivering. Sweaty. Hot. Near a black out. Spasms wrack my body 'til I think I see God.

Junior gives my pussy a kiss before he rises up and turns me over on my stomach. I lift up on my knees as he slaps my ass and slips his dick inside me.

I hiss and clutch the pillows to my chest as he starts sliding in and out. The sounds of my juicy pussy echoes in the room. "Fuck me. Fuck . . . me."

"Knew this pussy was good. I knew it. Damn!"

Junior bends over my back and reaches beneath me to squeeze my titties and tease my nipples as his balls slap against my clit with each hard thrust.

I bite the pillow.

He bites my shoulder.

I reach behind him to squeeze his ass and push him deeper into my pussy as I adjust to the feel of him.

"Let me ride it," I tell him.

His dick slides out of me with "whoop."

I squat over him and hold that dick up with my hand as I ease down onto it. Locking my feet under his legs, his mouth latches on to to my right breast as I start working my hips against his. Each "pop" makes the hard base of his dick rub against my clit. The feel of his tongue and lips on my throbbing nipples turns me on even more.

"You need this motherfuckin' dick, ain't it?" Junior asks as he reaches to grab my ass and slam my hips down onto his dick.

"Yes. Yes. Yes!" I drop my head to his sweaty chest.

That is just the beginning of the sexcapade. We fuck like crazy. Switching it up like crazy. Doggy-style, rodeo-style, straight-up style. On the sink. On the floor. On that rickety, scratched-up table. In front of the faded mirror. Against that mirror. Against the wall. Against the door. On the chair. At the foot of the bed. The head of the bed. On the sides. Frontward. Backward.

Me and Junior get stupid. Fuck it. This is my night and I want it every fucking way I can get it. This is my damn stress reliever.

"I'm ready to get this nut," he tells me as I'm bent over the TV clutching it for dear life as he pops my pussy and tries to blow my back out from behind.

I use my ass to back him out of me and lead him back to the chair to push him into it roughly. He stretches his legs out as I climb on that dick and wrap my arms around his neck.

Shit, if he's gone cum I'm gone get me another nut too.

I circle my hips nice and slow and his mouth gets twisted as he holds on to my hips.

"You's a bad bitch, Aisha. Damn, gurl. I gotta get some more of this pussy."

I just laugh. I feel the first waves of my nut and sit up straight to let my head fling back as I ride him. I feel his dick get bigger and harder. I bite my bottom lip and purr as I cum and cum and cum and cum. "Yes. Yes. Whoo. Yes."

Junior cries out like a bitch and tries to hug me close to him as his hips jerk with his own nut but I brush him off and raise my arms above my head like I'm riding an electronic buffalo or just riding a good-ass high.

Once I'm done I stand up on wobbly legs and stumble back from his ass.

Junior stands and falls into the bed, his filled condom still hanging from the tip of his drained dick. "Damn, I got to sleep that shit off."

"Yeah, uh-huh," I say, even as I start gathering up my clothes to get dressed.

"Just let me get a nap and I'ma fuck the shit out of you again."

"Uh, no," I tell him, dressed and looking beneath the blankets on the floor for my car keys.

Junior turns over on his back and looks at me in surprise. "Where you goin'?"

I see my keys beneath the table and snatch them up. I open my purse and pull out four fifty-dollar bills. "I'm going home. Now you know if you tell anybody about this that Maleek will either kill you when he get out or get somebody to kill you while he still locked up."

Junior looks confused.

I toss the fifties onto his chest and turn to walk to the door.

"You not taking me to my fuckin' car?"

"Call a cab," I call over my shoulder before walking out and slamming the door behind me.

I look down at my diamond-encrusted watch. It's just seven thirty. I have just enough time to make it home before Maleek's nightly call at eight. I can even talk to him longer tonight because after all that dick ain't no way I'm going to work tonight.

"You have a collect call from a federal correctional facility—"

I press one before the automated voice can even finish. I carry the cordless into the living room and curl my body into one corner of the couch.

"Whaddup, Queen?"

"Missing you like crazy," I purr. (Okay, not as crazy as before the money drama but he didn't need to know that.)

"Yeah, I miss you too, baby. I never knew I would get sick of jackin' off in this motherfucka."

And there wasn't but so many times I can masturbate. That's why I got me a little fuck-thru today. Whatever guilt

I feel rise up in me I push away. "Just don't think about it, baby."

He gets quiet.

"I'll be glad when this is all over," I say with honesty. Once Maleek's home—or I get together my own stable—it's a wrap on Diamond.

"You? Shit, me, too. I'm sick of this shit, Aisha. I'm sick of being in here."

"Don't worry, King. You'll be back home running these streets in no time."

"Back running them? Who said I ain't running shit now?"

I start to say, "Me, bitch. I'm saying it. Where the loot if you the head nigga in charge?" but I chill out on that. "Damn right and I better not catch nobody saying it," I say, soothing his ego and pride. I shrug my shoulder. Whatever.

"Listen, Aisha, if my trial . . . if I get time . . . if I don't get the fuck outta this . . . this shit—"

"Don't, Maleek."

He sighed—fucking sighed—into the phone. "Ten years is a long time, Ish."

"We gave that attorney all that fucking money." I sit up straight. "Oh, hell to fucking no on ten fucking years, Maleek. Hell to the no!"

"Aisha, I'm just keepin' it funky."

I jump to my feet, bumping the table and sending my wedding picture face forward with a crash. "Well, let's keep

it funky then. Why give them motherfuckas our life sav-
ings and you still sittin' in that motherfucker talkin' 'bout
ten years? We paid them all that dough just for them to
stand up beside you in fucking court?"

The line is silent.

I drop back down on the sofa and close my eyes as I
take a deep-ass breath to keep from crying. I'm so angry at
him. So disappointed in him. So hurt by him. There is so
much shit I've been dying to say to him the last couple of
months. Shit that weighs down the tip of my tongue.

I have to say them.

"You know, Maleek, if you didn't think the lawyers
could get you off or get you less time then why would you
blow our whole stash and leave me out here fuckin' broke,
busted, and damn disgusted. Everythin' you ever told me
to do I did. You moved in these nasty-ass fucking apartments and I stayed right here with you. I didn't fuckin'
complain. I ain't said shit. Now you left me here and I'm
still here waiting on you." Tears are streaming. My heart is
pumping. I slash my hand in the air like he can see me. My
throat hurt from hollering. "Preparing for ten years wasn't
leaving me ass-out with no money in this motherfucker.
That wasn't preparing for no ten years. Right now I feel
like you said fuck me, you know?"

The line is quiet again. He ain't have shit to say.

I drop my head to my chest as my tears drop down on
my thighs.

"If you wish to make a call please hang up and dial your number again."

He hung up.

I drop the phone to the floor and reach out to stand my wedding picture back up. The glass is broken.

23

Lexi

"On everything I love, *fool, if you don't get the fuck out my face I will bust your ass in this bitch tonight.*"

What the hell? I lift my head off the pillow and look around the dark bedroom.

"*You think I'm a let a female whup my ass?*"

I drop my head back on the pillow and laugh.

"Our neighbor upstairs wake you up, too," Luther says from behind me as his arms tighten around my waist.

"Yup. Give 'em ten minutes and they'll be humping like dogs."

"*You think I'm a let a man whup mine? Nigga, please. You got me mixed up with one of them dumb bitches you fucking around with.*"

"Oh trust me, no the hell I don't."

Two weeks ago a new couple moved into the apartment

above us. The Millers and their loud sexcapades moved on out and these fight-me-now-fuck-me-now freaks moved on in.

"What time is?" Luther asks, his voice still filled with sleep.

I peek one eye open and look at the alarm clock on the bedside table. "Six o'clock."

Luther set up in bed. "They fight all night and sleep all day while we working."

"Well, not me. I'm off today. Thank God for that." I turn and lay my head in his lap while he turns the TV on with the remote.

"That's your first day off since you got that new position, ain't it?"

I lift up to lean my body back against his chest. "Yeah, I make a little more money as a customer service manager but that eleven-to-seven shift and them classes for the house twice a week is killing me."

"You can pack your shit and go, Clevon."

"You want me gone so bad, Tammy, you pack it."

"If I touch your shit it's going right out the fucking window."

Luther raises the remote and turns the volume up on the TV. "It will all be worth it to get the hell up out of this oversized cardboard box."

"And miss out on the ghetto soap operas?" I nudge Luther and point to our bedroom windows.

Just as the sun was rising in the sky it's raining Clevon's clothes.

The kids been out of school for the last two weeks and since the day camp at the Y costing $150 a week per child—money we just didn't have—they spent most of the summer cooped up in the house under Trey's watch until me, Luther, or WooWoo get home. They happy as hell to hear I had the day off. As soon as they ate breakfast all of them went scrambling out that door with jump ropes, balls, and skates.

I tie a scarf around my hair before I throw on a pair of shorts and one of Luther's wifebeaters to clean the house like I'm on a mission. Mice and roaches are inevitable in a place with this many apartments but I try to keep our place free of places for them to feed or sleep.

Half hour later the smell of ammonia damn near knocks me out, so I open the windows and the front door. The window in my apartment looks out on the rear of the complex so I walk down to the end of the hall to look out the window at the kids playing. I'm almost back to my apartment when I hear a commotion and turn to see Aisha's door open as two big deliverymen carry in a steel side-by-side refrigerator.

"That girl crazy," I mutter to myself. If I had just a little bit of the money her butt blew on clothes and dumb shit

I'd be in my damn house, not filling up a project apartment with shit people in the 'burbs own.

And she had to be sitting on some money because her husband's been gone for a minute and her shopping hasn't slowed up any.

I'm in the tiny kitchen burning the hair off some chicken wings at the stove when my whole body kind of tingles.

"Dayum, girl, you fittin' them damn shorts."

I drop the wing in the fire and have to snatch it out before I whirl around. "What are you doing in here, Junior?"

He steps up and I step back, feeling the counter press into my behind. "The kids said you was up here and I came to bring you this."

He pulls the front of my shirt and drops something in it before I can blink.

I pull the bottom of the shirt out and money falls in my hand. I count it. Fifty dollars. "Junior, we got a thirteen-year-old and ten-year-old. The last child support check I got was three weeks ago. You never helped me get the sneakers or the cheerleading uniform. What I'm supposed to do with this?"

He sucks his finger and traces the outline of my dark nipple through the shirt. I hate the way it springs right to attention. I knock his hand away and cross my arms over my chest. "You spend more money than that on weed."

"Yo, I gave my demos to Tyrik and soon as I get my record deal I'ma take care of you and the kids."

I look up at him for a long time. Junior always talks about rapping a lot and even claims to be in the studio, but I always just took it for the joke he is. But now I see he's serious. He's living his life counting chickens before his eggs hatch (another wise one from Nana).

"First off, you don't have to take care of me 'cause I have a husband. All I ever ask you to do is take care of your kids, Junior."

"You know I still love you, Lexi," he says, his voice all soft as he lowers his head to mine.

My eyes lock with his and for just a second I let myself remember the Junior I fell in love with all them years ago.

He kisses me and I let him. My whole body feels electrified and I gasp as he grabs my hips and sits me on top of the counter. As my heart beats like a drum I spread my legs and he steps closer. My arms circle his neck and he kisses me deeper.

It has been so long since I felt so much energy. So much passion. I know all I have to do is drop my shorts and it will be so good.

His hands massage my ass and work up to tease my breasts as his lips work down to my neck.

God, it feels just as good as it did all those years ago. I used to think this man was made just for me.

But he isn't.

And it isn't ten years ago.

And it isn't worth losing what I have.

Or worth forgetting everything he ever does to make my kids—*our* kids—cry and feel neglected. Maybe even worthless.

I reach for his face with both my hands and pull it to me to kiss him softly on his full lips just before I put my hands on his chest and push him away. I jump down off the counter and move out the kitchen because I'm sure I can't stand the heat.

Junior follows me into the living room, his hard-on leading him. "Damn, Lexi. Why you keep teasin' me, li'l ma?"

I throw my hands up in exasperation. "You know what, Junior, you should be happy that I'm busting my ass to give your kids a home. You should be happy for me because I'm happy and I'm doing better than I ever have in my life and I found a man—a good man—who loves me."

"Oh, he do? You think that motherfucker loves you?"

"Yeah, I do. I think he loves me and you know what else? I love him, too."

He sucks his teeth. "Whateva."

"So to you this is a fuck. This is a game. This is Junior getting what he wants." I poke him in the chest as I speak, my eyes flashing. "But for me this is my life you playing with. This is your kids' life you messing over."

"This ain't no fuck or no game or no shit. I love you." He reaches out to stroke my cheek.

"Junior, you don't love nobody but yourself and if you don't grow up and get yourself together you gone turn around one day and find yourself by yourself." I turn and sit on the couch. "Molly's silly ass don't even deserve the way you dog her out."

"Oh, so now you and Molly best of friends."

"Nope. Not at all. So that should tell you how fucked up you treat her."

Junior waves his hand at me. "I don't want to hear this shit."

"Well, you better hear this. If you can't come here and respect your kids by keeping your promises to them, respect my house by calling before you come here, and respect my husband by stoppin' beggin' for *his* pussy, then you can't come here, Junior."

He twists his mouth and looks down at me with mocking eyes. "So now you perfect, Lexi? So now you a fucking goody-two-shoes? I done fucked the hell out of you plenty of times over the years whether I pay child support or not, whether I get the kids or not, whether you got a man or not."

I walk past him to the front door. "You know what, Junior? The dick is good. I ain't gone even lie. The dick is real good. But having a man in the home to help me raise all my kids, and moving the fuck up out Bentley Manor is even better."

"Lexi. Man, bitch, you trippin'." He walks past me to stand in the doorway. "When you come lookin' for this *real good* dick, I'ma make you beg me to fuck you."

Sex. That's all he focuses on? "Damn, Junior, you child-ish as hell."

"Yup, a big child who gets whateva the fuck he wants when he wants it."

I step back and slam the door in his face.

24

Aisha

The little cheap beeper I bought just for my tricks vibrates against the console of my car. I roll my eyes as I wait at the light. I don't even bother to pick it up. It's Stuart blowing it *and* my damn nerves is up.

I decided to cut it off with him last week and he been beeping me every day—damn near all day—since. He's too intense. Too caught up.

When I walked into the suite last week the lights were off. Candles blazed everywhere. A trail of red rose petals was leading into the bedroom where there were more candles and more rose petals. A full course candlelight meal was laid out on a table on the balcony. They were silk sheets on the turned-down bed with a white negligee laid across the foot. Stuart walked up to me carrying two flutes of champagne dressed in nothing but a silk robe.

Right then all kinds of bells and shit should've went off in my head. But it didn't.

I wore the negligee.

I ate the dinner with him.

I sipped the champagne.

I listened to him tell me how beautiful I was.

I even let him carry me to the bed.

I let him fuck me like I was his woman or his wife. All slow and shit with kisses on my shoulders while I moaned and squirmed and purred like he was tearing my pussy up. NOT.

I let him pay me extra just to eat my pussy.

It wasn't until after I left and was in my car headed home that I knew Stuart was taking shit to a whole other level that I damn sure wasn't feeling. Whether he got it or not, that was a wrap on Stuart.

I will miss the way he ate pussy. Shit, I was surprised how good his corny ass was at it. He had me cumming all in his mouth in no time at all. And he paid me for it. "Whoo," I say playfully as my pussy double-pumped at the memory.

I park my car on level 2 of the parking deck at Phipps Plaza. As I climb out the car I smooth the strapless jean dress I wore over my body before I push my shades down onto my face. I'm digging around in my hobo purse for my cell phone when a car pulls up beside me.

"Hi, Diamond."

I recognize the voice. Stuart. I drop my cell phone and twist my fingers around my box cutter instead. I keep walking like I didn't hear a thing.

When I hear a car door slam I make a left through two SUVs, determined to get away. I ran right into Stuart. What the fuck? He must've beeped me from his cell phone.

"Hi, Diamond," he says. "I've been beeping you."

I look left and right. We're alone as far as I can see. "Are you following me?" I ask him, the soft saddity voice he's used to is gone. I ain't gone lie, this the first time one of my tricks crossed over into my real world and I don't like it.

"No, I was on my way in the mall and I just happened to see you."

Is that true?

"I've missed you," he says, staring deep into my eyes. He licks his lips as he reaches out to touch my hand.

I shift from his touch and inside my purse I push the button to release the blade of my box cutter. This whole situation is creeping me the fuck out.

I have to get away. And if it takes a damn lie to do that then so be it. "You know I haven't been meeting you because I went out of town for the week."

"Can we go somewhere and talk?" he asks, shoving his hands into his pockets.

I cringe a little, not quite sure what this fool is gone whip out them pockets. "I can't right now, but yeah, we can talk when we meet this week."

"Good. I thought I wasn't gonna see you again." He smiles and looks relieved.

Hell, you ain't. "The way you ate up all this good chocolate pussy the last time?"

The echo of a car cranking surrounded us.

Boom . . . boom . . . boom.

I know that system. My eyes get big as my head swings in the direction of the bass. Kaseem's milk-white Caddy pulls out the spot just four cars up from us. Shit.

"I know him. He's a undercover. You better go," I lie with ease.

Stuart looks toward Kaseem and then back at me, obviously nervous. "So I'll see you Wednesday?"

"For sure."

He walks away and soon I hear his car squeal out the parking deck just as Kaseem slows to a stop beside me.

"Whaddup, Aisha?"

"Hey, Kaseem, what's up wit you?"

"Nothing." He eyes me from head to toe. "Who was that white dude?"

I shrug as I let go of my blade and pull my hand out my purse. "Some fool talkin' 'bout insurance or some shit."

"He was?"

I look at Kaseem behind the wheel of his whip. Still thug-sexy. "You spendin' up that money?" I ask, trying to change the subject.

He looks at me for a long time. So long that I kind of

fidget in front of his ass. "A li'l sump'm for this shorty I'm fuckin' with right now," he finally says, nodding his head toward his backseat.

There are a couple Gucci shopping bags on the seat. "That's more than a little sump'm."

"No less than what I woulda bought you if you ain't front on a nigga." Kaseem reaches to somewhere in the car and pulls out a toothpick that he sticks between his sexy lips.

"No, I just didn't wanna disrespect my man or your boy while he doin' time."

Kaseem sucks his teeth and reaches his head out the window to spit. I have to slide my left foot back for it not to land on my toes. "See you 'round, Aisha."

Boom . . . boom . . . boom.

And he pulls off.

I am looking so good for my ritual Friday visit to see my husband. I sit there waiting on them to bring him into the visitation room so he can tell me how fine my ass look.

His trial is set for next week and I have every intention of being there every day, sitting on the row behind him. I want him home. I want my husband back. I want my life back. The sooner the trial's over and done with the sooner I know exactly what I have to deal with. I hope for the best but I can't forget how defeated he sounds on the phone lately, like he already planning on getting the worst sentence possible. And although I still have some things I need to forgive Maleek for, I have some of my own dirt to forget. Still, I have no plans to leave Maleek. He is my husband and we been through plenty. If it's ten years' ride or die then I'm riding with him through this.

I look down at my wedding ring. I have to ask the Lord to forgive me for cheating on my husband. But a bitch like me has two choices and living a life less than what I'm used to is not an option for me. Maleek got me used to these nice-ass things so how can he expect me to settle for less now.

I'll have to step up my own hustle and trick out some other bitches. And with Stuart acting so psycho I'm considering setting up shop at a whole new spot like the Marriott. That fool has been beeping me every hour damn near since I missed our Wednesday. Straight psycho.

I smile as Maleek comes walking through the door in his prison uniform. I stand up waiting to feel those strong arms and his sweet lips even if for just a moment. Shit, that moment is all I have to live on.

"Hey, baby," I say, holding my arms open.

Maleek slides into his seat and crosses his hands on top of the table. He doesn't even look at me.

My eyes search his face as I slowly drop into my seat. I see the muscle working like crazy in his cheek. "Baby, what's wrong?" I ask, reaching out to stroke his hand.

Maleek grabs my wrist. When he did look at me his

eyes are red like fire and filled with hate. "I gave your no-good ass everything you never had and always wanted." He puts more pressure on my wrist and I gasp at the sharp darts of pain. "This how you do me? Out there sellin' your ass, you no-good bitch."

He knows. Oh God, he knows. Jesus. Oh, no. "What? Maleek, why you hurtin' me?" I ask, trying to pull my arm away as guilt fills me. I look around and I see the guards eyeing us.

"I feel like killing your motherfucking ass, Aisha. If I had a gun I could blow your brains out." The tears in his eyes scare me more than anything.

"Maleek, that's a lie. Who the hell you lettin' lie on me?"

"Don't lie to me!" he roars, putting more pressure on my wrist until it felt close to snapping in half.

"Ahh," I cry out, tears filling my eyes.

The guards surround the tables just as Maleek reaches across the table to clutch my throat. I wince at the pain and loss of air.

The guards all grab his steel-like arms. He finally releases me as one clubs him and I collapse to the floor. I use my feet and hands to push back from him on my ass.

People in the visiting room holler out.

I watch as it takes nearly four guards to drag Maleek kicking and screaming out the visitation room. I wince with each curse he throws at me.

"You no-good bitch!"

"Get the fuck out, trick!"

"I hate your no-good ass!"

"I could kill you, Aisha!"

I cover my ears with my hands and squeeze my eyes shut like I can make it all go away.

Strong hands grab my arm and pull me to my feet. I open my eyes to see a mean-looking guard. I feel all eyes on me. Feeling sorry for me. Laughing at me. Judging me.

"Right this way."

I just wrap my arms around my body, feeling cold and numb as I follow the guard down the hall.

"There go that no-good bitch now, Momma."

I look up to see Hassana, Mrs. Cummings, and Reema in the line of visitors. "What you doing here? I know your name ain't on the list." I spit at her, ready to pounce.

The guard steers me to the door.

Hassana laughs. "Watch her go in and see your husband if she ain't on the list. He sent for her."

Reema must feel bold with Hassana by her side because she shoots me a satisfied look. "He sure did."

I shoot all them bitches glares even as I walk through the door the guard holds open.

"Maleek Cummings's visitation privileges have been suspended indefinitely."

Just as the security guard closes the door I hear them heifers acting up.

But to hell with them. Maleek knew, and I thought my

game had been tight. Where did I slip up? Did Kaseem overhear in the parking deck and run back like a bitch? And did Maleek really tell them to bring Reema? Had her name been on his visitation list the whole time? Was this her first visit?

What the fuck did all this shit mean for me and my husband?

"Hassana, let's just go home."

I turn at the sound of Mrs. Cummings's voice and see Hassana and Reema trying to walk up on me with a sneak attack.

I cut between two cars and reach in my hobo for my keys. By the time I get to my car my trunk is up. I drop my purse in and reach under the spare tire for my box cutter just as they run up on me.

I whirl around and went straight to swinging at they ass. "Ya'll bitches want some of me? You either ride with me or get run the fuck over."

They jump back.

"Come on, Hassana, this bitch crazy," Reema says.

"You tough now that you got this big bitch with you. Fuck what ya heard. I ain't scared of neither one of ya'll asses together or apart." I jump at them again with my blade to let them know I'm not playing.

"Come on, Reema, I ain't got time for that dumb-ass ho anyway. I told my brother she wasn't shit."

Another day and another time I would have knocked

Hassana out for her mouth trouble but I didn't have the will or the strength. I sank down to the ground, leaning against the rear wheel of my car.

I feel my tears wet my cheek and I cry like a baby. I don't even give a damn who see me or who hear me. I'm tired. Broken. Beat. Scared. Mad. Ashamed. Hurt. Lost. Heartbroken. Alone. Helpless. Hopeless.

Desperate.

25

Devani

"Mrs. Tyrik L'Shaun Jefferson."

I love the sound of that shit. In the month since I'd dropped the baby news on Tyrik, it appears he's finally adjusted to the idea of becoming a father. Just as I'd hoped, Papa Jefferson has stayed on his son's case about "doing the right thing."

Pauline just cries a lot, but I'm sure she'll get over it. 'Course, I don't really give a fuck if she does or doesn't.

"You really believe that you're actually gonna pull this shit off?"

I glance over my shoulder to see my mother propped against my open door. Gone are the old, holey housecoats and raggedy-ass slippers. Now, she sashays around the house in Bebe's latest fashions and keeps her hair whipped as good as, if not better than, my own.

"Please try to keep the hate to a minimum," I sass with an amused wink. "I don't want to get too much dust on my shoulders. Tyrik is taking me out to The Palms 837 Club for my birthday."

Momma's brows arch just like I knew they would.

"A members-only club. I am impressed." She crosses the one arm and puffs from one of Koolay's potent-smelling blunts. Apparently the chunk of cheese I keep slippin' Momma is buying them a higher grade of weed. Hell, I'm catchin' a little buzz and I'm ten feet away from her.

Turning back toward the mirror, I wonder whether the Badgley Mischka dress is the right choice for the night. It's a beautiful, summer-white halter chiffon that bears a striking resemblance to the one Marilyn Monroe famously wore in that photo with the wind blowing up her dress. Plus, it did an incredible job of camouflaging my small pregnant bump.

"Uhm . . . I don't know about this one." I turn toward the bed and the piles of new clothes covering it. No more cheap knock-offs. Prada, Dolce & Gabbana and Chanel were all my body's new best friends. Trust, when I say I'm puttin' a hurtin' on that damn platinum card and lovin' every moment of it.

My style has grown so fierce that even that uppity Aisha has shot me a few jealous looks. I love that shit, too.

"I need you to run an errand," Momma says.

"What? Not tonight, Momma. I'm runnin' late. Get Koolay to do it."

"I would, but Miz Cleo doesn't like Koolay and I need to borrow her lasagna recipe for tonight's dinner."

I can't help but laugh when I glance over at her. "Are you shittin' me?"

"What? I decided to learn how to cook a few things."

I can't stop laughing.

"It's not funny. Just go and pick up the damn recipe!"

"Fine. Fine, Chef BoyarNegro. I'll pick up your damn recipe before I go."

"Thanks." She watches me for a few minutes. "So when you gonna get your ring?" Momma asks and takes a long toke.

The question widens my smile as I clear a spot on the bed. "Tonight."

Momma chokes.

I sit on the bed and reach for the candy-apple red Marc Jacobs pumps.

"Tonight? No shit?"

"Well, it's not written in stone, which by the way I'm hoping for at least three carats, but let's just say that my woman's 'tuition says it's tonight."

"Uh-huh." She draws another hit and her eyelids fall so low she looks more asleep than awake. "I'll believe that shit when I see it."

This just proves even your kinfolk can't stand to see a nigga happy.

"I gotta go." I stand and snatch up my purse. I mean,

damn. The day is almost over and she hasn't even wished me happy birthday. My own damn momma.

She steps back as I close and lock my bedroom door. "Ain't nobody gonna steal your shit."

"I know they're not. That's why I'm locking the door." I purposely brush my shoulders off in front of her and march through the living room. Koolay is puffing on his own fat blunt and "massaging" himself in front of the fifty-inch, widescreen plasma HDTV I charged.

"Koolay, put that shit away," Momma barks for the bazillionth time.

"Whaaat?" he asks, high as hell. "It ain't like she ain't neva seen no dick before. Hell, she selling that coochee to the highest bidder, though it probably ain't worth no more than a five-spot."

"That's five dollars more than your unemployed ass will ever have."

To prove me wrong Dumb-Ass digs a five-dollar bill out of his jeans and smacks it down on the coffee table.

Suddenly, Momma is on his ass like white on rice. "Nigga, what have I told you about puttin' the moves on my daughter?"

"Ow. Wait, baby, please. Ow."

"You gettin' the fuck up out of here—tonight!"

"Ow, wait, baby. We were just fuckin' 'round—right, Devani?"

I just laugh and walk out the door. After all, Momma is in her element.

Despite the seven o'clock hour it's still bright outside and niggas are roasting beneath the summer sun. A few teenagers have put up a portable basketball net and are dribbling in the center of the parking lot. One boy bounces the ball off the rim and the ball flies in the air and hits the back of my silver Lexus.

"Hey, watch it," I shout, mad at myself for breaking my own rule and driving my good car to this cesspool. My shout draws every pair of eyes toward me and soon all the men are in a sudden competition of who can outhoot and whistle at me the loudest.

"Hot damn." A nigga I don't even know struts up to me. "Where are you and your fine ass goin' this evening?"

"None of your damn business." I lift my head and stroll with an extra swing in my hips toward Miz Cleo's. I feel like a movie star as I move through the hood.

"My, my, my," Miz Cleo sings as I approach. "Don't you sure look pretty this evening."

"Why, thank you. My boyfriend is takin' me out for my birthday."

"Is that chiffon?" Miz Osceola leans forward and feels the material for herself.

"It sure is," I boast. "Tyrik buys me nothin' but the best."

"Uh-huh." Miz Cleo twists her lips with clear disapproval.

Just like I said. Niggas never want to see you happy.

"How come we don't ever see this boyfriend around here?"

I prop my hands on my hips. "Is that a real question?"

"I'm just sayin'," Miz Cleo continues, ignoring my sarcasm. "If a man truly cares for you, he would at least come by and meet your momma. That's just showin' respect."

"Humph," Miz Osceola mutters.

Miz Cleo turns toward her friend. "What? Ain't I speakin' the truth?"

"C'mon, now. You know these youngun' don't know nuthin' about respecting their elders. They ain't nuthin' but a bunch of selfish bastards."

"For your information," I cut in, "Tyrik has invited my mother out to his home plenty of times."

Both women turn their beady eyes toward me. "And?"

"And . . . she hasn't been able to make it," I lie awkwardly.

"Uh-huh." Neither looks as though they buy the story.

"Well," Miz Cleo says after a long silence. "I suppose you came for the recipe?" She reaches into the top of her bra and pulls out a small slip of paper and stretches it out to me.

When I reach and grab hold of the paper, Miz Cleo doesn't immediately let go. "You do know all that glitters ain't gold, chile?"

"Preach on it," Miz Osceola says like we up in church or something.

I pull on the paper, but it still doesn't budge. "Whatever you do, don't trade one hell for another."

I snatch the piece of paper out her hand, and then turn and walk away before I really show her the meaning of disrespect. I can't wait to see the last of those two old bitches. If they were so smart, why the fuck are they still in this rat hole?

When I return to the apartment, I literally walk in on Momma fuckin' Koolay's brains out on the sofa.

"Gross," I yell, throwing the recipe inside and slammin' the door. Children should never *ever* see a parent having sex. It fucks with you. Trust me, I know. I've walked in on them too many times to count.

I'm still disgusted as I burst back outside and storm toward my car.

A man's high whistle catches my ear and I turn to see Shakespeare strolling toward me. Before I know it, I'm blushing and performing a small pirouette for his inspection. "You like?"

"I love," he says warmly as his eyes gobble me up.

My gaze spots the journal in his hand. "Does this mean you'll write another poem about me?"

His brows arch. "How did you know about my poetry?"

"I have my ways." I can't believe how bad I'm flirting.

"Then the answer to your question is: yes." He flirts right back. "How can I not write about an angel?"

"Oh, you're good."

"Soon as you dump Tyrik's ass, I'll show you just how good."

"Then I guess that means I'll never know."

The familiar sound of police sirens fills the air and we both turn toward the gate as two cop cars whip into the complex.

"Oh, shit," Shakespeare mumbles. "I bet this has something to do with Smokey."

"He's out of rehab?"

"Yeah. Keisha and the kids came back, too."

Dumb-ass bitch.

Sure enough, the po-po stops in front of Smokey's building.

"I'll catch up with you later." Shakespeare starts jogging toward the police and I head to my car.

"By the way," he calls out. "Happy birthday!"

I don't believe it. He remembers—just like he does every year. Too bad he's always too broke to buy a present. "Thanks!" As I slide behind the wheel, I think what a shame I'm not a hopeless romantic. If I were, Shakespeare would've won my heart years ago.

"C'mon, girl. Stop daydreamin' and go get your ring." I reach over to the CD player and blast Tupac's "All Eyez on Me."

26

Devani

Dinner at the Palms' exclusive 837 Club turns out to be more than I dreamed of: excellent food, great wine, and good service. Tyrik is nervous throughout the night.

Tonight's the night, I keep singing to myself.

"You look beautiful," he says, yet again, as he reaches for my hand.

I take the compliment with a widening smile. "You keep saying that."

"That's because it's true." He kisses my hand. "What do you say we get out of here?"

I blink at the curveball he tosses me. Where the hell is my ring? "Sure." I continue to smile as I dab the corners of my mouth. "Where should we go?"

Twenty minutes later, we're back at his place and chillin'

in the outside Jacuzzi. It isn't exactly what I had in mind, but whatever. I'm just waiting for my damn ring. After a game of footsies and a bottle of champagne, Tyrik props me up on the edge and dives in for some pussy delight for dessert.

I swear, Junior might have the best dick, but Tyrik's tongue is second to none. Soon, Tyrik is fuckin' me every which way but loose in the living room, the kitchens, the staircase, the bed, the shower, and back to the bed. It's like his ass is on a mission or something.

Being eight weeks pregnant, my ass is worn the fuck out by the time it nears midnight.

"Happy birthday, baby," Tyrik murmurs as he spoons my tired ass.

What the fuck ever. Where's my ring? I've earned my ring.

"I got something for you," he adds.

It's about damn time.

Tyrik reaches over me and pulls open the nightstand drawer.

My energy immediately renews itself and I can feel my stomach loop into knots. However, the box he pulls out is definitely not a ring box.

"What's this?" I ask, sitting up.

"It's your gift," he says and plants another kiss on me.

What the fuck? I rip into the box and stare stupidly at a simple diamond bracelet.

"You like it?" He plants another kiss against my collar-
bone. "It's a little something to remember me by when I go
to Pittsburgh."

Remember him by? My fuckin' heart starts racing.
"Where's the ring?"

Tyrik pulls back and stares at me. "What ring?"

"My fuckin' engagement ring." I throw the damn jewelry box at his chest. "You're supposed to be giving me an
engagement ring."

"Whoa. Whoa." Tyrik slides out of bed. "I never said I
was going to marry you. Are you crazy?"

What? "Your father—"

"My father doesn't make my decisions. I'm a grown-ass
man. You got to be out your rabbit-ass mind if you think
I'm marrying some hood rat out of Bentley Manor."

Ah, shit. This nigga has straight-played my ass.

I'm swinging at his head before I can think straight. I
even manage to land a few good blows before he pins me
down. What's more infuriating is that he's actually laughing at me.

"I'm gonna kill you," I shout, squirming with all my
might. "I want my goddamn ring!"

"Don't ruin this, Dee. We had some fun, but that's all."

"You're not fuckin' leaving me here. I'm having your
baby."

"Are you?" he challenges. "Maybe we should talk to Junior?"

Oh fuck! "Tyrik, baby. I don't know what Junior told you but—"

"What? You thought you were going to just straight-play my ass? Is that it? Haven't you heard that blood is thicker than water or did you think your pussy is so good that Junior would keep that shit quiet?"

"No, baby. You gotta to believe me. Junior is a fuckin' liar."

Tyrik grabs a fistful of my hair and snatches me up off the bed. "You got to get the fuck up out of here. Thanks for the pussy, but it's time to go. And you can forget about takin' the motherfuckin' Lexus."

"Tyrik, baby—"

"And I've already canceled the credit card." He tosses my clothes at me.

Oh, shit. Think, Devani, think. "Tyrik, you're making a big mistake."

"No. I'm correcting a mistake."

He drags me down the stairs without giving me the chance to get dressed. "I don't care what Junior says," I bark back. "And you better bet your ass that you're going to take care this baby." One shove and I'm tumbling down the stairs with one thought: This nigga's tryna to kill me.

Halfway down the staircase, I manage to stop my fall. But when Tyrik starts down the stairs after me, I scramble for my dress a few steps away and then bolt the rest of the way down. "You're fuckin' crazy," I scream.

A sharp pain erupts in my lower abdomen. "My baby." I clutch at my belly and double over. I can't lose my ace in the hole.

I head for the door, barely remembering my purse on the foyer table. "This isn't over," I threaten. "You're taking care of this baby. Trust." I jerk open the door as Tyrik nearly catches up with me.

Naked as a jaybird, I bolt outside still cussin' him the hell out. For an added "fuck you" move, I race to my Lexus and hop inside before he can do anything about it. I lock the door just as Tyrik catches up. He bangs on the door and window while I finally slip the dress over my head.

"Get the hell out of the car." He grabs hold the top of the roof and begins rocking the damn thing. "Get the fuck out."

"Fuck you, motherfucker! I'll see you in court!" I turn the engine over and slam my bare foot onto the accelerator and peel off into the night.

Minutes later, another sharp pain bolts across my lower stomach and I'm suddenly in a state of hysterics. I fucked up. I fucked up bad. The only thing that can save me— save my life and still get me the hell up out of Bentley Manor is the child growing inside of me.

Lord, please don't let this be Junior's baby.

The fact that I'm praying isn't lost on me. But damn if I can't help it. My tears are flowing so hard it's difficult to see the road, so I ease off the gas pedal. I try'n plan my next move but now all I can think about are the what-ifs. What if I'm wrong and this baby really is Junior's?

Twenty minutes later, I reach Hollowell Parkway and I can see the iron gates of Bentley Manor in the distance. My hell. My prison. Maybe Momma will know what I should do next.

At the sound of screeching tires my gaze shoots up to the rearview mirror and I'm instantly blinded by an SUV's high beams.

"What the fuck?"

The vehicle speeds up and my heart leaps into my throat. I slam my foot back down onto the accelerator and fly past the Circle K.

The black SUV jumps into the wrong lane and catches up to me. I turn my head to glance out my window, prepared to flip this motherfucker off, when I catch sight of Rufus in the passenger seat—a split second later, I see the gun.

Pop! Pop! Pop! Pop! Pop!

My hand falls from the wheel and my foot slips off the gas pedal as my brain tries to process what just happened. I still see Rufus as the SUV continues to peel off into the distance. There's an eerie sound of steel hitting iron and a white bag explodes in my face.

What . . . what's happening?

Pain answers me. It's suddenly pulsing from every part of my body. I glance down but don't understand why my white dress is now red.

"Devani! Devani!"

Shakespeare? What the hell is he doing here?

I lift my eyes and see his hand reaching through the broken glass window. When did that happen?

"Devani! Oh my God! Somebody call for help!"

There's horror and sorrow in his voice and I wonder what's wrong. I blink but when I open my eyes, I'm cradled in his arms.

"Hold on, Devani," he sobs. "Help is on the way."

I realize that he's crying for me and I reach my hand out to tell him it's okay—that I'm all right; but my arm is so heavy and I'm so so tired . . .

27

Molly

Pop! Pop! Pop! Pop! Pop!

My eyes snap open at the familiar sound. Not again.

Once upon a time the sound of gunfire would send me scrambling to the nearest corner, quaking and sobbing about what I've gotten myself into by living in this hellhole. Now, I'm more annoyed than anything else. I have to get up early to meet my mother for breakfast at IHOP in Woodstock and then I have a doctor's appointment.

"Somebody call for help!" a man's voice drifts outside my window.

Lazily I roll over and stretch out my hand. It's soft, cold . . . and empty. I shoot up in bed and search the darkness for my husband. Where in the hell did he go?

Before I know it, I'm dashing out of bed and searching

the apartment like a crazed woman. Given the size of the place, it doesn't take long.

This doesn't make sense, but then I remember the phone call Junior received not too long ago. I was pissed that someone was calling and waking us up, but Junior assured me it was nothing and to go back to sleep. Now I wonder what was so important he had to creep out.

"Oh, God. He's been shot." My brain leaps to the illogical conclusion and I race out the front door with my stomach twisting in knots and my heart in my throat.

I burst into the night in my pink jersey nightgown and join the Bentley Manor's regular night crawlers. The people with common sense remain in their apartments—I should be in mine. I don't know where the shooting took place, but I just fall in step behind the drunk, the high, and the curious.

There's an empty space next to our Chevy Caprice and it confirms that Junior is gone. As I near the complex's entrance I finally see a silver Lexus squished against the security gate like an accordion. I know it's wrong, but I actually stop and breathe a sigh relief. It isn't him. Junior had borrowed Tyrik's black SUV so I can use the Caprice tomorrow.

Before I can turn around, a familiar voice cries out, "Devani, no!"

Devani? Come to think of it, I did see Devani leaving the complex in a silver car this evening. I resume walking toward the gate, pushing my way through the crowd of sour-smelling men.

And then I see them.

Shakespeare is sitting on the glass-covered street, crying and rocking Devani's blood-soaked body.

"No, no," he moans repeatedly.

There's so much raw pain in his voice and his face that it feels wrong to witness such anguish, but it's also hard to turn away. My gaze lowers to Devani's still face and tears burn my eyes as I remember the child she was carrying.

An innocent life . . . gone.

"Let me through, goddamn it! Let me through!"

Heads swivel toward the hysterical voice to see Devani's mother shove her way through the crowd. Poor woman.

She collapses next to Shakespeare and pulls her daughter away from him.

I can't watch anymore. I turn and navigate my way back out of the crowd and return to the apartment.

If Junior wasn't involved with the shooting then where in the hell is he?

"I told him if he can't get what he needs from that fat-ass wife of his that he was welcome around my way any damn day of the week."

Goddamn it. It's been more than two months and I still can't get Geneva's words out of my head. I pick up the cordless phone and dial Junior's cell phone. With each ring

I grow more worried, anxious, and pissed. When Junior's voice mail comes on, I slam the phone down and back-hand the sudden tears streaming down my face.

Where is he?

"Honey chile. Open your eyes and see what's in front of you."

I return to bed and empty my tears into the pillowcase. Hours later as my face dries and my head aches, I hear the front door open. I don't move or even call out. When he creeps into the bedroom, my back is to the door and my eyes are wide open. He doesn't bother to turn on the light; but I hear the swish of clothing and the rustling of sheets before he slides in behind me.

I want to lash out, interrogate where he's been—but I also know what will happen. He will leave me . . . and I'm not sure I can handle that.

Junior inches close until his body spoons me. "Molly, are you up?"

Silence.

He leans forward and plants a kiss against the back of my head and slides his arm around my hip.

For now—it's enough.

The International House of Pancakes, otherwise known as IHOP, in Woodstock is teeming with customers. Since I didn't get any sleep last night, I'm a zombie as I walk up to the hostess stand. Before I can inquire whether my party has arrived, I see my mother waving at the back of the restaurant.

"Never mind," I say to the hostess. "I see her." Drawing a deep breath, I pray for strength and march toward my mother.

At fifty, my mother is a beautiful, size-two bottle blond with smooth, taut skin she acquired from a talented cosmetic surgeon. Her designer clothes are the epitome of high fashion and her makeup is flawless. I can feel her laser blue eyes scan my round body through her dark shades.

"Good morning, Mother." I curve on a plastic smile and deliver a quick peck against her cheek.

"You look like crap," she says, removing her shades.

"I'm doing well. Thank you for asking," I answer, pretending to be unfazed by her comment.

"Good morning, ladies," our flaming-hair waitress says in greeting. "What can I get y'all?"

"Coffee," Mother says.

I know it's the only thing she'll order, but I, on the other hand, am starving and I know my mother is picking up the tab. "I'll have coffee, too. Can you also put in my order for a stack of buttermilk pancakes, two eggs with cheese and a side order of bacon? Thank you."

My mother waits until we're alone to say, "You're never going to get rid of that weight eating like that."

"I've lost twenty pounds, and besides, my husband doesn't complain."

"Why should he? You're his sugar momma, after all. Or should I say: I am?"

Here we go. "Momma, don't start."

"Molly, give it up and come home. How much longer are you going be that nigger's whore?"

I lean back against the chair and fold my arms. I'm really not in the mood for this shit, but unfortunately I need a favor.

"Come home, Molly," she urges again. "Your father is sick."

The news stuns me and I sit up straight. "What's wrong?"

Her gaze lowers as the waitress returns with our coffee. We remain silent until she's gone.

"Massive heart attack—last week."

"And you're just now telling me?"

She doesn't answer.

"He still doesn't want to see me." I guess.

"He doesn't know what he wants, Molly. But it's time to end all this foolishness."

Knowing that even after suffering a massive heart attack that my father still doesn't want anything to do with me breaks something within me and another rush of tears spill down my face.

"Molly," my mother snaps in a harsh whisper. "Not here."

"I changed my mind," I say, pushing back my chair and climbing to my feet. "I'm not hungry after all."

"Molly, please sit down."

I ignore the request and turn on my heel. When my father said I was dead to him, he obviously meant it.

I'm out of the restaurant before I know it and fumbling for my car keys.

"Molly." My mother is suddenly behind me. "Don't do this. Both of you are just stubborn as an ox. I want this to end. I want my family back."

I wheel around to face her. "Junior is my family, Mother. Is he welcomed, too?"

Her horror and repulsion is instant, but in the next second she covers with a smile. "Molly—"

"I have to go, Mother." I slip the key into the lock and open my door.

"Wait." She grabs my arm and digs through her purse for an envelope. "Here. I know you need this."

It's money. Money Junior and I need—badly.

"Thanks, but no thanks. We'll manage." I slip in behind the wheel and start the car.

My mom leans down into the open window. "Don't be foolish." She tosses the money into the car. "When you're ready to come home—alone, we'll be waiting." She slips her shades back on and strolls away.

A baby is going to improve my marriage. I'm convinced of this more now than before. I know Junior doesn't spend too much time with Trey and Danina, but I know that things will be different with our baby.

I'll make sure of it.

I'll teach our child how to see beyond color. I'll shower him or her with unconditional love and support for whatever they decide to be and for whomever they decide to love. I drive around the Atlanta perimeter for a few hours to clear my head and to waste time before my doctor's appointment.

I had a complete physical last week, but scheduled this follow-up appointment for a referral to Southeastern Fertility Clinic. Medicaid doesn't cover infertility, but I'm sure I'll be able to work some angle with my mother for the money. Of course, Junior will have a fit if he finds out what I'm up to.

But that will require him to come home.

The check-in girls at the doctor's office greet me with smiles and I hand over my Medicaid card for them to make a copy to file my claim. Ten minutes later, a nurse appears and calls my name.

"That's me," I say, standing and looping my purse strap over my shoulder. I follow the nurse down a long hallway to an office.

"Dr. Ferguson will be with you in just a moment."

"Thank you." I sit down in a leather chair across from a massive mahogany desk and wait. Why are doctors' offices always so damn cold?

My bored gaze jumps around the room to notice silver-framed pictures of Dr. Ferguson's picture-perfect family and to the various diplomas covering the walls.

"Sorry to have kept you waiting." Silver-haired Dr. Ferguson enters the room with a brief smile and then walks around to take his place behind the desk. "You're here to discuss infertility, right?" He opens my medical chart.

"Yes." I scoot to the edge of my chair and nervously fold my hands in my lap.

"Alrighty." He adjusts his wire-framed glasses on the bridge of his nose and reads intently at something in the chart. "Ah, it looks like we got your blood work back from the lab today." He pauses.

Suddenly I don't like the change in his expression. "Yeah. Is there a problem?"

Finally his gaze lifts to my own. "I'm sorry, but your test result reads positive for HIV."

28

Aisha

I haven't seen or talked to my husband in two weeks. His father called that next day after the scene at the prison and tells me I should be getting my divorce papers soon. Afterward he let me know he's been eyeing me for a sec and he'd gladly pay for a shot of ass or two. Now ain't that some shit? Still stuck on stupid, I carry my ass to that prison set on convincing my husband it's all lies. Desperate to save my marriage. I found out my name was removed from the visitation list.

My marriage is over and I ain't had nobody to blame but myself. But it also means that when it comes to money I ain't have nobody to rely on but myself.

I glance over at my moms as I pull my Benz to a stop at the red light. "Wanna go to IHOP when we get finished at the apartment?"

She shrugs her shoulders and didn't once look away from the window. "I ain't really hungry."

I'm headed back to Bentley Manor for the first time since all this shit went down. I been holed up in my momma's apartment because I know the streets is hot with what they assumed to be my downfall. My momma is disappointed in me, my brothers is fighting damn near every day to keep niggas from talkin' shit about me, I lost my husband, and my name is dirty as hell, but I still have more money than any of these busted, broke-down bitches can even hope to see. So I'm finally getting the fuck out Bentley Manor. Maleek brought me here and left my ass here. Now he's gone. His trial is over and he got those ten years just like he feared. I ain't have no reason to stay in that dirty bitch no more.

I found a nice three-bedroom town house in Kennesaw, Georgia. It was thirty minutes from Atlanta, we didn't know a soul there (thank God) and the rent is $900 a month, but fuck it. I'm moving my family and me out of low-income housing. We deserve it. Now all we needed was the first and last month's rent and the security deposit. No problem, but that meant a trip back to Bentley Manor sooner than I first planned. My stash is big enough to float me for a year if I cut back on my shopping. Since I ain't sure about going back to turning tricks, that gives me plenty of time to figure out just what the hell I'm gone do.

Maybe go to college, because I'm just being real when I say I know a five-dollar-an-hour job will run my ass crazy.

One thing I did hope for is to run up on Reema's skanky ass. I ain't done with her. She's still a bold bitch to carry her ass to that prison when I already had to check her about my man. This ain't even about Maleek. It's about checking a bitch for stepping out of line with me and try-ing to play me close.

If Maleek wants a knock-off woman when he had the real thing then that's his choice. Knowing he is fucking with Reema made it easier for my ass to get over him . . . well, to at least get closer to the point where I'm over him. Maleek and me spent a lot of years together. Yes, I fucked Junior. Yes, I sold my ass to take of myself and him. But I love that nigga and I hate that I hurt him.

I slow the car to a stop in front of the entrance to Bent-ley Manor. There's a nice-ass Porsche parked up the street a bit. "I need to be driving that."

"You know I wish I had taught you that money and material things ain't the beginning and the end, Aisha."

The anger in my momma's voice surprises me and plenty of smart-mouth comments come to mind but I swallow them all. I will never disrespect my mother. In-stead I look out the driver's window waiting for traffic to lighten up so I can turn.

Blood and broken glass is still on the street. Signs of the

murder. I saw on the news this morning that somebody shot up Devani's car last night. I didn't really know her or even notice her. She wasn't on my radar but it's fucked up to think of anybody dying like that. People are crazy.

I hate to even drive through her blood staining the street like she ain't shit but a memory.

Being that it was early morning, the parking lot of Bentley Manor is empty. Not even Miz Cleo and Miz Osceola nosy selves have made it downstairs yet. No kids out enjoying another hot summer Georgia day. That's why I came this time of the day. I'm gonna start packing up my shit and grab my loot so I can kiss this run down mother-fucker good-bye.

I pop my trunk and go out. I start lifting out the flat-tened cardboard boxes and my momma climbs out and holds the door to the building for me.

"This don't look no better than Hollywood," Momma says as she walks down the hall behind me.

I just laugh but my laughter stops when I see the word WHORE spray painted on the door to my apartment. I drop my head.

Momma throws her arm around my shoulders. "Aisha, I don't agree with what you did but you just did what you thought you had to do and everybody makes bad choices. Don't let nobody knock you down for making a bad choice."

And that's why I love my momma and I don't regret being able to take care of her.

We walk into the apartment and it doesn't feel like my spot. My home. My place. My space. This is a small piece of the world that me and Maleek carved out together. Now that our world together is over it's time for my ass to get ghost, too.

"Ma, I left the tape downstairs. I'll be right back."

"I'll start in the kitchen," she calls back.

"A'ight." I think about it and go back to the couch to grab my box cutter from my purse. I slide it into the back pocket of the jeans I'm wearing, just in case I run up on Reema's ass.

As I walk down the hall and into the stairwell I hate how alone I feel. No friends. No man. Besides my mother and brothers it's just me. I feel kind of stressed with all the shit going on in my life and I ain't gone lie that it would be a relief to have females my age to talk to, get advice from.

"Diamond."

I look up into Stuart's face. He looks all jacked up. His suit is wrinkled. He has a shadow of a beard. His eyes are bloodshot. He looks sweaty. Crazy. Wild.

I turn and try to run back through the door leading to the hall; he lunges and catches me. I cry out as we fall forward.

"Diamond, why are you running from me?" he whispers in my ear. He grinds against my ass and strokes the side of my face.

I cringe at the smell of bad breath and liquor. God, I have to get to my blade.

"I missed you so much." He kisses my cheek and strokes my hair.

I force myself to relax. "I missed you too," I lie, hoping he'd give me just enough slack to do what I have to do.

I want to holler out for help but what if that pushes him over the edge and nobody even bothers to answer—or worse yet, my momma comes running and gets hurt instead?

"I've been waiting for you. I thought something happened to you." He strokes his hand up and down the side of my body. "I was going crazy until you finally came home this morning."

Going crazy? Bitch, you is crazy.

He's been stalking me. *Oh God, this whacko been fucking stalking me.*

I hate the tears that well up in my eyes. I swallow them back. "I was locked up. I solicited a cop," I lie, thinking on my feet. "I just got out this morning."

He keeps on stroking me and grinding his erection into my ass. I feel nauseous. What the fuck I got myself into?

"Can we get up? You're crushing me, Stuart."

He shifts to the side of me but his arms are still around me even as I twist around on my back. "Let me take care of you. I'll put you up in your own apartment. I'll buy you all the jewelry and clothes you ever desired, darling. It'll just be me and you. You're too good to sell yourself like a whore or live in this filth."

Darling?

Like a whore?

"How did you know where I lived?" I ask, curiosity kicking my ass.

"That first night we spent together I followed you home."

Son of a bitch.

"At first I couldn't believe you lived here. So I followed you the next week, too."

A chill ran up my spine as I look up into his eyes. They are odd and missing something. I can't explain it but it scares the shit out of me. I force a smile. "You did all that for me?" I ask, before I lick my lips all nice and slow the way he likes.

His pale blue eyes dip down to my mouth. "God, I missed that tight black pussy. I can't wait to stick my cock in your sweet little cunt."

Okay. Uhhg!

He lowers his head and his cool thin lips covered mine.

I let him kiss me. As soon as his tongue slips inside my open mouth I bite down on it hard as hell and draw blood. I spit against the wall as he releases me. I shove my body back to the wall behind me and raise both my sneakered feet to kick him away from me. One of my feet lands straight in his face. The other smashes his fleshy nuts. He howls in pain and bends over, clutching his nuts even as he struggles to stand.

I jump to my feet and dig out my blade as I turn and dash to the outer door of the building.

"You black bitch!" he yells just before he grabs a fistful of my hair.

No the hell he didn't. I turn and swing my leg to kick his ass in the face again.

He reaches up, catches my foot and yanks me forward.

I grunt as I fall on my back and my head crashes against the step. He steps toward me and I start slashing the air with my blade to keep him back.

"You fighting me and I offered to take care of your hood-rat ghetto ass!" he roars, his face changing before me as it twists with rage.

He lunges forward. I swing.

Swish.

The blade slices his chin. His eyes widen as blood pours from the gash, dripping down onto the legs of my jeans.

He rams his fist into my face and I taste blood in my mouth. I blindly swing again.

Swish.

"Agghh!" he hollers out, clutching his left eye with one hand as he grabs my wrist with the other, banging it on the floor. I try to hold on to it. I really try. But he keeps on until my grip loosens and the box cutter drops with a clang to the floor.

He picks it up in a flash and raises it high above me.

Just for a second, with the flesh of eye and cheek bleeding so much his entire face is glossy red with his blood, I think he's the devil himself.

"Lord, help me," I pray in a whisper just before he brings the blade down upon me.

Swish. Swish. Swish. Swish.

Each slice of the flesh on my face brings out a cry from me as I struggle against him with what little strength I have left.

My face feels raw. My tears sting as they run down my bloodied cheeks.

Somewhere I hear footsteps. A woman cries out.

The cuts stop and I feel the relief of his heavy body suddenly off mine. The door to the building opens and closes.

"Aisha!" I hear my mother cry and then I feel the sweetness of her arms around me.

The last thing I hear is "Call 911! Somebody please. Call 911!"

29

Lexi

WooWoo called me. For the second day in a row the newspeople were back at Bentley Manor. First Devani and now Aisha. Must be a full moon or something with all the mess going on. All that violence makes you feel like your own world isn't safe. Like it can spin out of your control at the snap of a finger.

It makes me want to be home with my family, so I leave work a couple hours early. I want to sit them down and maybe talk to the kids and answer any questions they have. I didn't want them to think that violence is supposed to be a normal part of their lives.

When I pull up in my car I see that Luther's home. Good. He's real good with talking to the kids.

I grab my purse and lock my car door. Miz Cleo and Miz Osceola wave me over to them but I'm not really in the mood for gossip, so I just wave back and walk on into the building.

The smell of ammonia is so strong. To cover the stench of her blood.

I can't move from the door. I wince as I imagine the terror Aisha went through in this very stairwell. Still clutching my Wal-Mart jacket I take a deep breath and force myself to walk real fast to the door leading to the hall of first-floor apartments. I almost feel like the attacker is on my heels. But that's silly. He's long gone by now with only a witness reporting a red Porsche peeling away right after it happened.

I pause and look at her door. I wonder if Aisha ever heard of the book *The Scarlet Letter*. We read it in high school once. Like the woman in the book, someone branded Aisha. Hers was on her door and the WHORE is so vulgar. But then prostitution isn't exactly a walk in the park.

I already complained to management about getting the door repainted. I didn't want my kids to have to keep passing that every damn day.

I walk into my apartment and drop my keys and purse on the dinette table in the kitchen. The house is quiet. TV off. No kids running around playing. No food cooking.

I walk back to the bedroom because maybe they all watching TV in our room. I pause at the bathroom when I hear the shower going.

I tiptoe back to the kitchen and pick up the phone. "WooWoo? Hey? You got my kids?"

"Yeah. Luther asked me to watch them 'til you get off. You home early?"

I nod as if she can see me. "Yeah, I took off early. You can send them home."

"They watchin' one of them Madea DVDs."

"Well soon as it's over you can send them home."

"Hey. Lexi? You okay?"

I shrug. "I didn't really know Devani and Lord knows Aisha looked down her nose at me, but all that mess that went down is kinda getting to me."

"I feel you. I'll walk the kids to your door myself. Okay?"

"Okay."

I kick off my shoes and walk into the bathroom. "Luther, I got off early. What you want for—"

My words freeze at the sight of my husband's betrayal.

Like the loud slamming of doors they all come rushing back to me.

Junior cheating with my friends and my enemies.

Boom!

Junior kissing that girl the morning after Valentine's Day.

Boom!

Evan smoking a glass dick.

Boom!

Klinton standing there with his wedding ring on.

Boom!

Raq being carted out the house in handcuffs.

Boom!

And now this.

I feel sick to my stomach as Luther and Junior are both frozen. My eyes take it all in. Two hard bodies. Two hard dicks. My husband fucking my ex. FUCKING . . . IN . . . MY . . . BATHROOM!

Boom!

I go barreling into the bathroom. I don't know who I hit and I don't care but my fists and feet just keep landing blows after blows after blows. Water from the shower soaks me as I fight both of their no-good asses. Luther slips and goes sliding down onto his back in the tub. I reach right down and box him in the mouth.

Junior jumps over me to get out the shower. His condom-covered dick swings like a pendulum and slaps me in the face. I swing backward to land another blow on him.

"Stop, Lexi," Junior hollers.

"Lexi, stop it," comes from Luther.

For one crazy moment I freeze. I'm down on my knees in between them. The smell of their anal sex is still thick in the air as I look between my husband and the father of two of my kids. I could literally hear something inside me snap.

I jump to my feet and shove Junior's ass onto the toilet as I dash from the bathroom. I head straight for the metal lockbox at the top of the closet.

The front door slams and then Luther walks into the bedroom wrapped in a towel. "Lexi, let me explain."

I close my fingers around the cold metal and whirl pointing the gun at his chest. Raq bought it for me and it's been locked in that case ever since. Until now. "Sit down," I order him, using my free hand to knock my wet hair out of my eyes as my soaked clothes drip and make a puddle at my feet.

"Lexi—"

"Sit down!" I holler, my face wincing as my pain fought through the numbness.

I keep him in front of me, shifting my body around the room as he sits down on the edge of the bed. I keep my eyes and the gun aimed at him as I lean down to snatch up the extension cord on the floor behind the TV stand. The television crashes to the floor.

Love has become hate.

Trust is replaced by betrayal.

Another damn man in my life bites the fucking dust and I am so sick of it all.

I move closer and look anywhere but in his lying eyes. "Lay on your stomach."

"Lexi—"

I cock the gun as one tear races down my cheek. I wipe it away angrily.

He lies down and I tie his ass up with the extension cord, keeping the gun right by me in case he makes a wrong move. "I really tried my best to be a good wife to you. I wanted this to work. I thought it was going work."

"I'm sorry, Lexi."

I roll his naked body onto his back with my foot before I pick up the gun. "I try to make the best life for my kids and I keep fucking up."

"Lexi, it's not what you think."

I laugh hysterically and cock my head to the side to look at him with an almost peaceful expression. "Oh, 'cause I think I just caught my husband getting fucked in the ass by my baby daddy. Is that not what I saw?"

He turns his face away from me.

I look down at him as my heart breaks into a thousand pieces. A vision of Junior sliding his dick inside of Luther's ass flashes like a bolt of lightning.

Slap! I slap him and my mouth curls downward. His head snaps to the left. "I keep picking the cheaters."

Slap!

"The crackheads."

Slap!

"The thugs."

Slap!

"Now a dirty down-low brother."

Slap! Slap! Slap!

"My dumb ass done had 'em all."

His cheeks are red as I continue to slap his head back and forth like I'm possessed. His eyes are angry as he looks at me.

"You wanna hurt me?" I ask. "What? You ain't hurt me

enough? All you motherfuckers ain't hurt me enough? Huh? Huh?"

I climb on the bed and straddle him as I snatch his chin up with my hands. "You like sucking dick? Huh? You little bitch you."

"Stop this shit, Lexi."

I put the gun to his mouth. "Huh, here you go. Pretend this is Junior's dick and suck it," I say, breathing heavy as I lean in close and push the gun between his lips.

He presses them together tightly to stop the gun from going any farther.

"Suck it before I blow your fucking brains out. You ain't using them anyway fucking your stepkids' daddy in our house. In the shower they wash in. You dumb bitch." I hate the desperation in my voice but that's how I feel.

The barrel of the gun hits his teeth.

"Show me how you suck Junior's dick."

He closes his eyes and a tear races down his cheeks as he begins to suck the barrel of the gun.

I sit back and look down at my husband. My anger turns to such pain. Who is he? Who did I have around my kids? How did I miss the signs?

I lick the tears and snot that crosses my lips as his jaws caved while his mouth slides up and down the barrel.

"Luther, I trusted you. I trusted us. I swear I could just kill you right now."

I jerk the gun from his mouth as I get up off the bed and sit on the floor with my back pressed to the wall.

My marriage is over. My picture-perfect family is a joke. My baby daddy and my husband are fucking gay. I have to explain to my kids why yet another man is gone from their lives. Why do I keep failing my kids? Why I keep failing myself?

I feel so stupid for believing in Luther and our marriage.

I feel betrayed by Junior.

How long was it going on?

How long has Junior been on the down low?

Did they always use condoms?

Did Luther ever come at my sons with this gay shit?

The thought of that breaks me. I pull my knees to my chest as my shoulders shake with my tears. I hate my life.

I stand back up. Tears stream from my swollen eyes as I move to stand over him. I point the gun at his head.

He doesn't deserve to live.

"What the hell going on here?"

I hear WooWoo's voice but I never take my eyes off Luther lying there hog-tied and scared as I prepare myself to blow his fucking brains out.

"I didn't deserve this, Luther," I say to him softly as my finger shakes on the trigger. "My kids didn't deserve this."

"Momma."

I hear my babies cry out.

I feel WooWoo come up beside me. She puts her hand on top of mine. "Lexi, the kids. Don't do this in front of your kids."

I look to my right and my face crumbles as more tears fall. They're all gathered in the doorway. Trey is holding Imani in his arms as she cries and reaches out to me.

I can't do this in front of my kids. "Untie him, WooWoo."

I lower the gun to my side but I keep it ready. I know now this man is a stranger. "Get out, Luther. Stay away from me and my kids. I mean it."

He walks to the closet and throws on clothes. When he reaches for a suitcase I shake my head.

"I will pack your shit tomorrow. Just leave. Now."

I hear the kids asking him what happened as WooWoo walks him out. I take the gun and lock it back in the metal case before I crawl into bed in the fetal position. I feel so cold. One by one I feel the warmth of my kids' bodies as they all climb on the bed with me.

I love my kids. I adore my kids. If I have to struggle by my damn self to take care of them then I will. I have to.

None of us can stand to go through another damn breakup.

30

Molly

"Positive . . . for HIV?" I ask in a voice that doesn't sound like my own. "There must be some mistake." Please say it's a mistake.

Dr. Ferguson's pensive gaze drops back down to my chart. After a moment, he removes his glasses and lifts his sorrowful gray eyes.

"But how? I-I'm no drug addict. I don't sleep around. I've only slept with one man my whole life—my husband."

My husband.

"I told him if he can't get what he needs from that fat-ass wife of his that he was welcome around my way any damn day of the week."

I am sick to my stomach.

"I hear what you're saying, girl. I had a piece of that choco-

late ass a couple of weeks back. Brother is a straight freak, but I just love how he calls me 'li'l ma.'"

"Mrs. Jefferson, have you ever had a blood transfusion or—"

I stop listening to remember every night that Junior stayed at "the studio," didn't answer his cell phone, and even how he snuck back out the house once we'd gone to bed.

"Mrs. Jefferson?"

The doctor's voice penetrates my thoughts and I blink up at him.

"I know this information is coming as a shock. But it's very important that you understand what I'm telling you. Untreated HIV disease is characterized by a gradual deterioration of immune function. Most notably, crucial immune cells called CD4-positive T cells. A healthy uninfected person usually has eight hundred to twelve hundred CD4-positives per cubic millimeter."

"How many do I have?" I ask suddenly, wanting him to get to the point.

He pauses for a moment and then continues, "During an untreated HIV infection, the number of these cells declines. When the number falls below two hundred, a person is vulnerable to opportunistic infections and cancers that typify AIDS, the end stage of HIV disease."

AIDS? "How many do I have?" my voice quivers out of control as more hot tears trickle down my face.

"Three-ten." He slides a copy of the report over to me.

"Oh my God." I take the report and try to read it, but the tears are coming on stronger now and I can't make anything out.

Dr. Ferguson continues with his spiel, but I don't hear a word of it. Afterward, he fills out a referral form to a specialist and asks whether I have any questions—and I can't think of a single one.

When he escorts me to the door, all the nurses at the nurses' station glance up and I feel like the star of a freak show. With my lab results and referral clutched in my hands, I bolt out of the office bowling over anyone who gets in my way.

Once at the car, I fall completely apart.

Morning turns into afternoon and then into early evening and I still can't manage to get the damn keys into the ignition, let alone the start the car. All I can do—all I'm able to do—is mourn my life.

Three-ten. My T-cell count echoes in my head. My death sentence.

More and more cars leave the parking lot as the doctor's office closes. Some time around seven, Dr. Ferguson pushes through the glass doors and heads toward a red Saab—the only other car in the lot.

He stops when he notices the Caprice. Our eyes meet, despite the distance, and at last, I'm able to start the car.

✧ ✧ ✧

Somewhere between Cleveland Avenue and Hollowell Parkway, my tears finally dry and waves of anger crash into my veins.

I've been living a lie.

I *am* that dumb ass bitch those project bitches whisper about after they've fucked my husband.

My fucking husband!

Geneva's laughing face floats in my mind. *"Yes, girl, I rode that big, black cock until I got saddle sores."*

Laughter, and then, *"I told him if he can't get what he needs from that fat-ass wife of his that he was welcome around my way any damn day of the week."*

My hands tremble on the steering wheel. How many women has it been in the last three years—five, ten, twenty—even more than that? Suddenly my mind is a computer and it has no trouble pulling up dates of when Junior was too tired to make love, and some times when he did, I detected the taste of something—or perhaps someone else—on his dick.

How fuckin' sick is that?

Another wave of nausea hits me and I pull over to the side of the road and open my door just in time to vomit. When my stomach is empty it's all I can do to endure the pain of my dry heaves.

I'm dead. He killed me.

The muscles in my abdomen cramp and twist and still I heave. Cars zoom by and threaten to decapitate me, but after ten full minutes I'm able to pull myself back into the car and slam the door.

My anger festers and soon my thoughts turn to revenge. Just thinking about all I've given up to be with this man, to love this man—and for what?

When I think about how I begged him not to leave me . . .

No. It's not going down like that. I'm not going to be played like that.

I glance over to the passenger seat and my lab report and a lightbulb clicks on in my head. Shifting the car back into drive, I hang an illegal U-turn and flip off the cars honking at me.

Ten minutes later, I park at Kinko's copying center and march up to a pimply-face teenager behind the counter.

"Do you have a Sharpie?"

Todd, according to his nametag, reaches over to a penholder and hands me a black Sharpie. I quickly circle my name at the top of the report and then write in big block letters: MY HUSBAND JUNIOR GAVE ME AIDS!

"I like to make a thousand copies of this."

Todd looks down and reads the message and looks as though he's afraid to touch the paper.

This is what my future holds.

"Please," I add. "And do you have any tape?"

Finally he takes the lab report away. Fifteen minutes and a hundred bucks later, I walk out with my copies.

The tires screech as I whip our big-ass hoopty into Bentley Manor and I don't give a fuck that a few crackheads are barely able to jump out of the way as I plow toward my apartment building.

I sling my purse over my shoulder and then grab the stack of lab reports and tape and then climb out of the car. It's a quarter to eight and the sun is setting and I paint on a bright smile to the first group of women I come across.

"Good evening, ladies," I say and ignore the eat-shit-and-die looks they give me as I cram my report in to each of their hands. "I think you might find this interesting."

As I walk off to the next tenant, there's no mistaking the gasp of horror behind me. And so it went. Some laugh and some look downright ill, but I continue to hand out the report, and even tape a collage of them inside each building.

"Good evening, Miz Cleo and Miz Osceola."

The old women look at me strangely. Undoubtedly, my uncharacteristic good mood is throwing them off.

"Evening, Molly," they answer in unison.

I quickly hand them a flyer and keep moving.

"Oh, my Lord!" the women exclaim behind me.

After the last building, I still have a healthy stack so I just start tossing the report up in the air and letting them fall on the sidewalk and street. I know I look like a crazy woman, but I'm so far past giving a flying fuck about what people think.

When I storm into my apartment, it's no surprise that my loving husband isn't home. I glance around the little shit hole and a second round of boiling hatred burns inside of me.

I lash out and overturn the cheap furniture from the living room to the bedroom. When I'm through with that, I grab some garbage bags from the kitchen and start cramming my clothes and belongings into them. When I reach up to the top of the closet, I freeze when my hand lands on the last box in the back the closet.

The gun.

The rest sort of plays like a movie in my mind. It's more like I'm watching someone who looks like me opening the shoebox. I'm not sure what I'm thinking or if I'm thinking at all. I do take my time loading the weapon, even test the weight in my hands.

No. I'm not thinking. I'm just doing.

I'm putting the gun in my purse. I'm loading the bags into the car. I'm leaving Bentley Manor. I'm going home to die.

I'm at the gate. I'm looking both ways on Hollowell Parkway before pulling out.

And then I see him.

"Honey chile. Open your eyes and see what's in front of you."

Junior is walking up the cracked sidewalk from the Circle K, laughing . . . with his arms around Geneva.

I'm watching.

They're laughing.

He stops and leans forward to kiss her.

I shift the car into park and reach for my purse.

They're kissing.

I open the car door and I walk over broken glass toward them.

They're kissing.

I'm close.

They're kissing.

I'm aiming.

They're kissing.

I'm crying.

They're kissing.

Junior looks up. "Molly—"

I'm shooting. I'm shooting. I'm shooting.

Miz Osceola

I wake up *that morning and just feel like things are gonna be different. Change done gone come. Life is ready to move off pause. Or at least I hope so.*

I've seen a lot during my forty-plus years at Bentley Manor. Good times. Bad times. Better times. Worse times. Drugs, poverty, anger, hopelessness, and helplessness has a way of making life "interesting." Still, nothing I ever seen here could have prepared me for what all went down last month. Nothing.

For the first time in a long time I thought about leaving, but I didn't. The death and the pain nearly aged me twenty years, which is twenty more than I got to spare. All of it touches me so close 'cause I wasn't lucky enough like Cleo to have kids of my own. These people at Bentley Manor is like my children. My family. Besides, I can't leave Cleo. She's my homey, like the young folks say.

And I know it bothers Cleo, too. Me and her see a lot and we talk a lot about it but neither one of us has said one word about any of it to each other. We sit in each other's apartment but we haven't made a move to go downstairs and sit like we used to. Still we see and we know. If not talking about it is some crazy way to make us forget, then fine, mum's the word.

But we still see and we still know.

Three murders. One vicious attack. Prostitution. Drugs. AIDS. Adultery. Men sleeping with women and men.

Sex, drugs, and violence.

Humph. And them women on them TV talkin' 'bout being desperate. They didn't even know the half.

Aisha. Her momma pulled up in a U-Haul a couple of weeks ago. Her and two teenage boys started moving all Aisha's stuff out her apartment. Lord, all the clothes, TVs, highfalutin furniture and things they brought out that place. Looked like a going-out-of-business sale at Macy's. I had got Cleo and we went down and let her know we was sorry 'bout Aisha getting hurt. It was kinda funny how as hot as it was the momma just held on to this ratty-looking wool coat and said her daughter would be just fine. Such a pretty girl and now her face all cut up. Thank the Lord she's alive, though. Far as we know they ain't catch that white man who did it to her, but the Lord has final say.

Kaseem busy spreading the word about Aisha prostituting herself and Reema adding fuel to the fire about how she has Aisha's husband. Big deal bragging 'bout a drug-dealing jailbird who just got sentenced to ten years. Whoopdee damn do! So many people here at Bentley Manor is glad to see Aisha fall since her head was always so high. They saw what they wanted to see. I saw a little girl trying to buy her way to importance.

Just like Devani. Yeah, that one still makes me weep. Especially when I see how broken up her momma is. Can't be easy losing another child—especially the way Devani died. Sometimes I dream about her and that baby of hers. And I even pray for Tyrik that the Lord give him some sense. A damn waste is all it is. A waste. But if you do the crime you do the time, so he went from the NFL to the PEN. Rather kill her than take care of her. Ridiculous. Too bad Devani was so blinded by that money that she couldn't see the love Shakespeare had for her—love he ain't gone ever get back now.

And poor, poor Molly. That child ain't the first person I seen deal with that wild mix of undying love and the pain of betrayal. And Lord knows he put that white girl through some shit. Tried to give her a hint but love made her blind. Loving Junior too much led her to kill him. And she was wrong. Even a scoundrel like Junior didn't deserve to die that way. No doubt about that. But Cleo and I still clutched each other tight that night as the police put her in handcuffs. We seen the papers she handed out about having that AIDS. We knew the hard and painful road she traveled to become a murderer. Heard her parents wouldn't even come get her belongings from out the apartment. So the managers set what little stuff she and Junior had out and the vultures 'round here picked them bones clean in less than an hour.

Well, Junior. Junior was Junior. Sometimes the life you live and the way you treat people dictates the way you die. And Lord knows we seen that boy in a man's body do some crazy stuff through the years. Some downright crazy stuff. Hell, what could be more sick than sleeping with the man married to the mother of your children? To be honest, Luther was hardly the only man Junior slept with here in Bentley Manor. You'd be surprised what the eyes of two old ladies see late at night while people think the shadows hidin' their secrets. Everything done in the dark comes to the light.

Now Lexi wounds run deep. Every scar in her soul caused by the betrayal of some man. But sooner or later she has to learn that she caused a lot of them wounds herself, always in search of men. Five kids. Not a daddy in sight. Husband gone. Marriage over (thank God). The father of two of her kids brutally killed. Yeah, she got a helluva uphill struggle to make sure she get right and them kids don't turn out wrong. Her sister told me Lexi bought a small house outside Atlanta somewhere. Guess that's a step in the right direction. Only time will tell.

Funny thing about time. It will tell. It will be on someone's side. It's all someone needs. It will heal all wounds.

I make myself a big glass of ice water and shove my pack of cigarettes into the pocket of my shorts. I walk to the hall closet and pull out my chair and my bat before I leave my apartment and walk down the hall a bit to Cleo's place. I knock twice with the end of the bat and wait. I hear her gospel music playing.

The door opens and she looks down at my chair, my bat, and my jar of water. She turns around and doesn't say one word. When she comes back she has her chair and her slugger too. She locks her door and we make our way on downstairs.

We just settle in our chairs when a big U-haul turns into the parking lot. Me and Cleo look at each other before we look back at the truck.

It's a young woman and two kids.

"Wonder what her story is?" Cleo asks.

I shrug.

All we have to do is wait and see.

Acknowledgments

God, I thank you for blessing me with my life. Every up and down, every bit of good and bad got me here. I know you walk with me as I go even further.

To my family: Thanks for understanding when I have a deadline and I have to shut myself up inside the world of my books.

To all the readers, bookstores, and book clubs (especially the Niobia Bryant News Yahoo group)—thanks times a million for your support.

Tony: Thanks for understanding when I was too tired to cook dinner. You would cook for me, make a run to Checkers (the #4 with a tea is the BOMB), or make me walk away from that computer to go relax and chill at a restaurant. That's love and I have a lot for you.

Ma: Thanks to you for teaching me how to be a woman. You are the greatest example.

Caleb, my big brother: I love you so much and you make me proud.

Daddy, Granny, Claudie, Aunt Marion, Little Marion, Aunt Mugger: Watch over me from heaven.

My aunts: Rogers, Marsha, Marie, Mae, Dottie, and

Dab "Zsa Zsa." My uncles: Lloyer, Jim, Pete "Slim and Trim," Ernest "Dickey Boy," Randy, Donald "OG." I love ya'll to death.

My cousins: Cheryl—you read my books more than ANYBODY in the whole family and I love you for that. Shine and Londa, you two stay on phone patrol. Felisha, Andre, Chuck, Bobby, Marvin, Derrick, Stacy, Angie (thanks for reading all my books, too), Gina, Tony, DeAngelo (I love you, Rat), Blair (The Big Bammer), Sade (Miss Saddity), Pam and Auriel (Ya'll crazy), Terry (I'm so proud of you), Brenda, Shane (I thought you were gonna e-mail me, heifer), Bobo (I love you, cuz), Brandon, Michelle, Connie, Bam, Gina, Kenny (aka CRUNCH—boy, you crazy), Trav, Keion, Monte, Eric, and Tracy (you are too laid-back, girl). Ebony, Felicia (Where are you, cuz? I love you), Donna, Nasir, and Dashon. (I ain't forget ya'll.)

De'nesha bka Adrianne: Thank you for your talent. You really impressed me with your pen. Two Sagittarius got together to do a book? We're both a little bruised during the process but in the end I am so in love with this book. I couldn't have done it without you.

Deidre Knight (The Knight Agency) and Claudia Menza (Menza-Barron Literary Agency): Thank you ladies for such a great deal. We all worked really hard on this one. Here's to continued success.

Cherise Davis, Meghan Stevenson, Celia Knight, Jamie McDonald, and the rest of the Simon & Schuster/Touchstone team: Thanks for guidance and help. Cherise, you really kicked this manuscript up a notch. Thanks.

Kim Louise: Thank you for your ear and your addictive calmness. Bryant & Louise Productions coming at you in 2008!

Thanks to the ladies at Morrison's Creative Trends: Thanks for the laughs, the book talks, and the hottest hair in the Dirty South.

Thanks to Compliments Hair Studio in Irvington, New Jersey, on North Maple Avenue—*the* hottest hair salon on the East Coast (www.myspace.com/compliments hairstudio).

If I forgot anyone blame my head and not my heart.

Peace.

—Meesha M.

Dear God, I'm so jealous that you and Granny are probably kicked back and having a grand old time. Watch her though; she'll hide your keys! But seriously, thank you God, for blessing me and answering each and every one of my prayers even when I didn't care for the answer. To my sister Channon, for always having my back and being my shoulder to cry on. (Girl, keep your dancing butt home sometimes.) To my other sister, Charla, perhaps the funniest person I know, for dubbing me Chef Boyardee Negro. To Mom, we may not always get along but hey, we're stuck with each other. My beautiful niece, who always brings a smile to my face as long I'm not babysitting more than two hours at a time. To Kathy Alba, thanks for being my best friend for twenty-odd years and always coming through in a pinch. Charles Alba, thanks for taking care of my girl—and hell no, I ain't paying you two dollars.

To the ByrdWatchers fan club: You've always been so loyal and thanks for encouraging to me to do what I do. To Angie Clark: Miss those late office work hours—NOT! Luanne Segars, Tammy Reynolds, Donna Davis, Alda Townsend, Tiffani Johnson, Kathy Pope, Pat and Robert Barrett. My favorite cousins: Josephine Johnson, Melanie Rogers, and Remel Rogers.

To my film production company 5onfilm: Michelle Auda, Jef Blocker, and David Walters. Plus Eddy's Kids group: Lydia Phillips and Andy Ausley. Also to Bridget Anderson and Shirley Harrison for being my writing warriors.

A big, big thank you to Deidre Knight of the Knight Agency for sticking with me for the past ten years. The minute you heard about this idea you were all over it. I love you for that. To Cherise Davis at Touchstone, for being extremely pumped about this story and making us see it in a whole new light.

And to Meesha aka Niobia—we did it. I don't know how but we did it. Thanks for putting your foot in these stories. I'm proud of what we've accomplished.

—De'nesha

About the Authors

MEESHA MINK is the pseudonym for Niobia Bryant, a national bestselling and award-winning author with nine works of fiction in print in multiple genres for multiple publishing houses (Kensington/Dafina and Harlequin/Kimani Press). *Desperate Hoodwives* is her first work of sexy urban fiction but definitely not her last. Currently the author splits her time between her hometown of Newark, New Jersey, and her second home in South Carolina. For more on Meesha visit: www.myspace.com/meeshamink and for more on the author's works under her real name visit: www.niobiabryant.com.

DE'NESHA DIAMOND is the pseudonym for Adrianne Byrd, a national bestselling author of twenty-four multicultural romances. Adrianne Byrd has always preferred to live within the realms of her imagination where all the men are gorgeous and the women are worth whatever trouble they manage to get into. As an army brat, she traveled throughout Europe and learned to appreciate and value different cultures. Now, she calls Georgia home. For more information on De'nesha Diamond visit: www.myspace.com/christianwrites, and for more on the author's romance work visit: www.adriannebyrd.com.

Both authors can be reached at the official
Desperate Hoodwives website:
www.hoodwives.com.

Drama never stops in the hood,
and it's no different for the women
at Bentley Manor.

Turn the page to read a sneak peek
of the second book by
Meesha Mink and De'nesha Diamond

Shameless Hoodwives

coming from Touchstone Books
in July 2008

Miz Cleo

Bentley Manor. My hell. My prison. My home.

It's been a few months since that terrible trouble with Devani, Aisha, Lexi, Molly, and, 'course, Junior. Some people still buzz about the whole mess. Me, I just shake my head and keep on keepin' on. The thing is: Trouble and Bentley Manor always go hand in hand.

This place started off as a regular Atlanta apartment complex, but in the late '70s it was the ghetto, in the late '80s, the projects. Now it's the hood.

My best friend, Osceola Washington, and I laugh about that sort of stuff. We joke about how we were Bentley Manor's first Desperate Hoodwives. Together, we try to keep an eye out on things 'round here—but it don't do no good.

Folks gonna do what they wanna do.

For nearly forty years I've whittled the time away workin', strugglin', and watchin' my dreams pass me by; but with the Lord's help, I manage to hold my head high. Life is short, as they say.

Well, it is and it isn't.

Seventy-one years I've been blessed to be on this earth. I've buried parents, siblings, children, and even a husband. The young folk think hustlin' is new.

It ain't.

I've put in my hustlin' time, worked three jobs to support and raise four children. I don't know whether I've done a good job, though. I lost my oldest daughter to drugs, my two boys to the prison system, and I have no idea where the other one is.

Over the years, I've seen just about everything under the sun, which makes me wonder why I didn't see this comin'. No point in being angry about it.

What's done is done.

As I lie here on this floor, watchin' the blood pour out of me, I feel a certain peace about all that's gone on before. One thang for sure: When you're dyin', your life does flash before your eyes. Now, I can't help but wonder if I coulda prevented what just happened.

Maybe I could've and maybe I couldn't . . .

Takiah

I can't believe I'm moving back to Bentley Manor, but where the hell else am I going to go? All my life, I ain't had a pot to piss in or a window to throw the shit out of.

Jesus, listen to me. I got to do something about my goddamn language before I show up at my grandmother's door and she slaps the taste out my mouth.

I shift in my seat because I can't feel my ass anymore. I don't know what the fuck I was thinking, jumping on a Greyhound bus in September for seventeen hours—and with a six-month-old baby at that. I should have just fucked Dwayne so he would have fixed Kameron's Buick. Then I could've just driven me and Tanana down from Washington myself in one-third the time.

Now I've just about had it with shitty looks and shitty diapers. All these motherfuckers on this bus can kiss my ass as far as I'm concerned. I paid my money just like everybody else.

Tanana squirms in my arms and I swear to God, I hold my breath, praying she doesn't wake up wailing again. I just need some peace and quiet a little while longer. My nerves are shot and I need a hit so bad I can taste it.

After a sec, she settles down and I sigh in relief. I don't have any more bottles to feed her and she's wearing the last Pamper. Now, I'm just hoping my grandmother doesn't turn us away when we get there. Hell, I hope she's still alive.

Fuck. Why didn't I think to check before I got on this bus?

Princess

I don't talk much. I guess I don't really have much to say, or better yet, I don't believe there are too many people who give a shit about what I have to say. Or think. Or believe. Or feel.

So I get shit off my chest through my pen. Songs. Poems. Journal entries. Doodles. Notes.

Living up in Bentley Manor there is always plenty to see and write about. There's mad drama all day, every day. Like all that mess that went down a few months ago with Junior and Molly . . . and Devani . . . and Lexi . . . and Aisha. Damn, the body count was high as Iraq or some shit.

But that's Bentley Manor. You never know what's gonna be on and poppin' up in this raggedy motherfucker.

My stomach grumbles. I roll off the bed and leave my bedroom to walk into the kitchen. Last week my momma dipped for a few days and left me with not one red cent in my pocket to catch the bus to school or any food in the fridge. The only time she kept food up in here on the regular is when one of her men was around. No man, no food.

I don't know what the hell the roaches and mice surviving off of. For real.

And when she did buy food there wasn't shit but frozen dinners or pizza, Little Debbie snacks out the ass, and lots of cereal. I can't remember the last time my momma actually turned on the stove.

My momma is dead wrong for this shit. *Humph!* My momma dead wrong for a lot of shit.

I walk back to my room. I'm trying not to think of Big Macs and fried chicken as I sit on the windowsill in our second-floor apartment. I sit here a lot and I see mad shit going down. Shit people care that you see and wish that you don't see. Every day up in this piece is like watching my own ghetto soap opera. Lifestyles of the poor and shameless.

Not that I don't have stories of my own. I have plenty. Memories. Nightmares. Flashbacks. A bunch of shit I *wish* I could forget. Shit I wish like hell never happened to me.

More strange hands than I can count have been over my body before I even had a real body. Either them trifling motherfuckers were feeling me up, fucking me, or fucking me up.

I'm just seventeen and I know I done seen and been through way more shit than any seventeen-year-old should. Way, way more.

I feel tears rising but I swallow them bitches back, 'cause I learned early that tears didn't do shit for you. They didn't stop a grown man from taking your virginity when you were eight years old. They didn't stop your own father from beating the shit out of you like you were a stranger in the street. They didn't make your mother believe you when you told her that another one of her string of sorry-ass boyfriends been pinching on your titties and ass.

Fuck tears.

I pick up my journal from my lap and open it. The first thing I see is a doodle of my name. Not my real name, Jamillah Unger, but my nickname, Princess. I use my finger with the bit-off nail to trace the flower pattern I drew around my name. They call me Princess because my mother's nickname is Queen.

Humph! That chick ain't know shit about being no queen and she damn sure ain't never treat me like no princess. When my mother looks at me she ain't see shit but a child-support check. My daddy used to beat both our asses. He's a major asshole but he's a major asshole with a decent trucking job that pays his court-ordered support like clockwork. To me that's the only reason I'm still up in this piece. No Princess, no check.

My thin, fake-wood bedroom door swings open suddenly.

"Princess, where Cash say he was goin'?"

I turn my head to see my tall and curvy redbone mother standing there. Figures the first question out her mouth would be about her latest no-good boyfriend, Cash. Fuck asking your only child about her day. Fuck making sure I went to school today. Fuck checking to see if I ate. Fuck me. I get the picture loud and clear.

Woo Woo

Ever since my crackhead momma left me and my sister Lexi with our nana I've been calling Bentley Manor home. My spot. My hood. I learned some of the best and worst shit I know right up in that crazy-ass complex.

I learned how to whup ass and talk shit there. At twelve I sneaked and smoked my first cigarette in the stairwell of our building. At fourteen I smoked my first blunt at my friend Sasha's apartment. At fifteen my hot ass finally got some of that good stuff in boys' pants (thank God it got better with age). The first time I lived alone was when I took over my grandmother's apartment in Bentley Manor. When I graduated high school and then technical college my ass was right up in the Manor.

Shit, I remember plenty of late nights when we all would hang out in the parking lot drinking and smoking weed, talking shit and telling jokes. In the summertime we would get water guns like big-ass kids and chase each other in and out of the apartments.

But there been some bad shit too. Some real bad shit. Murders. Violence. Drug busts. Newborn babies thrown away like trash. Robberies. Crazy shit.

I still get sick when I think of how close my sister came to killing her faggot-*ass*, on-the-down-low-*ass*, no-good-son-of-a-bitch-*ass* husband. Emphasis on ass since that's what he likes so damn much. Walking in on Lexi holding that gun on Luther almost made me shit my damn pants that day.

Yeah, I've had some good- and bad-ass times in Bentley Manor, but I always thought once I was out of that motherfucker I wouldn't come back. Hell, my nana been dead going on ten years. I ain't seen my bitch of a mother in God's knows when. My sister moved her kids into their own house outside Atlanta. I moved out my apartment the same day Reggie proposed three months ago. I left so fast that I didn't get all my deposit back. From the hood to the burbs where life is all good. And I thought that day was the last day I would see Bentley Manor.

But I do go back. It's always late at night while most people are asleep. So no one can see me. So that no one will know. I park my car down the street and walk into the complex to head straight to Hassan's apartment.

Just like last night.

I shiver as I think of the things he did—*we* did to each other. It was worth it. Fuck it. Even though I overslept because I didn't want to leave his bed or his arms, it was worth it. I was almost late for one of the most important days in my life . . . but it was still worth it.

And it was significant because it was the last time I would ever allow myself to see that nigga again. So hell yeah, last night was worth everything I risked.

"Aleesha . . . Aleesha?"

I shake myself from my thoughts. "Yes?"

I hear a slight rumble of laughter behind me.

"I *said*, do you, Aleesha Moore, take this man, Reginald Carver, to be your lawfully wedded husband?" Reverend Yarborough asks.

Keisha

I fell in love with Smokey back when we were in high school, back when the hardest thing he smoked was a couple of blunts. Believe it or not. He was once cute himself. Six-two, lean, and the captain of the basketball team. Hell, I was the captain of the cheerleading squad. Back then, it just made sense for us to be together.

Then came the bum knee.

Then the never-ending pity party.

Then shortly before graduation, I got pregnant.

Two hours after I received my diploma, I was standing in Fulton County courthouse, getting married. My momma cried through the whole ceremony. Wailing about how I was screwing up my life. At the time, I thought I was doing much better than her. She'd never been married and claimed a different man was my father damn near every year of my life.

I was doing good. I had a ring around my finger.

Joke's on me, especially after the first year Smokey

turned to crack, he'd slipped my precious ring off my finger while I was asleep and sold it.

In my mind, we were like Whitney and Bobby. I was going to love him to recovery. Our vows meant the world to me. Sure, there had been a few times when I'd get mad, pack up the kids, and head out to my sister's house out in the suburbs, but I would always come back. Somebody has to look after Smokey.

At least my sister, Cheryl, made it out of Bentley Manor.

My ass will probably die here.

Hearts break, lives shatter, and lies prevail—but four more women at Bentley Manor are determined to get out of the ghetto by any means possible. They won't all succeed . . .

Shameless Hoodwives

COMING IN JULY 2008

TOUCHSTONE
A Division of Simon & Schuster
A CBS COMPANY